Art of Convenience

MICHELLE CARRERO

Copyright © 2024 by Michelle Carrero

All rights reserved.

No part of this book may be reproduced in any form or by any electronic or mechanical means, including information storage and retrieval systems, without written permission from the author, except for the use of brief quotations in a book review.

Cover Artist - Staci Hart at Quirky Bird Covers

Copy Editing/Proofreading - Kristen's Red Pen

Formatting - Grace Elena Formatting

❀ Created with Vellum

For all the Camila Sanchezs out there— you are worthy of the things you want.

And for Lauren. Look silly, we did it.

Playlist

Hey Ma - Cam'ron, Juelz Santana, Freekey Zeekey, Toya
Love in This Club, Pt. II - USHER, Beyoncé, Lil Wayne
all the good girls go to hell - Billie Eilish
skinny dipping - Sabrina Carpenter
JEANS - Jessie Reyes, Miguel
ocean eyes - Billie Eilish
I Wanna Be Down - Brandy
Piss Me Off - Johnny 2 Phones
Pony - Ginuwine
Too Many Nights - Metro Boomin, Future, Don Toliver
People I Don't Like - UPSAHL
upsides - Nic D
Be Your Love - Bishop Briggs
High - Sivik
Happy - Kyle Hume

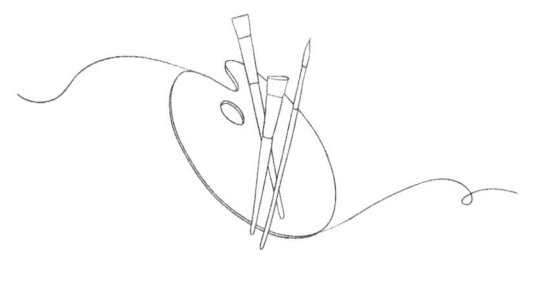

Camila

"Wait—is Josh the guy you broke up with because he wouldn't titty fuck you?"

"Ugh, God no! That was Damien." My best friend rolls her eyes and scoffs. She says his name like she's trying to hold back her disgust but a slight smile tugs at the corners of her lips. "No. Josh is the one that had halitosis."

"What?" I squeal, trying to hold in my laugh.

"Bad breath."

"Yeah, Taylor. I know what halitosis is, I just didn't know you broke up with someone because of it." She gives a small shrug with her shoulder, unable to keep the smile off her face and I can't help but shake my head and laugh. "How did we get so far off topic here?"

"You're the one that brought up the non-titty fucker! And for your information, I didn't break up with him because he wouldn't do it, I broke up with him because of his reason."

Just yesterday I was having my first out-of-body experience, and absolutely not in a good way. Now I'm here. In Taylor's old Honda, driving eight and half hours to Vegas having what some people would deem an inappropriate

1

conversation. Others might call us crazy, but honestly, this is just our normal.

"Mmm...and what was the reason, again?"

"Mila, he literally said *'Why would I want to do that when you have three perfectly good holes?'* verbatim."

I try to make a shocked face, but I can't control the laugh that rips through me.

Driving down the freeway passing mile after mile of desert, I begin to zone out. The dry, vast nothingness out the window is a far cry from Miami. We grew up living next door to each other and have been inseparable since sixth grade. Her parents traveled a lot for work, and being an only child she spent a lot of time at our house, so much so that my younger brother even refers to her as his other sibling.

We've been with each other through everything. From middle school dances to packing up her car and moving across the country to attend college in San Francisco together. My parents were a little hesitant about that decision, but up until yesterday that had been the most wild thing I had done in my life.

"What are you thinking?" Her head tilts and she briefly looks at me with a raised brow.

"I was just thinking... what if I suck up my pride and go craw—"

"NO!" She cuts me off, aggressively shaking her head at me. "Absolutely not. Camila, listen to me. You were miserable at that job, they treated you like shit and they don't deserve you." I keep my eyes focused outside while I twist the gold pendant across the length of my necklace chain. "Look," she lowers her voice. "I know that you have this deep-seated desire to make your parents proud but I'm telling you, they wouldn't be happy to know that their daughter has been working at a job she hates for the last five years."

I always say, 'Things in life that are absolute; death, taxes, and Taylor telling it like it is.'

She's not wrong. I worked my ass off while in school to get my business degree so that I could do something my parents would be proud of. But secretly I wanted something for myself, so I minored in art as well. A career in the arts was risky, it wasn't a solid safe bet like accounting or financial advising. So for the last five years, I've worked for an investment banking company—albeit at the bottom of the totem pole, and at times for some real assholes. But when I told my parents I got this job even though I would have to work my way up, they were proud of me.

So every day, even though I continued to hate my job, I went in. I forced a smile and said "Sorry, sir," "Thank you, sir," and "Of course, sir" a thousand times a day. I spent day after day battling the anxiety that came with just the thought of going to work. Sitting at my desk with my legs bouncing uncontrollably beneath me. A permanent stomach ache. And I'm fairly certain I could also blame my boss and the stressful work environment for my beautiful, thick hair starting to thin out.

However, yesterday when I was standing in front of my boss, in his tacky office that had a mild mustard aroma, something inside of me broke—more like snapped.

MR. HALL IS ON HIS THIRD TYRANT OF THE DAY AND CAN'T be bothered to close his office door. No. He wants to make an example out of me and I won't be surprised if it is something he'll get off on later. Remembering the way my face heats in embarrassment as he talks to me like a literal child in front of all my co-workers. I am 50 percent embarrassed that he is screaming at me again knowing everyone outside his office is listening, but I am also 50 percent grateful he at least left the door open so I won't suffocate in the mustard smell.

I watch his nonexistent lips move. His large arms that he tries to pass off as muscle wave around and the crease deepens between his thinning eyebrows, but there is a ringing in my ear.

What the fuck am I doing?

"Do you think you can manage that, Ms. Sanchez, or should we hire someone off the street to get it done instead?" His voice sounds as if I am underwater.

I blink and shake my head. Am I experiencing vertigo?

"Ms. Sanchez," he shouts.

That is always his go-to—to threaten me, to push me harder. And because of the type of person I am, I almost always comply. But for whatever reason, that tactic isn't going to work today.

As if I am hovering above us in his office I watch myself say, "I think…I think finding someone else to get it done instead would be best."

He stares at me blankly for what feels like thirty minutes but in reality is probably only fifteen seconds. He is likely waiting for me to snap out of the alternate universe I have fallen into. He blinks once, and both of our eyes trail down to his desk where his fat knuckles knock on a stack of papers. "Very well," and then with a flick of his wrist, I accept his dismissal.

I beeline straight to my office and I take the two steps to round my desk and sit down in my chair. The cushioned fabric seat gives warmth to my cold body. The space is rather empty for someone who's been in the same four walls for five years, but I slide the two photo frames I do have into my oversized bag and before I know it I am typing up my resignation letter. I hand it off with sweaty palms to Mr. Hall's assistant and the corners of her lips turn down as I wave to her before stepping into the elevator.

I somehow manage to make it home, even though I have no recollection of how I got here.

"Mila? Is that you?" Taylor yells from the bathroom.

My eyes have gone dry and the dizziness is still persistent. I sit my bag down on the floor of our tiny apartment, unable to form the words to answer her question.

"Okay if it's not you, Mila, and it's a robber, just know that the clothes by the door are covered in dog shit. I had a very sick pup whose owner didn't want to cancel their grooming service today. Also, all my jewelry is fake," she continues to yell from the bathroom.

I walk like the tin man up to the bathroom door, "I quit."

"Fuck yeah!" Taylor sits up from the bath covered in bubbles, splashing water everywhere.

"No. Taylor, how did I do this? What have I done?" Immediately the shock starts to wear off and panic begins to set in.

"Camila, look at me." Her voice is stern.

"I love you, but you're in the bath, I think I can wait to look at you until you're out and in your robe," I say, rubbing at my chest.

"Okay don't look at me, but listen. That job was tearing you down, and every day when you left for work I manifested it would be the day you quit. This is a good thing, a great thing. You will figure something else out, we'll figure it out together, okay?"

I don't know what else to say so I just nod my head in agreement.

"Great. Let me dry off and then we'll pack."

I finally look at her, because I can't tell if the shock has completely scrambled my brain or not. "Pack for what?"

"Are you serious? Don't you remember the end of your first week of work when you came home crying and I told you that you could quit and we could go Vegas and forget about it?"

Yes, my brain is definitely not keeping up with her anymore. "Are you talking about a conversation from five years ago?"

"Is that how long you've been at that shit hole job?" Her eyes go wide.

"Yes."

"Okay then yes. Look, it doesn't matter how old the conversation is. The fact is, we're celebrating. Go pack."

"Tay, I can't celebrate this."

"Okay..." She bites her lip and nods her head. "Then we'll go to get our minds off it and come back refreshed and ready to make a new plan. I know the world stops turning when you don't know the next move."

Taylor, my optimistic best friend.

"I think you're the only person to ever use the words Vegas and refresh in the same sentence," I say with a small smile.

"Go pack. We leave first thing in the morning." A wiggle of her eyebrows is her only response.

"THANK YOU, TAYLOR," I SAY. "YOU WERE RIGHT."

"About stopping for the breakfast burritos this morning?" she asks, leaning across the center console.

"All of it. The breakfast burritos and an eight-hour drive to Sin City are exactly what I needed."

"Damn right!" She slaps my thigh. "You're going to come home from this weekend a whole new woman."

My only plans are to enjoy a weekend with my best friend and not think about the colossal mess that will be waiting for me back home. I look back out the window, and promise myself that for the next two days I won't think about any of it.

"Okay wait. Did you really break up with Josh because he had bad breath?"

"That and he still used a flip phone."

I fold over laughing and then reach over to turn up the music.

Miles

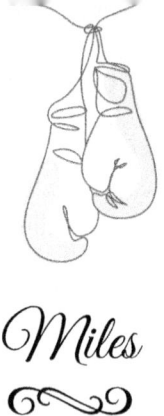

I just got the promotion I've been working towards for the past ten years, followed by the verbal ass-whooping of the century. Did I bluff a client into signing something I needed? Sure. But that's not illegal; I might toe the line sometimes, but I never cross it. It's one of the things that's made me one of the best lawyers in San Francisco. I get shit done that needs to be done and this time was no different. Unfortunately for me, my managing partner, Samantha, doesn't always agree with my tactics.

The sun is at its highest peak in the sky as I look out my corner office window. The city below is bustling. The people on the streets look no bigger than ants from all the way up here. My office is quiet save for the clock ticking on the desk behind me. But my quiet time is quickly interrupted. I can smell my annoying, cocky friend before he even says anything.

"Dude. Name partner? When were you going to tell me?" Jonas practically shouts from behind me.

"Close the door, and sit down." I swivel my chair around, one arm hanging on the back, the other resting under my chin. "It's not official until Monday, but I got word last night."

"Son of a bitch." He shakes his head with a wide grin.

"Yeah, but Samantha found out about how I bluffed Rick on the Davenport case and she just tore me a new asshole." I open my laptop with a raised brow.

"Well good, your old asshole was getting disgusting."

I wad up a piece of paper and throw it at him. He deflects it with ease, laughing and running a hand through his perfectly styled dark blonde hair.

Jonas doesn't get called a pretty boy for no reason. He might be as tall as me, and he can throw a punch in the ring, but our comparisons end there.

He's about as friendly as they come, so it was a shock to everyone when we became fast friends in college. Our differences only presented themselves further when we both applied to the same law school. Jonas was practically a shoo-in for Stanford with both his parents being alumni. His father was still teaching there and his mother was a board member. I, on the other hand, had a retired Major League Baseball player for a father whom I hadn't talked to in years, and a sick mom.

I was desperate to get out. Desperate to make a better life for myself so I could take care of my mom. I've always believed I was the best at everything and that there was nothing I couldn't do. When I had a goal in mind, I not only reached it, but I fucking obliterated it. I proved that to myself when I got into Stanford. But that's when I started to spiral. I took my anger out on Jonas at the time, and I might still be the same grumpy asshole I was back then, but I'll never not be grateful to Jonas and how he helped me during that time.

"Okay, on a serious note, congratulations, Miles. This is fucking *huge*." He leans back into the leather couch, crossing an ankle over his leg. "You might not be the most approachable guy here but you're a winner and you never fail to get the shit done."

I know he means well and he's right, I have worked hard for everything I have, but I've had to. But beneath a thick slab of skin, I feel a tiny prick of guilt at his words because I also know he believes he has everything *he* has because of his good looks, and his parents' influence.

"Thank you." I meet my friend's eyes, and we exchange a nod. "Now I just have to play it cool for a while, let Samantha calm down so she doesn't change her mind before it's announced."

"Sam's no joke. Her bite matches the bark and then some, but she would be..." he pauses leaning over the arm of the couch to look out the glass doors, making sure no one is around before whispering, "an idiot, to change her mind."

I hang my head back on my chair and spin around to face the window.

"Plus, you've been doing the same shit the last ten years. It's not like she doesn't know how you operate by now, it's what makes you the best."

"Yeah, she'll get over it." I clear my throat, shaking the mental fog. "I think I just need to blow off some steam."

Jonas puffs out a long breath, the sound of the clock ticking fills the room again followed by his fingers tapping against the leather couch. I spin around once more and I'm met with a shit-eating grin spread across his face and I know exactly what he's thinking because it's the same thing he suggests anytime either one of us has any minor inconvenience.

Shaking my head, I lean forward on my desk and point my finger at him. "Don't even say it."

His smile drops and he purses his lips together while

nodding his head, looking around the room. Just as I sit back in my chair, like an uncontrollable child he shouts, "Vegas?"

"What part of *'I need to keep my shit together'* did you not understand?"

"So we'll just go till Sunday instead of Tuesday." He drums his hands on the coffee table before jumping up and heading to the door.

"Jonas!"

One hand is already on the door, his phone in the other, he doesn't even look over his shoulder as he says, "I'm texting Lola to have the jet ready for us by nine."

"Jonas!" I bark again.

"Relax, dude. We'll have a chill night, nothing wild, a few strippers and some blow. Child's play." He shrugs. I know he's joking but there's no talking him out of it once I'm left staring at his backside as he walks down the hall. He passes the giant metal letters mounted to the wall: Smith & Mitchell. I'm reminded of my unofficial accomplishment. And as long as I don't do anything to fuck it up, next week that wall will shine with Smith, Mitchell, and Cameron.

JONAS

You up?

ME

I know you didn't just send me a 'you up' text.

JONAS

Soak it in. I can't imagine you ever getting another one.

> **ME**
>
> 👍 👍
>
> **JONAS**
>
> It's the first Saturday of the month. Half-off pancakes at the cafe if we get there by 9.
>
> **ME**
>
> You make 7 figures. Why the hell are you harassing me out the door for half-off pancakes?
>
> **JONAS**
>
> It's one of the ways I get my kicks.
>
> **ME**
>
> I don't want to know about your kicks. I'm going back to bed, leave me alone.

INSTEAD OF SETTING MY PHONE DOWN AND GOING BACK TO sleep I open my work email and busy myself for a few minutes.

Boom Boom Boom

It sounds like the task force is at my door. *What the hell?* I move swiftly out of the king-size bed. Not bothering to find a shirt, I hurry through the living room, clipping my hip on the side of one of the green couches. I squeeze my eyes shut and breathe a silent *fffffuck*. Just as my hand grasps the doorknob, I'm met with a hideous falsetto.

"How could you use me like this? You said I was the one! Did last night mean nothing to you?"

I rear back from the door, my eyes narrowing as I try to get my ears to work harder.

"You just want to use me like toilet paper, I get it. Well, let me tell *you* something. You will never find anyone who will lick that ass better than me."

My eyes threaten to pop out of their sockets when I

realize whose voice that is. The door nearly flies off the hinges when I rip it open, grab Jonas by the back of his neck, and throw him inside my suite.

He holds up his hands in mock surrender, "Okay, I'm sor —." He drops his head trying to hide his laugh which only causes my scowl to deepen. "I'm sorry. But since you're up, can we go get pancakes now?" He points to the door behind me.

"You're an idiot." I adjust myself in my gym shorts that are twisted after I flew out of the bed and move to the kitchen to assess the coffee situation.

Jonas only shrugs, "Just another way I like to get my kicks. Annoying you." He makes his way further into the living room and falls down onto the daybed by the window that overlooks the fountains below. "Put a shirt on, so we can go, the Ubers here take forever," he yells across the open floor plan.

I run both hands through my hair and look at Jonas, the picture of unaffected, before giving up and walking back to my room to change.

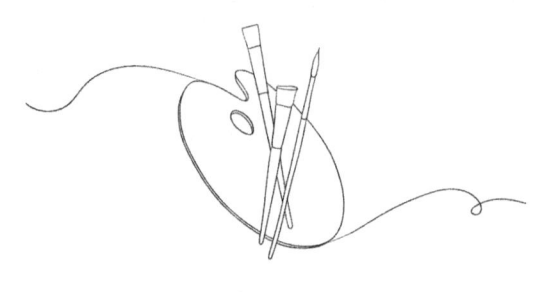

Camila

The dry sun is beating down on my skin and sucking the life out of me. Although to be fair, it could also have something to do with all the Adios Motherfucker drinks we downed last night. I gag a little at the memory.

"Remember when we were supposed to just go to a nice dinner and have an early night last night?" I look over at Taylor, squinting out of one eye.

"Honestly, this is better," she says, keeping her eyes shut as she basks in the sun. "We only wanted to have an early night *last night,* so we could day-drink *today*, but in this heat? Who would want to do anything but lay out at the pool anyway? Now we're in recovery mode so we can go hard in the paint again tonight."

Yes, the point of this trip was to forget about how I quit my job with absolutely zero backup plan. Last night the drinks did the trick and today I'm too hot and too exhausted to give it any thought. The only thing on my mind now is wondering how I can eat and take a nap at the same time.

"I'm going to need a nap, and you're going to need more

sunscreen." I reach my arm over, poking my finger into her shoulder. Her light skin is currently holding a light tan but I know from many beach and pool days that at any moment it could turn red.

"I should have brought that pizza down with us," she ignores me.

"What pizza?"

"I found a slice of pizza in the mini-fridge this morning." She turns her head to look at me now, the first movement she's made in an hour and I throw my arms over my face as my chest shakes with laughter.

"Damn, I wish I remembered eating pizza. I hope it was from that retro place." My stomach grumbles in response to the thought. "Run back up and get it," I tease her.

"I would, but after wearing those shoes last night, my dogs are barkin'." She lifts her leg towards the sky, holding her thigh with her hands while shaking her foot.

"Alright, I've got a few more minutes out here then I'm done." It's only the beginning of May, so I guess by Vegas standards it's not really that hot. But when you've spent the last eight years in The Bay Area, where it's pretty much always windy, and even when it's warm there's a slight chill, the 84°F feels like the middle of the sun.

"Okay. Fifteen more minutes, food, nap, food, club. Sound like a plan?"

"Ready, break," I clap.

"The music in here sucks."

"Definitely not the vibe," Taylor says, curling her lip.

"You want to finish these drinks and then bail?" Before the words have even made it to her ear, Taylor chugs the contents of her mixed drink.

"Your turn," she says, smiling and eagerly nodding her head towards me. I'm already feeling the buzz and my drink is still three fingers tall but the eighties love songs mashed with techno beats are more annoying than fun right now. I bite down on my straw and suck down the rest of my drink while Taylor gives me a five-second countdown. "Nice." She takes the glass from me and dumps it on an empty tabletop nearby.

I swivel around looking for the best way out of the patio bar, spotting a door right past a group of men to my right. The space is so cramped, I have to squeeze between the men and a long high-top table. "Excuse me," I say. More out of habit than anything because it's not like they can really hear me.

"Hey," the tallest guy of the bunch shouts at me. His breath reeks of stale beer and he's yelling louder than necessary. "Where ya headed?" I don't respond, but still give a polite smile as I push past him. I stop and turn back to face him when he's put a hand up in front of Taylor. In her heels, she's as tall as he is. "That's alright, I'd rather bring you home anyway," he says to her.

She tilts her head and flashes her full, beautiful smile and I just know in a matter of seconds this poor guy is going to be licking his wounds. "Baby, if you had three wishes from a genie, you couldn't take me home," she says before patting him on the head. I cover my mouth to stop my laugh from flying out as she passes the guy and we make our way outside.

As we walk down the Las Vegas strip for what feels like an eternity, I have to hold on to Taylor's arm so I don't fall over laughing. Aside from the matching scars on our forearms, from a rafting incident gone wrong while night swimming one summer, we couldn't be more opposite.

Her sea-green eyes and pale skin are a stark contrast to my dark eyes and year-round deep summer tan. Never mind the fact that she has a good five inches on me in my 5'4" frame, but her confidence matches her height—and then some. You would think after fifteen years together I would have picked up some of her wild, carefree spirit but I'm starting to think there are just certain parts of myself that will never change.

The alcohol has been holding up its end of the bargain. For one weekend, I wanted to not be plagued by my anxiety. I wanted to live a weekend free of feeling that tightness in my throat. No headaches or stomach aches. I wanted to forget the dreaded feeling of being every bit the disappointment that I feared I would be to my parents. I've been a pack mule with the amount of stress I've carried from that job, and quitting it might have just worsened the load. But right now, I won't think about that. I won't think about any of it. I focus on the feeling of the alcohol warming me as it works its way through my system and tells my brain that everything is fine. At this moment, my only concern is for my feet because I look around and realize that Taylor has been leading us the opposite way of our hotel.

"Oh my God, Taylor! Our hotel is the other way." I stop in the middle of the overly crowded sidewalk.

"Be so for real right now Mila, we're not going back to our hotel yet." Her feet stop a few steps ahead of me when she realizes I'm no longer by her side. "The night is still young." Her arms fly up over her head and she accidentally whacks a man with her clutch. "Oops, sorry," she shouts after him before turning around to face me. "There's still plenty of time to make bad decisions." Her hand reaches out to me and where she fails at wiggling her eyebrows she succeeds in flashing me her wolfish grin.

"Great." I groan with a forced smile. "So, where are we going now?"

"You know the lady that I do the meal prepping for?" Taylor has fifty or so odd jobs, so it's hard to keep up with all her gigs, but with a slightly confused expression I nod along anyway. "Well turns out, her husband's company opened this new club, and I texted her on our way here. She was able to get our names on the list. Apparently, it's super exclusive and practically impossible to get into."

The hotel bed is calling my name but I can tell she's excited so I rally. "I'm going to need a Vodka Red Bull," I say pointing a finger at her.

"How about three and a kamikaze to top her off?" We link our arms together and stagger off down the strip.

TAYLOR GIVES OUR NAMES TO A MAN WHO LOOKS LIKE HE could be security for WWE and we walk right in, past the line, up the stairs, and into the most extravagant roof-top club I've ever seen. With the sun having set hours ago, it creates a dark indoor nightclub feel. Cool blue and purple lights dance above and the music is so loud I can feel it vibrating in my chest. We lock hands and have to make our way through the dance floor to get to the bar that sits on a raised platform in the middle. Taylor flags down a bartender to order our drinks as I lean against the bar taking in our surroundings. Next to me, a woman is shouting at her crying friend, "He's such an idiot, screw him, seriously!" And even though I'm in no position to judge, I'm glad that's not my situation tonight. I give the crying woman a pinched smile before noticing she's holding her heels in one hand and a drink in the other.

Pata sucia.

I continue scanning the club and my eyes catch on a bachelorette party in one of the VIP areas. Dicks everywhere. Penis headbands, penis straws, sunglasses with a vibrator in the middle. One woman is even waving around an ejaculating penis wand. I have no idea how she managed to sneak that in here, but good for her.

Taylor's blonde head of hair whirls around with all of our drinks in hand. "Cheers, bitch!" She screams over the loud music. I take the cocktail, set it down on the bar with one hand, and hold out the shot glass with the other. "To us, and our last night in Vegas, may tomorrow be filled with maximum buffet options and minimal headaches." We cheers our glasses and throw them back.

The alcohol burns my throat as I force myself to swallow. I place the glass on the bar and my hands hold the edge briefly as I try to stop the spinning that happens from throwing my head back so fast. When I look up, the room still spins until a pair of the darkest eyes I've ever seen are the only thing in focus. The music around me drowns out and the hum of my heartbeat fills my ears. I wet my lips and immediately feel heat rush from my face to below my waist. I tell myself it's just the alcohol.

I should look away, but it's like I'm frozen in place. I vaguely register that Taylor starts dancing next to me or against me, I'm not sure. I drop his gaze for a moment, as I try to focus on my friend who's now doing some variation of the Jersey Turnpike dance. But I can still feel his eyes on me, burning the side of my face. I take one quick glance back at him and it causes my breath to catch in my chest.

I quickly bite down on my bottom lip and I finally turn away. I'm too drunk to be eye fucking a stranger from across a nightclub.

Miles

THE BATHROOM ATTENDANT OFFERS ME A PUMP OF SOAP AND then goes back to straightening the condoms and Advil packets. Some guy who looks like he's never seen the sun a day in his life comes up next to me at the sink, reaching for a mint before he's washed his hands. *So fucking foul.* I take the towel the attendant offers me and drop a hundred-dollar bill in his tip jar.

As I make my way back to our private section, I find that Jonas seems to have met a new lady friend, which is on brand for him. Women flock to Jonas. I tell him it's because of his good looks, but he claims it's because my scowl scares all the women towards him. I'm no stranger to women, I just don't have the time or the desire to have a relationship with one. After seeing how it worked out for my parents, I can confidently say I don't ever want that. My relationship with women is simple: sex only. One time, no repeats, no relationship before or after. It sounds harsh, but I always make my intentions clear before moving forward. And this has always worked out for me. So I don't plan on changing my ways.

I enter our section just as Jonas and a woman in a red

dress peel their faces off one another. I slide past them and lift the nearly full bottle of Vodka out of the ice bin.

"Miles, this is uh—"

"Ava," the girl supplies.

I reach out to shake her hand, "Nice to meet you, Ava," I lie. Because I really couldn't give two shits.

I finish making my drink and sink back into the dark corner of the couch, busying myself with my phone.

"My friends are over by the bar, I could grab them and bring them over." Despite the darkness, I still notice the way her eyes are glazed over as she watches me. Her eyes trail down my body while her fingers run along the buttons of Jonas's shirt. I don't want to be a cockblock but I'm not interested tonight.

"Aly was it? I'm good." I tip my glass to her before getting up and walking over to the glass wall that looks over the strip at the end of our section. I swirl the liquid around my cup, causing a mini tornado before throwing the whole thing back in one large gulp. Jonas is a big boy, he can handle this night on his own. I'm too old for this shit. What was supposed to be a chill night with a few rounds of poker last night turned into complete debauchery. I give it another two minutes zoning out at the city, pretending as if I've never seen anything more interesting than the twelve million lights it takes to light up the strip before I move to make my Irish exit.

My phone is sitting on the table but Jonas and Red Dress are back to making out so I slink by and snatch it up. When I stand to pocket it, my eyes connect with a little brunette across the room. She looks like a deer in headlights but I don't turn away. And even though my eyes are locked on hers I don't miss the way her dark brown, almost black, hair flows wildly down her back. My hand twitches while holding my empty glass with the desire to tangle my fingers in that head of hair, to wrap it around my wrist and…

"You good, bro?"

Jonas's voice pulls me from my thoughts but I still can't tear my eyes away from her. She's staring back at me, her mouth slightly parted. Her friend bumps into her in a dance, and even from halfway across the room I can see her deep inhale. She pulls the corner of her lip in between her teeth as if she's attempting to hide her smile. And somehow even in this crowded as fuck club, I feel a cool breeze wash over me as soon as she looks away.

"I'm headed to the bathroom," I announce.

"You just came back from the bathroom?" Jonas holds his arms out confused.

"Yeah, I must have broken the seal," I say, distracted.

"Or you're just old."

I scratch my forehead with my middle finger and give him a smirk before heading out into the crowd.

The early 2000s hip-hop booming has turned into background noise as I make my way through the swarm of people. It's not hard to keep my eyes on this girl. I'm more concerned with how difficult it is to keep my eyes off of her, actually. They're still posted up at the bar and it feels as if I'm walking in slow motion, but the closer I get, the more I can't mistake how stunning she is. Her face is dewy, likely from being in a crowded club. She looks about a foot shorter than I am, but she doesn't look small or weak. Her black skirt hugs her hips and ends just past her ass, and immediately I notice her sculpted thighs. Everyone talks about the boob guys and ass guys, but no one talks about us leg guys. Something about her toned tanned legs in those high heels has my dick twitching against my zipper.

I close the last few feet of distance between us. With her

back to me, her hips dip and sway to the music. The metal of the bar is cool under my forearm as I lean against it, signaling for the bartender. I should say something instead of standing here like a creep watching her dance, but when she tosses her head back shaking her hair, I'm hit with the most intoxicating smell. The bartender comes rushing over with two handfuls of shots for a group of women to my right.

"What can I get you?" he yells over the music.

"Whisky. Neat."

To my left, the swaying has stopped. I take note of how her spine is now straight and no longer moving. When the bartender returns with my drink, he throws a napkin down and slams the drink on top of it. I take the drink and throw another hundred on top of the now-soaking-wet napkin.

I turn to face my mystery girl who is now watching where my hand clutches my drink. Her eyes follow as I bring the glass to my lips, and I use the opportunity to stare at her unabashed. I swallow the amber liquid and bite down the mistake I've made of mixing my spirits.

My lips part and I lean in towards her, while at the same time, she rests a gentle hand on my shoulder and presses up on her toes. "Why would you brave that crowd to come over here when you have your own private bar up there?" She pulls back, eyes twinkling.

"Because I couldn't ask you what your name was from over there." I mentally bitch slap myself. I couldn't come up with anything better than that? She doesn't seem to mind though, her head dips quickly but not before smiling and pulling that lip between her teeth again, and if I thought my dick was twitching before, he's full-on trying to head north now.

Angling her head towards me she says, "I'm Camila."

"Camila, I'm Miles. Nice to meet you." I extend my free

hand to her and she lets out a small laugh as she places her hand in mine.

"This might be the most formal encounter I've ever had in a nightclub."

I don't know how to tell her that I don't typically introduce myself to women in nightclubs, that the extent of my words start with *"Let's go"* and end with *"I'll call you a car."* So instead I take another slow sip from my drink as she opens her mouth ready to say something before her friend pops up over her shoulder waving her drink around.

"Hey! Did I see you come over from the VIP area?" she shouts.

Without taking my eyes off Camila, I respond to her friend. "I did. I can't guarantee my friend is decent over there now, but would you like to come up?"

Her friend answers for her. "Duh. We love a good VIP couch! Lead the way, big guy."

Camila winces and mouths a silent '*sorry*'. And fuck, is she cute.

And when have I ever thought a woman was cute? I mentally shake my head and give her a reassuring smile before placing my hand on the small of her back and pointing her forward toward our section. The walk isn't that far, and after I discreetly adjust the raging hard-on going on in my pants, all I can focus on is where my hand meets her back. The touch is feather light so I'm taken aback by the heat emanating off of her melting into my skin.

As we make our way up the four stairs that separate the VIP level and the general floor, Jonas is sitting on the couch alone nursing a drink. I don't have time to question where Red Dress went because his head perks up as soon as he sees me with Camila and her friend. "Hello ladies," he drawls. "Welcome, can I make you a fresh drink?"

"You could make me two." Her friend holds up two wiggling fingers.

"Lovely," Jonas purrs. "I'm Jonas, and I see you've met my grumpy friend, Miles."

"Nice to meet you, Jonas. I'm Taylor, do you dance?" she asks, taking the drinks from his hands. Jonas looks at her, smiling like a kid who just hit the winning numbers on *The Price Is Right*, and I know he and Taylor are about to hit it off because Jonas doesn't come to the club to hang out in the corner and look cool. The bastard loves to dance.

"Is the pope a catholic?" he asks in a terrible British accent.

Her eyes go wide and her jaw drops. "Was that your Ginger Spice impression?"

"Yes! No one ever gets that!"

"You're kind of funny." She tilts her head, with a crease forming between her eyebrows.

"Don't be so surprised, babe."

"Well, usually good-looking guys are corny. You know? Like they never had to be funny."

He grabs his chest as if he's deeply offended and to Taylor's credit, she pays him no mind. She rolls her eyes and turns on a heel, heading off to the dance floor, and to no one's surprise Jonas quickly follows after her like a lost puppy.

I'm finally able to turn my full attention back on Camila. "So, what are you celebrating, tonight, Camila?"

She looks away with an expression I can't quite place before turning back towards me, "A new adventure, I quit my job," she says with a false vibrato.

I've been at the same firm since I graduated law school. My boss—and mentor—paid my way through law school knowing I would be a return investment for her when I came to work for her firm. People will put in decades of their lives at a firm in the hopes of getting where I've been, and come Monday where I will be. Although I have no idea what it's like to celebrate leaving any kind of company, I can play along for her tonight.

"Well then, cheers." I lift my glass to her and a tight smile forms on her face before she clinks her glass against mine. Our eyes lock for a brief moment before we both throw our drinks back in unison. If I thought looking into Camila's eyes from across the room was doing something to me, I wasn't prepared for what sitting this close to her would do. It's causing the most foreign sensation to pump through my body but I pour another drink and ignore it. When I sink back into the couch the lights above cast a purple glow over her. As if my hand has a mind of its own I reach up and tuck a stray piece of hair behind her shoulder. For a moment her lips part and I wonder if that was too much, I follow the way her chest rises higher before slowly lowering. Finally, she brings her glass to her mouth, covering up her smile.

"And you? What brings you to Sin City?"

Instead of saying '*My boss just gave me the promotion everyone in my position works their entire lives for, but I continue to make shit choices and if I make any more, she's likely going to fire me rather than put my name on the door, so I'm here with my idiot friend to blow off some steam*' I say, "The drinks." And hold up another glass to her before downing it.

A FEW DRINKS—THAT I DIDN'T NEED—LATER, THROUGH blurred vision I make out Jonas and Camila's friend falling all over each other trying to make their way back up the steps. Camila and I are still sitting in the dark corner but she seems lighter, more at ease. It's likely the mass amount of alcohol we've consumed. Taylor comes running over waving her arms in front of us, the movement making me borderline cross-eyed. "Jonas wants to go see the fountain before the sun comes up. Are you two coming?" Her words slur but she shouts them with confidence.

I look to Jonas whos standing behind her giving me his best *don't you fucking dare* eyes. When I don't say anything, Taylor turns her head around to look at him, and he quickly hits her with his megawatt smile.

Before I can respond, Camila grabs my bicep with both her hands. "Wait! We didn't even get to dance yet," she cries. I don't dance. But when she looks at me with a pouty lip and pleading eyes, for some reason I couldn't deny her even if I wanted to.

I place my hand on her smooth thigh and give it a squeeze, "You two go ahead, we're gonna dance a little." I wave them off. "We'll meet you there."

Taylor raises a brow at Camila and she nods her head, silently telling her it's okay. They exchange a quick hug and Taylor points a firm finger at me, "Okay...we *will* see you soon, then." I don't miss her threatening tone but I like that she's protective of her friend. I give a mock salute and as she turns around Jonas places his hands together at his chest and bows his head. I'm sure he thinks he's on his way to hook up with this girl, but once they head out Camila turns to me and laughs.

"He's going to need more than a prayer to hook up with Taylor." Camila pushes off the couch, reaching a hand out to me. I stand, taking it in mine and our fingers intertwine as she leads us down the confetti-covered stairs to the dance floor. The strobe lights above us do nothing to help my hazy vision. In fact everything not only looks like we're all moving in slow motion, but it actually feels that way too.

We could have stayed up in our own little section but Camila drags us right to the middle of the crowd. The combination of all the bodies, loud music, and alcohol should be a sensory overload right now, but if someone told me we were the only two people in this room right now, I would believe them. She stops when she finds a spot, wraps my hands around her waist, and pulls me in tight behind her as she sways her body to the music. With every beat, she circles her ass into me and I'm sure she can feel how hard I'm growing behind her.

With my arms wrapped around her, I slowly bring one hand down and spread my fingers out across her thigh. I'm suddenly extremely aware of my own heartbeat. With every movement of her body, my thumb continues to rub up and down the length of her leg which feels smooth as silk under my touch.

Camila tilts her head to look up to me over her shoulder, the neon lights reflect off her distant but still gleaming eyes. She smiles, bringing her arm up and wrapping it behind my neck. All the air is sucked out of my lungs and it has nothing to do with the Vegas heat. When her head falls back onto my chest I lean down whispering in her ear. "You ready to get out of here, Camila?"

Camila

MY BRAIN IS AWAKE BUT MY EYES JUST CAN NOT FOLLOW suit. There is immense pressure at my temples and my mouth is so dry it feels like I could spit dust. At this point, I'm glad I can't open my eyes because I'm positive the room would be spinning.

Okay, Camila, just relax. Inhala exhala. As I take a full breath in, I'm hit with a refined and rich scent that causes the blood to start pumping through my body. I take a few more deep breaths before I realize Taylor smells like desert rain and cactus flowers, not whatever this woodsy—albeit comforting—scent is.

With my eyes still tightly shut, I begin trying to piece together last night. *Drag show, vodka, piano bar, vodka, dive bar where they threaten to cut off men's ponytails, vodka, rooftop bar, vodka. Dancing with a complete stranger who made every hair on my neck stand up when he touched my thighs, more vodka, leaving with said stranger. Fountain, Elvis, ice cream, Walgreens.*

The last few parts I'm only seeing snapshots of. Slowly peeling one eye open, I work through my disorientated brain to piece together my surroundings. I'm beyond grateful for the thick Vegas black-out curtains that are keeping this luxurious room dark when the sun would otherwise no doubt be blaring through the large windows. *Luxurious room.* I move to sit up, slowly, looking at the marble walls that surround the windows. *Luxurious room.* Beyond the bed, my eyes have to work hard to see past the doorway that opens up into a sitting room with a kitchen beyond that. *Luxurious room.*

This isn't my room. My heart rate increases to an alarming rate, and I can feel the bile creeping up my throat. *Inhala exhala.* Twisting my spine, I look over my shoulder. I'm greeted by a shirtless man with a body carved by Michelangelo himself. A close-cropped scruffy beard covers his face with the exception of where his full lips are coming through. His eyes are closed and it's a wonder how he ever has the strength to open them with the weight his long thick lashes must carry. Before I move to get up, I steal a peek at him—from the top of his unruly dark hair, down his thick corded arms to his large hands—and immediately I know I'm going to be sick. Sitting shining on his left hand is a gold band wedding ring.

What a fucking pig. I'm completely dressed, thank God. I don't have to rummage around looking for my clothes. I want nothing to do with a man who comes to Vegas and cheats on his wife. Although to be fair, I'm fairly positive we did *not* hook up, seeing as how I'm completely clothed and the only thing he seems to be missing is a shirt. But still.

As slowly as I can muster, while also trying not to throw up, I begin sliding out of the bed when a gruff voice startles me. "Normally I would be grateful you're trying to sneak out on me, and in most cases, I would pretend to still be sleeping while you did so, but since we didn't even have sex, I won't count this as a one-night stand."

Ugh, the nerve of this guy.

Since he's awake and I no longer have to move like I'm avoiding laser beams, I plant my feet firmly on the floor and stand. My fingers pinch the bridge of my nose as I try to stop the room from spinning before making my way to the edge of the bed. "Okay well, here's the thing," I clap my hands together in front of my body. "I'm so glad we didn't have sex," I say, pointing my clasped hands towards him. "I appreciate you not taking advantage of me, but I can't think of anything more disgusting than a man who cheats on his wife so…" In an unexpected event, he rears back as if I've slapped him across the face and then proceeds to look me up and down.

His scowl deepens. "I agree. I can't think of *anything* more foul than cheating." He enunciates the word 'anything' as he motions toward me.

I'm so confused by this whole conversation, and with the mass amounts of vodka still coursing through me right now, the last thing I want to be doing is having a conversation with this guy. He tilts his head and raises his eyebrows, his arm still stretched out to me. I look down and feel lightheaded when I spot the same shiny gold band on my left ring finger. I bolt to the bathroom, tripping over a high heel along the way, throw my face into the toilet bowl, and spill my guts.

Thick fingers hastily grab my hair and pull it away from my face. While a large hand rubs slow circles around my back. It takes me another minute to register what's happening and no sooner than that, I'm throwing up again. When I feel like there's nothing left, and I can be calm and rational I sit back and stare up at the beautiful man who I did NOT have sex with, but instead, just watched me vomit. Twice.

Mortified, confused, and on the verge of having a full-blown panic attack, I rest my back against the cool porcelain of the soaker tub behind me. "Okay." I exhale a deep breath. "So are you telling me, prior to last night, you were *not* married?"

"No. I am not married. I've never been married and I never plan on being married."

My cheeks fill with air before I blow it out and point to his hand. I watch as the color immediately drains from his face. "Is there room in that toilet bowl for me?" he asks.

I close my eyes and tip my head back to rest on the tub.

Miles—I think is his name—leans against the counter with his arms crossed taking a few breaths before bringing one hand up to rub his eyebrows. He must be a doctor because he is beyond calm when he says, "Tell me exactly what you remember."

I'm about to start listing off the same list I had made in my head maybe ten minutes ago when my phone starts buzzing on the floor just outside the bathroom door.

"Do you want that?" he asks me.

My face must read as shocked and panicked as I feel because Miles pushes himself off the counter, and steps outside to grab my phone. A shock zips through me when his fingers brush mine as he sets it in my hand. I offer him a tight-lipped but grateful smile because the only thing that could have made this more embarrassing was if I had to crawl across the bathroom floor in front of him to retrieve my phone.

The buzzing stops and the screen lights up with a missed call from Taylor. Several missed calls, actually. Before I can call her back my phone is buzzing again.

"Taylor…" I answer.

"Babe! What happened? You never showed up at the fountain which, by the way, they apparently stop running the show at midnight. Since when? I don't remember that." I put her on speakerphone as she continues to ramble about how she had to talk Jonas out of taking his clothes off because he wanted to go swimming. Opening my photo album, the last few photos and videos I have, although mostly blurry, confirm exactly what I feared happened. "Neither one of us knew what hotel he was staying at, and I tried calling you literally all night. Anyway, he stayed in our room if Miles is looking for him, but he said he can get us tickets to the best breakfast..." she continues talking as I turn my phone over to show Miles a picture of us at the wedding chapel... with Elvis.

Thirty minutes later and I've only just pulled myself up off the bathroom floor.

After reassuring Taylor that I was fine and would meet her in an hour to pack and check out, Miles sent the photos from my phone to his.

With my shoes clutched tightly in my hands, I walk out to the impressive living room. The velvet couch is soft under my legs when I sit down and begin working the buckles on my heels.

"Well, the good news is, these rings are bullshit," Miles says, stepping out of his room while pulling a shirt over his head. A small smirk hits his lips and I realize I've been caught drooling over his abs and the thick cut of the V lining his hip bones. I brush my hair back out of my face as he pulls the gold band off his finger. He holds the ring out to me between his thumb and forefinger. And then he crushes it.

"How—"

"It's plastic." He nods to me. "Check yours, I'd be willing to bet they were bought from the same gumball machine. Or keep it on." He shrugs his shoulders when I don't take it off.

"Just washing your hands two or three times, it's liable to turn your finger green though."

I look down at the little gold band and rip it off as if it's just burned me. Not for fear of it turning my finger green but because I can't believe I hadn't taken it off already.

"I'll have someone look at the photos and figure out where they were taken. Check out the chapel and see how legitimate this whole thing is."

I want to be concerned with how calm he is, but I've not said more than ten words in the last thirty minutes. It's like my brain can't choose between fight or flight and I'm stuck in freeze mode.

"What if it is?" I finally bring my eyes to his. "Legitimate, I mean. What if it is?"

"Then I'll have it taken care of." Again, just a casual shrug. The picture of unfazed.

I don't blink. I just stare at his back as he moves around the loveseat and heads into the kitchen.

"The coffee here is trash, but do you want some anyway?"

My cold fingers wrap around my phone on the marble coffee table. I stand, fighting the urge to limp in my shoes, and I head to the door, passing Miles in the kitchen on my way. Twisting the handle and giving it a pull, I turn around to face him. "I have to go," my breathy voice comes out no louder than a whisper.

Miles walks over, and pulls the door back, leaning his shoulder against it. "I'll be in touch."

I don't blink. I don't even look at him. I muster up the ability to nod once and then I head down the hallway.

If being in the car on a Sunday, driving home from Vegas hungover was bad, doing it after having accidentally gotten married is fucked.

"Just so you know when I said 'still plenty of time to make bad decisions,' I meant like spending $15 on one slice of pizza bad, not getting married to a stranger bad," Taylor says.

If I had the energy, I would reach over and hit her. But I just stay staring out the window.

It turns out Miles is in fact not a doctor, but a lawyer. Which would explain how he managed to be so unbelievably calm about the entire thing. I, on the other hand, came to Vegas to forget about the fact that I quit my job and to ignore my problems for two days and I'm leaving with a problem bigger than I could have ever imagined.

A sigh escapes me as I continue to look out the window, unable to even respond.

Taylor reaches across to me, grabbing my hand from my lap. "Mila, babe, it's going to be okay. Miles will figure it out, according to Jonas, 'Miles Cameron is the best lawyer in San Francisco,'" she says, in a goofy baritone voice. "He's going to take care of it. And honestly, he was hot as fuck."

That brings my attention from the vast nothingness of outside to finally look at her. "And what does that matter?"

"There could be worse things." She shrugs her shoulders with a devilish smile and I spend the next few hours making a list of things I can think of that are worse than waking up married to a hot stranger. Number one: trench foot.

Miles

Talan should already be waiting for me in my office. I texted him after the plane ride from Hell last night letting him know it was urgent. Jonas knew something was up, but thankfully he was still too hungover to annoy me about it and instead, he just slept the whole way back.

Walking through the offices of Smith & Mitchell this morning, my head is high. I should be walking with sweaty palms, and uncombed hair, given the terrible sleep I got last night, but today I'm going to do what I do best and get shit done. Talan to his credit is waiting outside my office door by the time I reach him. I motion to him, "Inside, now."

"Good morning, Mr. Cameron. Today is the big day." I like Talan enough, he's helpful in the sense that he always gets what I need, and even more, I like that he keeps my business private. Which is exactly what I need right now. Discretion.

When I finally figured out which chapel was responsible for allowing two completely intoxicated strangers to legally bind themself together, I went down there and secured all the paperwork. I couldn't be sure if the woman at the front desk was there the night before, but unfortunately for her, she was there yesterday morning and caught the brunt of my wrath.

I called a car to drive me back to my hotel, and for the first time, my facade about this whole debacle slipped when I saw the signatures—if you could even call them that. It's obvious we were very intoxicated. My knuckles turned white as I gripped that paper before slamming the file into the seat next to me.

All I could think about was the sheer panic in Camila's eyes. My body physically reacted to how scared she was and that alone was almost enough to unnerve me. I've worked with people in a million and one different situations. People cry, scream, laugh, panic, and find immense relief around me every day. I might not be a people person, but it comes with the job and I know how to fake it. I didn't become the best at what I do by getting caught up in other people's emotions. But yesterday morning, when I looked into Camila's eyes, I felt something tight in my chest that I couldn't recognize. I knew I needed to be the one to keep calm for the both of us.

So on the flight home last night, I reminded myself who I am, and what I'm capable of. And I have to deal with this on the day that they're supposed to announce my promotion. Fuck. Me. "Not a great morning, but you're going to help me fix it, Talan," I say, sitting down at my desk and opening my laptop to start the day as if it's any other.

"Yes, sir."

I explain the situation to Talan. Everything that happened the other night—or at least that I can remember—and everything I found out yesterday morning at the chapel. When I don't hear a response, I look up to find him staring at me, wide-eyed.

"Talan?"

"Yes, of course, Mr. Cameron." He shakes his head and

pulls out his phone. "I'm on it. I have a friend down at City Hall." His thumbs begin typing away. "We'll have this cleared up in no time."

"Thank you, Talan." I nod to his dismissal.

I work through lunch, but I catch Talan trying not to break out into a sprint, heading towards my office doors.

"Mr. Cameron, I spoke to my friend this morning and she was able to expedite the annulment, we just need to have these papers filled out and returned to her in sixty days and she'll be able to get it filed, and it will be like nothing ever happened." His chin is lifted high and he's beaming ear to ear as he waves the papers around. I sink into my chair and my muscles relax for the first time in twenty-four hours.

I've never been a man that shows a lot of emotion but I throw my hands up in the air and spin my chair around looking out my office window. I let out an exhale so deep it threatens to rattle the window. "Thank you, Talan."

"Would you like me to drop these papers off to *your wife*, personally or should I send them in the mail?" I don't have to see him to know he's proud of his little joke. And now that I have that weight off my shoulder I let out the closest thing to a small laugh.

"I'm sorry, your wife?" Samantha's booming voice has me very nearly jumping out of my skin. A ringing sounds in my ears, I stop breathing, and I'm certain I see black spots in my vision. Is this what a stroke feels like? Am I about to turn my chair around and admit to the woman who just told me, a little over forty-eight hours ago, that if I don't keep my shit together there will be no promotion? The promotion that they're supposed to announce to the entire office in less than two hours? Absolutely the fuck not.

Quickly, putting my courtroom face on, I turn around, "Samantha." I smile. "Nice to see you. Sorry I missed you this morning, but it's been nonstop in here." I gesture around my fairly empty desk.

"Cut the shit, Miles. What *wife* is Talan referring to?"

"This is awkward." I ignore the hammering at the back of my skull and she stares at me waiting for me to dig my own grave. Not today. "Look, Sam, I didn't want to make anyone uncomfortable, but I guess we're here now. Remember that trip I took to Kauai last year, that everyone made a big deal over? My first vacation in eight years?" She continues to stare blankly at me. Okay, definitely not going to make this easy on me. "My wife, Camila, wanted to do a small wedding, just her immediate family and my aunt came. I didn't want to tell anyone in the office, in case feelings were hurt. You know how it can be sometimes." I give her a playful wink.

"A year. You expect me to believe that you've been married a full year, and no one here knew?"

"Talan knew." I raise a hand to Talan who now looks like he's posing naked for a live painting class.

"And this, Camila? She's never come to a single fundraiser or event?"

"Why would she? I barely go to any of those events myself." Her eyes narrow in on me, "But you know what, I'll see if we can make the next one," I lie.

Samantha stalks over to me with the grace of a snake that just found a wounded rabbit.

"Oh, I'm sure you will."

I fight to not audibly gulp because if there's one thing I never do, it's show my tell. Samantha starts to retract from my desk and I'm still holding on to that breath and fake smile when she stops at the door and turns back to me. "Oh, and Miles? I came in to let you know that Smith had a family emergency to take care of this morning, so we're postponing announcing your official promotion until after the gala."

Through my tight-lipped smile, I manage to get out, "Not a problem."

"No. But it will be if I find out you're pulling some more shady shit." Her smile is sickly sweet but I keep my face neutral while she struts out of my office. She's halfway down the building before Talan and I both blow out a long breath. I roll my eyes and look at Talan, who looks like he's either about to be sick, or wants to run away and hide. I don't know and right now I don't really care.

"Mr. Cameron, I'm so sorry, sir, I had no idea she…"

I lift my hand, cutting him off. "It's fine Talan. I'll take care of it."

"What should I do about the papers?"

"Set a calendar reminder for fifty-nine days from today, I'll talk to Camila, but make sure that in fifty-nine days, you get those papers to her, no matter what."

"Yes, absolutely. I'll make sure of it. But, I'm sorry, sir. Why fifty-nine days?"

"Because it gives us just enough time to get the papers signed and turned in before the sixty-day mark, but also enough time for me to convince Sam that Camila is actually my wife."

Yep. Definitely having a stroke.

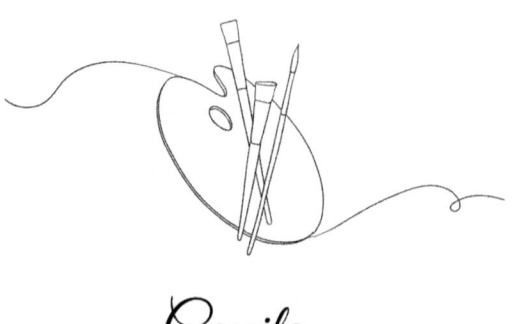

Camila

"Let's begin."

Confused, I look around the dimly lit room. One large ficus tree sits in the corner. Three out of the four walls that surround me are brick, with the fourth wall being a window overlooking the bay. I sit cross-legged on my mat, the thin material giving little cushion between me and the cool hardwood beneath me.

Mira, my yoga instructor, brings her hands together at her heart. She hasn't asked any questions about why I'm the only person here or why I'm here midday when I usually attend the first morning class.

Every class follows the same physical steps. Breath awareness, warm up, a series of postures, and a final resting pose, or savasana at the end, typically accompanied by some powerful words of affirmation or poetry. However, every class leaves me with a different mental clarity. Some sessions are better than others. Today as I round my back down to my mat to take my final resting pose, I have found zero comfort.

I cannot connect my mind to my body when my mind is racing elsewhere.

Mira's soft voice floats above me, "In your mind, repeat after me. I am enough."

I fucked up.

"I am a powerful creator."

I quit my job.

"Where I am right now is perfect."

I got drunk and married a stranger.

"I am worthy of love and belonging."

What have I done?

As I roll over, push myself up to a sitting pose, and bow, Mira looks at me, concern etched in every crevice of her wise face. Likely she can tell her affirmations were completely lost on me today. Since I don't want to talk about it I begin rolling up my mat. "Where is everyone today?"

"Midday can be a strange time. Some days many arrive, others only one."

I nod my head and move to gather the rest of my things.

"A different time for you to be here today, friend." It's not a question but I'm not oblivious to the curiosity in her voice.

I offer her a tight-lipped smile as I force my mat into my bag. "I have somewhere I need to be in fifteen minutes. I thought stopping here first would help me."

"And did it?"

I don't know if I would recognize help if it smacked me in the face right now. But it's not Mira's fault. And I can't stand to think that I would upset her, so I muster up a forced smile and bow my head. "Yes. Thank you." I turn on my heel and head towards the door.

"Camila." Her voice is still soft but commanding.

I pause before looking over my shoulder at her.

"Trust yourself to make the best decisions for you."

I don't allow myself to think the negative thought that wants to dance across the forefront of my mind when I know she's likely telling me this because she can sense everything I've been feeling.

THE SALTY AIR BRUSHES ACROSS MY FACE, TANGLING MY HAIR behind my head. The smells at the Wharf all start to blend together. From chocolates and fresh pizza to the Pacific Ocean splashing up beneath me.

Tourists move about all around me but my gaze stays focused looking out across the bay towards Alcatraz. I can clearly remember a family trip we took out here when I was a senior in high school. My dad ordered tickets for all of us to do the Alcatraz tour, but he accidentally ordered tickets for the night tour instead of the day one. My mom was too scared to go, so my dad had to bring us by himself. Taylor had come with us on that trip and we spent the two days after the creepy excursion tormenting my younger brother, Sebastian. It was on that trip that we decided we would apply to college here. My parents weren't happy with that decision, I'm sure they assumed it wouldn't pan out the way I had planned. I'll never forget their faces when I told them I was moving.

Originally, my only plan was to go to school, get a degree, get a successful job, and make everything that my parents went through for their children worth it. I've only ever wanted to live a life that would make them proud. And ever since I moved out here nine years ago, I've followed through on all those plans.

And yet somehow here I am. Staring out at the same bay that once held my dreams, but now with the dreadful feeling that maybe they were right. My options at this point are limited. I can't go back to that job, to a man who tore me down at every opportunity. I might be so lost that I don't know my own needs and or even my own desires right now, but I know enough to know that I will never go back to that job. That leaves almost an even more unbearable option. Going home.

I try to think of the disappointment on my parents' faces, when I tell them I quit my job, and have no idea what I'm doing, but my stomach bottoms out at the mere thought. I have meager savings that will only hold me over for a short time so unless I figure something out now, those fears are going to become my reality very soon.

I never would've thought that sitting on a bench waiting for the man I accidentally married would pale in comparison to another problem in my life, but here I am. When I got a text from an unknown number this morning that simply said, "Meet me at the Wharf at 5. -MC" I physically shook my head at how I hadn't even been thinking about that problem. I guess on the drive home I had a lot of time to think. And one thought that continued to circle was how calm Miles was. How—relatively—calm he kept me. So when he said he would take care of it, I trusted that.

I've never been married before, hell, I've barely had a relationship, unless you count casually dating in college and a boyfriend in high school for two months. I dated one other guy shortly after college but he broke up with me when he found out I had been faking my orgasms. I didn't think that would be the appropriate time to tell him I was positive most of the women he had been with had been doing the same.

But if Miles is ready to meet me, only twenty-four hours later, it must not be that difficult to have taken care of. Now if he could only fix my other issue too, then I might be willing to agree to his self-proclaimed title of *Best Lawyer in the City*.

Miles

Walking up to the pier, I'm momentarily distracted from my game plan by that untamed head of hair blowing in the wind. Distracted enough that I almost get run over by a hot dog truck. "Hey, man!" The driver throws his arm out.

My nostrils flare, but now isn't the time to pick a fight with the hot dog guy. My molars grind together as I storm across the walkway, making my way over to the pier where Camila is sitting on a bench. I don't know why seeing her knocks me so off balance but I need to regroup. I repeat the plan over again in my head. *Convince Camila it would be for her benefit to play the part of a happily married couple.*

This is no different than what I do every single day. Day in and day out, I get people to do what I need, and if I have to bluff, dupe, or blur some lines in the process to get it done, then that's what I'll do.

There's a deep wrinkle between her eyebrows. She's had time to let the full weight of what happened sink in now. The shock has no doubt worn off and I'm sure she's in full-on panic mode now. Unfortunately for me, that's only going to make my task more difficult. I straighten my tie with one hand and comb my fingers through my hair with the other. Schooling my facial features to remain calm, I close the distance between us.

"Camila."

Her head snaps up to me. And even though she's squinting from the sun and the breeze, I'm still taken aback when I look into her dark, coffee-colored eyes again. She looks casual in her leggings and an oversized, distressed, navy hoodie and my first thought is that she still somehow looks just as beautiful as she did two nights ago, dressed to the nines in a packed club. My second thought is, I hope that's not another man's sweater.

Where did that come from?

"Hi." She offers me a smile and raises her eyebrows at me. Only now do I realize I've just been standing here staring at her like an idiot.

I take the seat next to her on the bench and she follows my every movement with her eyes. "So," I pause, *clock in, game time.* "I wanted to meet you here because I had my assistant look into our situation and he said it's really not a big deal, however, it looks like legally we'll be married for the next sixty days or so, and then we can be granted an annulment and it will be like none of this ever happened." I remain stoic, my voice void of any emotion. I'm waiting for her to freak out, cry, or scream. To tell me that we need to find another way. But she surprises me by nodding her head and looking back out across the water.

"Okay. I guess that makes sense." Her voice is distant. Tired. "I don't know anything about marriage licenses' and annulments but you're the lawyer, so I trust you."

"You do?"

"Should I not?" Her head snaps back to face me.

"No, I mean, yes, you absolutely should. It's just rare for me to meet someone who gives their trust so easily."

A tight line forms from her lips and she offers nothing else but a shrug of her shoulders. What is happening? Who is this girl and why is she not freaking out? Holy shit. I might actually pull this off. Camila's hands are tucked inside her sleeves, which she's twisting into tight knots. The breeze has started to pick up, maybe she's just cold. I expect to see relief wash over her, especially after accepting this lie so well. But that deep crease is still there. This is it, this is my opportunity now.

"I know it's not ideal but it will be okay and it will be taken care of. In the meantime, I was..." I pause as she shakes her head, pulling her lips in between her teeth. Tiny beads of liquid form in the corners of her eyes. "Hey," I'm slightly thrown off by an unusual twisting in my chest. It's the same feeling that happened the other day when she took off running to the bathroom. I have no idea what I'm doing, or why I'm doing it, but I find myself lifting my hand and rubbing small circles across her back. I don't know what's more alarming, the fact that I can now identify this feeling as a need to comfort her or that I'm doing it like it's the most natural thing in the world.

"No. It's not you. I'm sorry. I don't mean to be crying in front of you like this." She sniffs, waving a hand in front of her.

"It's alright, you *are* my wife," I joke trying to make light of the situation because even though I watch people cry almost daily at my job, I've never felt a need to comfort any of them.

She tilts her head and gives me a look like *you, asshole.*

"When I told you I was celebrating quitting my job, I lied. I was actually trying *very* hard to forget about that fact for a night. Hence the mass amounts of alcohol." She tilts her head and her hands fall between her knees.

I give her some time and wait for her to continue.

"My parents…They have very high expectations for me." She hesitates, wiping her eyes with the back of her sleeve. "Anyway right now, I'm slowly running out of options. If I don't figure out my next move soon, I'm going to have to go home with my tail between my legs, and to be honest, that thought makes me feel as sick as waking up next to a stranger and finding out I'm married."

I appreciate her attempt at a joke but as I sit staring at this beautiful woman, listening to her cry makes me wonder if I shouldn't just call Talan and have him bring the papers down here right now. The last thing she needs is me conning her into being my fake wife for *my* benefit. I can feel the scowl on my face as I look out across the water. I have to remember everything I've worked for these last few years. Everything I've done to get to where I am and *why* I've done it. Those thoughts are all it takes, and I hear myself saying, "We could help each other out…" Her fidgeting body stills next to mine. "We could pretend to be married," I clarify.

"We are married." She huffs a small laugh and bumps her knee into mine. The movement is so casual but for whatever reason I'm hypersensitive to every touch from her. I look at her finally and say, "I mean, you could move in with me. You know, while you figure out your next move. You wouldn't have to tell your parents you quit your job."

I swear my heart feels like it's going to beat right out of my goddamn chest as those eyes fight against the wind to stare at me in utter disbelief. After a moment, Camila throws her head back and barks out a laugh. She grabs my arm with one hand where the warmth of her fingers burns through my suit, and wipes away the tears now streaming down her face with the other.

Too distracted by her hand on my arm, I just wait for her to calm down. When she finally looks back at me she sobers instantly. "Oh my god. You're serious?"

I nod, take a deep breath, and hold it in. I don't know if I'm more annoyed that she's laughing at me or because I can't bring myself to be mad at her for it.

"Well I'm not sure telling my parents I got drunk and married a man I just met is going to go over any better than telling them I'm a failure." Her fingers tangle with her necklace before pinching the gold pendant that hangs there and she begins zipping it side to side. "Although in the eyes of Mr. and Mrs. Sanchez, sadly, I think they might prefer the first option." She brushes the stray hairs that are wrapping around her face now. "This is too much for someone with my kind of anxiety," she murmurs to herself before looking back at me. "That doesn't explain what you would get out of this situation though?"

I'm down, but I'm not out. I can still come back from this.

"I work at a law firm." I shrug my shoulders. "It's not going to be hard for people to start figuring out that I'm legally married and, to be honest, it will look terrible on my end if people find out and I have to explain that I accidentally got married." That is at least one truth I can admit to.

"So, you would lie to them? You want me to lie?"

"It's not *lying*. Technically we *are* married. And will be for the next two months. It would just look better for me if the person I was married to actually looked as if she were my wife. And really, this is more for your benefit. Maybe I feel bad about what happened, and I'm looking for a way for you to benefit from this mistake. Some time to not worry about anything except finding a new job sounds pretty helpful to me." I've already said more than I should. Every good lawyer knows to only give necessary details and move on quickly.

Camila puts her head down in her hands, knees on her elbows, and shakes her head. It's the longest minute of my life, but I don't say anything else. I let her process, I'm confident that I've got her. Until she lifts her head and says, "I don't even know you. I can't move in with you and pretend to be married to you. This is absolutely insane."

It's hard to argue with logic. And this is exactly why some situations call for a trick here and there.

"Think of it as a mutually beneficial business arrangement. You don't want to tell your parents that you quit a job or admit defeat and move home, and I don't want any of my colleagues to find out I'm married and think it's fake." Bringing up her parents was a low blow on my end, I'll admit it. But I'm not looking at her like Camila, the girl I couldn't keep my eyes (and hands) off of for a night. I'm looking at her like Camila, the girl who holds the key to getting my name on the door.

"Don't you think this sounds kind of…complicated?"

The only thing that would complicate this situation is feelings and since I have no interest in those, I'm confident this arrangement can work out for the both of us.

"I don't think so. It will be strictly business. I have no interest in ever being in a relationship, so if that's something you're worried about, you can take it off the table. And look, I might skirt the truth about some things, so there's no point in lying about the fact that I obviously found you attractive the other night but as the marriage license shows, we both had too much to drink. I'm able to keep things completely professional between us from now on, and if it makes you feel better, I can have my assistant draw up some sort of contract for us. A business agreement if you will."

Camila doesn't say anything for a long time.

Is this what my partners feel like in a courtroom when they lose? I've never experienced a loss like this before. I'm about to get up and leave. She clearly thinks I'm insane. And at this point, I'm right there with her. I don't know what I was thinking.

Placing my hand on Camila's knee and giving it a light squeeze, I throw out one last hail Mary. "Hey, you know what? Never mind, don't worry about it. Do me a favor though, and get me your parents' address in case I have to send the paperwork there."

With that, I give her leg one last bump with my knuckles and stand to leave. I cannot believe I'm giving up on this. She's still sitting there staring at where my hand just left her leg as I walk around the bench, pausing to look around so I don't run into anything or anyone this time.

"Wait." It's barely more than a whisper but Camila's voice stops me dead in my tracks.

That's twice today now that I've stopped breathing. Turning around to face Camila, the wind blows her hair in all directions now. "Okay," she breathes.

And my heart all but falls out of my ass. "Okay?" I ask.

"Okay."

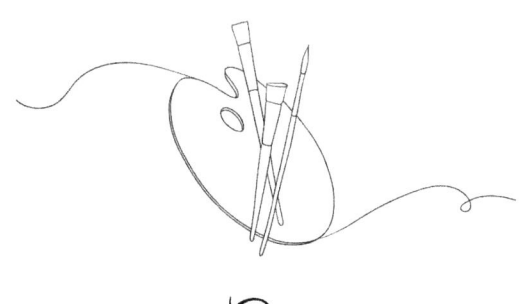

Camila

My eyes are puffy but have adjusted to the dark room. The only light is the blue glow emitting from my laptop that's cracked open and playing my 'Let Me Be Dramatic' playlist. I'm sitting on the blanket-covered couch in my living room trying to figure out how I got here. And I don't mean here on this couch, I mean *here*, as in my life. This time last week I had a job. A job that gave me Sunday-Friday headaches because I was in a constant state of anxiety. But I had a job. My parents were at home not having to worry about me; they were proud. And now here I am, an accidentally married, jobless disappointment, waiting for Taylor to come home to see me staring at a blank TV.

The jingle of keys rattles just outside the doors and I have only a split second to wonder what kind of reaction she'll have to my newest and greatest surprise.

"Ooompfh." Actually, she's not even going to notice me after running into all those boxes in front of the door.

"Hey, Mila," she says cautiously. "What's ah...what's going on here?"

Looking over at my best friend I must have the word

terrified written on my forehead because she comes rushing over to sit beside me. I believe there are many different kinds of friendships but there's a certain comfort that comes from a friendship like ours. One where we can be ourselves, completely vulnerable. So as soon as I feel her arm wrap around me and pull me into her side, I let it all out.

I tell her about my fear of having to move home, meeting with Miles, his idea to play out this marriage for a while, how I agreed to move in with him, and how he agreed to pay our rent so Taylor wouldn't have to worry about it. Oh yeah, I made him tack that on at the end. The moment I'm done word vomiting and I look into those big green eyes, it confirms to me that this idea is even crazier than I initially thought.

Something about Miles's face, even with that permanent scowl, made me feel safe though. It made me think this plan could work and that maybe it wasn't as crazy as I initially thought. As soon as I agreed, he told me his assistant would work out the details to have my things packed up tonight and movers would come by, along with his driver Wills, to pick me up and move my things in later tomorrow.

"And what is he getting out of this?" Her skeptical face tells me she thinks I've agreed to be his Pretty Woman.

"I think he's mostly just doing it to help me out because I cried in front of him," I confess. "But also, I don't think he wants his coworkers to find out. I guess it doesn't look good to be the guy that's married but…not really."

"So all you have to do is pretend to be married to the hottest grump on the West Coast?"

My bottom lip is raw from how hard I've been chewing it. I look around our tiny one-bedroom apartment with all its color and random art. From street vendors and swap meets to some of the most exquisite galleries around the world. Blankets, floor pillows, and flowers litter the place. The most expensive things we own are kitchen appliances and tools that Taylor calls her babies. I call them the cities' shiniest pickpocketers because on more than one occasion she's bought an appliance before paying rent and we've had to make up the money somewhere else. But she loves to cook, and it's one of the only things she's stuck to doing as long as I've known her, so I let her indulge in it.

Our space isn't a lot, I have a twin bed in the bedroom, and Taylor sleeps on the pull-out couch in the living room but it's *our* space. It's filled to the brim with things we love, and now just thinking about leaving her here, I start sweating and I have to squeeze my hands to stop them from trembling.

As if she can sense my panic, Taylor scoots closer and begins rubbing my shoulder. "Camila, I'm not going to lie, I am a little concerned with who you are and what you've done with my best friend."

"I am too," I say honestly.

"But I'm gonna be honest, it doesn't seem like that bad of a gig—"

I pull away from her grip. "You can't be serious?"

"I am *nothing* if not always serious," she deadpans and I have to fight the urge to roll my eyes. "But, are you worried about how complicated this could get?"

Immediately I shake my head, "No. Obviously, I was attracted to Miles the night we met, but he made it very clear that he is not now or ever looking for a relationship. This is only a business deal to help us both out."

"First of all, who said anything about a relationship?"

"Well since I'm not known for a casual hook-up…"

"Yet!" she points a finger at me and I fix her with a stare.

"Ever. Anyway, I only agreed so I wouldn't have to call my parents and tell them I would see them sooner than Christmas this year because I quit my job."

"Listen, babe, I would sell pictures of my feet covered in peanut butter before I let you move home and face the supposed wrath of Elena and Diego. "

I swipe her with the back of my hand. "Peanut butter?" I squeal. "You're disgusting. And I hate to break it to you, but you would need to stop investing in food processors and start investing in some pedicures for that business to pop off."

"Hey!" She holds up her tired-looking feet. "First of all, don't knock other people's kinks, and second…people would pay for deez toes," she says, wiggling her toes back and forth.

I laugh at her and feel some of the weight starting to leave my chest. I heave a sigh and lean back into the couch.

"Listen, Mila, it's basically two free months for you to focus on nothing but what your next move is. And who knows, maybe without the pressure of needing to find something in some stuffy office, you might be able to find something you actually enjoy."

I don't know that I'll ever get that lucky. But I give her a smile anyway.

"Thank you, Taylor." I embrace her and she gives me one of her too tight hugs.

"Anytime."

Her hand still rubs my back. "You're not just saying all this so you can sleep in my room for the next few weeks, are you?"

"Such a skeptic, you are. But I'm definitely sleeping in your room." I laugh and pull back. Her hands hold my shoulders tightly and her eyes focus on mine. "But I also meant what I said about figuring out your next move with the hot lawyer. It sounds like a no-brainer."

It sounds so simple when she says it like that, but I know that living with Miles Cameron is going to be anything but simple.

Squinting up into the setting sun, I crane my neck all the way back, till I find the top of the high-rise building. "Excuse me, Miss."

To my left one of the movers is trying to get by with a handful of my boxes in hand. "Sorry." I move to step out of the way before following the next mover into the building. He holds the door to a private elevator, I look left and right.

"Miss?"

"Oh. Um..." I turn my face into a smile. "Thank you."

The ride up is quiet and long. My stomach flutters and I can't stop tugging at my sleeves. When we finally make it to the top and the doors slide open I'm confident if my jaw fell any lower it would shatter on the light-washed wood floors beneath me.

I step through the entryway, into the largest space I've ever seen in the city. Bright orange light beams through the floor-to-ceiling windows that make up the entire back wall.

The minimal living room takes on a hazy golden color. My fingers glide along the back of the oversized sectional as I move over to the windows. The Golden Gate Bridge acts as the centerpiece of the space. In between the concrete fireplace and sectional sits a low lightwood square table with only a small potted plant sitting on it. Despite looking like a model home and no one actually living here, it is unbelievably calming and inviting.

To the left of the elevator is a beautiful chef's kitchen with an island the size of my old bedroom. More natural wood and sleek dark iron fixtures accentuate the room. There are exposed shelves with beautiful handcrafted ceramic mugs and vases. The entire open floor is serene, with natural elements covering the space from top to bottom. But my eyes go straight to the wall above the dining table. Hanging above the built-in bench is one of the most colorful and exquisite paintings I've ever seen. It's an oil painting with vibrant greens and gold. Full of texture, making up banana palm fronds. A stark contrast to the rest of the space but no less stunning.

I've been standing in front of the palm leaf painting for a while when I notice the movers coming down a set of stairs past the kitchen. I follow them but stop short when they all get back in the elevator, offering a quick wave before the doors slide close.

The cold brush of the kitchen island sends a chill down my arms as I brace myself against it. "Now what?" I whisper to myself.

"They were told not to touch your things, so you could unpack if you wish."

A scream escapes me as I jump back clutching the counter tightly behind me. An older woman with jet black hair that's only just begun to gray comes to stand next to me, dropping a basket of kitchen towels on the island.

"I'm sorry." I place a hand on my chest. "I didn't realize anyone else was here."

"That's alright, honey. No one else besides me usually is." She smiles, shaking out one of the linens.

I scratch my forehead and then reach my hand out towards her. "I'm Camila."

She takes my hand and gives a rather firm shake for someone her size. "Rosa," she replies with a smile. "I'm leaving once I've finished these linens, but there's dinner in the fridge for you and I'll show you to your room on my way out."

"Oh. I should probably wait for Miles to come home." Even though I'm confused about what the proper etiquette is in this situation. This situation being that I just moved into my fake husband's penthouse.

Still smiling, Rosa shakes her head. "You'll be waiting a long time. Mr. Cameron doesn't usually come home until very late. I'll show you to your room, and then you'll eat."

I hope my face isn't betraying me and shows more gratitude than confusion as I nod my acceptance.

Rosa has left me in a beautiful guest suite and I'm noticing a theme with minimal decoration. The room has two walls of floor-to-ceiling windows, an oversized forest-green bed across from them, and a side table with only an empty vase and lamp. There is a beautiful large oak wood empty dresser and hanging above it is another remarkable oil painting, this one of elephant ear palm fronds. I step into the ensuite bathroom and roll the dimmer switch, lighting up the spa-like space that appears like it's never been used before. I knew Miles had to be well off and obviously I didn't expect to be sharing a room with him in this sham marriage, but I wasn't prepared for this level of extravagance either. I make my way back into the bedroom, sit down on the floor, and open one of my suitcases. I brace my hands on the frame of my luggage when for the first time, what I'm actually doing begins to sink in.

HAVING ALREADY SHOWERED BEFORE I LEFT MY APARTMENT, all I had to do was put away some clothes and toiletry items. I told the movers not to pack any of my art and left most of my personal items behind as well. I tiptoe down the stairs, in case

Miles has come home and I didn't hear him. When I reach the second to last step my heart rate picks up. *Inhala exhala. He invited you here, stick to the plan. You're fine.* My ears strain to pick up any sounds other than my heavy breathing. I would have just stayed up in my room all night to prolong the inevitable, but my growling stomach forced me out. I peek around the corner into the kitchen and the muscles in my shoulders relax when I realize I'm alone.

The quiet air in this place is defining. I open the music app on my phone and press play on my 'Girls Night In' playlist.

I welcome the cool air of the fridge on my face as I look to see what Rosa left for dinner. I'm not sure if it's from the long day I've had, or if Rosa really is just that incredible, but I find glass Tupperware of the most delicious-looking lasagna I've ever seen with reheating instructions on top.

I stand at the kitchen island, one foot propped up on my other leg as I scoop bites of pasta onto the homemade bread. Movement out of the corner of my eye causes me to pause with the perfect bite halfway to my mouth. Miles steps out of the elevator and stops dead in his tracks with that signature scowl. It really should be intimidating but it's having an oddly different effect on me. It's at this moment that I realize maybe I shouldn't be down here.

"I'm sorry," I begin.

His eyes scan my body up and down before shaking his head and he moves towards a door off to the right of the elevator.

"I wasn't sure when you would be home, and Rosa told me to eat," I say looking around.

"I'm glad you were able to get settled in." He drops his bag inside the door before closing it again. "I'm just not used to someone being here when I come home."

My playlist is still going and it dawns on me then, that I'm wearing pink silk pajama shorts and a tight black cropped tank top. He moves slowly to the opposite end of the island and I'm frozen in my spot. The only thing moving is my heart as it erratically bounces around my chest. I don't miss the way his eyes roam over me. Pausing a brief moment at my bare legs and then a longer moment at my breasts, which I absolutely do not need to look at to know that my nipples are welcoming him home as well. The way his eyes trail my body is almost obscene. Something about his gaze heats my body in a way that's absolutely foreign to me, but for whatever reason I couldn't move or turn away right now if I tried.

His thumb runs along his bottom lip before he clears his throat and pulls his eyes from me, taking my breath with them. I wait in loud silence as I watch him get his food from the refrigerator. While it heats, his fingers grip the knot of his tie and he pulls it loose. A moment later his jacket is gone and he starts rolling up his sleeves. If he's going to be brave enough to let his eyes roam over my thighs and breasts, I'm not going to be shy about staring at his forearms—tan with dark hair dusting them.

Three words. Forearm vein porn.

Now it's my turn to clear my throat. "You have a beautiful home," I blurt out.

"Thank you. My designer was pretty upset with me, she could never shut up about how much more she wanted to do with the space."

"No. I like it." I say looking around. "It's very…you."

"Quiet?"

I laugh, feeling a little more relaxed. "I was going to say *polished.*"

The corner of his mouth lifts half an inch. Not a full smile, but holy shit, if he looks that good wearing the tiniest smirk known to man, I'm not ready for a full-fledged grin. Before I go down this road of ogling him again I try to think of something safe to talk about. "Umm, and the paintings." I point to the one above the dining table. "They're gorgeous. Who are they by?"

His brows pull together and immediately that half a smile vanishes entirely. "I don't know."

I'm getting whiplash. First by my body betraying me under his gaze. Then all it takes is for slight movement from the corner of his lip and I feel it in my chest. Now we're back to grumpy Miles and it's making my stomach turn. I'm never going to survive this.

"So, how is this going to work? Am I going to be like Belle and be locked in my room for the next two months? It's a lovely room, don't get me wrong, but if you want to convince people at your work that I'm really your wife, do I need to drop off your lunch or something?"

He walks around the counter until he stands only two inches in front of me. I hold my breath when he lifts his hand up to my neck. The thick pads of his fingers spark against my collarbone when he runs the chain of my necklace between his fingers. I suppress the urge to lean into his touch when he adjusts the gold clasp to the back.

"Something like that." His words are soft and lazy when he drops his hand back to the counter. All I can do in this moment is pray to whoever will listen, that this man who makes a living off reading people, can't see that I've completely stopped breathing. His eyes narrow in on my neck before he looks away and I remember that I'm here because I've made every choice with zero thought the last few days, and I need to get my head back on straight.

I straighten my spine and lift my chin. "Okay then. I'm heading to bed." Internally I roll my eyes at how my breathy voice betrays my false confidence. I have to actively slow my pace as I head towards the stairs so Miles doesn't think I'm trying to run away.

"Camila." His voice startles me and I pause, slowly turning around to see his eyes studying me. "Don't stay locked up in your room." He shakes his head as if he was going to say something else and I blink once before heading off to my room.

The sheets and duvet cover on my bed are tucked in tight along all the edges. When I slide in I feel like it's giving me a comforting hug. The pillow is crisp and cool under my face and before the darkness consumes me, I'm left wondering how I'm supposed to get back to myself while living with a man who has me thinking and feeling things that are completely foreign to me.

Miles

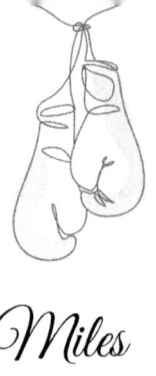

"Okay, great, so McClellan will take the lead on that." Samantha sits at the head of the conference room table, closing a binder of papers. "The last point I have for you this morning is if you have yet to get your tickets for the fundraiser gala next Saturday, please see Mark up at the front before you leave today."

Jonas bumps my knee under the table and I snap my head towards him where he's giving me the *what the fuck* eyes. I've been sitting in the world's most boring mid-week meeting for over an hour. That's not even fully true, I don't know if the meeting was boring or not. I have no idea what this meeting has been about because I haven't been able to stop thinking about my new house guest. Every time I try to tell myself to focus, it's because I've caught myself thinking about Camila and how she looked standing in my kitchen. I'm not surprised by my attraction to her, after all, it's kind of what got me in this situation to begin with.

I am however surprised that I haven't been able to stop thinking about her. When I slid that dainty chain across her neck last night, I'm positive she held her breath for a few seconds. I definitely shouldn't be thinking about her this way, since she's living with me and that will only complicate things. But when I saw her mouth part like she wanted more from that touch, for a moment I wanted to give it to her. I imagined pulling her into me and crushing her lips with my own, holding her face with one hand while the other tangled in her hair. I could imagine her hands trailing down my stomach, her fingers sliding along my waistband. That touch would be enough to make me lift her up by her ass, her legs wrapping around my waist, arms around my neck as I walked her back to the couch without breaking the kiss. And then I remembered the line: *Get shit done but never cross the line.*

Everyone else has filed out of the room except Sam who is still sitting at the head of the table. I gather my things and head towards the door. I get one foot in the hallway before her commanding voice stops me. "Miles." I turn to face her. "I look forward to meeting your wife at the fundraiser next weekend." I give one nod before passing a slack-jawed Jonas on my way back to my office.

I can feel Jonas hot on my heels as we enter my office.

"Okay so… do you want to tell me why Samantha thinks that my best friend of sixteen years is married, or should I start the amputation now? Because let me tell you, on the list of things I had planned today, giving up my left nut would have been on that list before finding out you were *married?*"

I open my laptop and begin pulling up files. "I need you to send me the notes from the meeting," I say, ignoring his question.

His eyes widen as he looks at me like I've grown a second head. "One, I didn't take notes. And two, are you going to answer my question?"

"I might have zoned out, but I saw you typing the whole time."

Jonas digs the palms of his hands so far into his eyes that if I had the energy to

spare, I might be concerned for him. "I was typing out the lyrics to a Pearl Jam song, asshole. I didn't want to look like *you* and be completely obvious I wasn't paying attention." He throws his hands in the air. "Now dude..talk!"

The thing about Jonas is he might be a pretty, party boy, but when your ass is shoved in a corner, he's the only guy I would trust to be by my side.

THINKING BACK TO THE SUMMER BEFORE I STARTED HIGH school, I can remember running home, in the hot afternoon sun. I was flying up the stairs, taking the steps two at a time up to my room. I stopped in the doorway when I found my mom packing. Not that her packing was unusual, my dad traveled a lot for baseball, but she was packing my things. When I asked what was going on she said we were leaving and staying with my Aunt Grace for a while. I could tell my mom was upset, and we had always been close so I knew I could have asked at the time, but she seemed so hurt, beyond talking. So I silently started packing my things alongside her. We left that night and never went back. She later explained that she and my father would be getting a divorce, but that when he was home I was more than welcome to spend time with him, which I did. It wasn't until the following summer I found out they had gotten a divorce because my father had been cheating on her. I refused to see him after that. I resented him and even if my mother could forgive him, I couldn't.

By the time I got to law school, my mom was battling her second bout of breast cancer and wasn't doing well. I would fly home on the weekends that I could and we were lucky enough that my aunt was around to help out as well. My dad reached out a few times, but I never answered. Though I know my mom talked to him, I later found out he was the one paying for her medical treatments. But I still had no desire to have any kind of relationship with him. I was angry that my beautiful mother with the kindest heart was suffering while this asshole got to live a long healthy life with his new wife.

My father always engrained the mentality "do whatever it takes to be the best" in me. When I was younger I wanted to be the best to make him proud, As I got older I wanted to be the best to shove it in his face that I got here without him. That he couldn't claim any of my greatness. He had to watch me become successful and know that he had no part in any of it. But the worse my mom got, the more I struggled. I began suffering in my classes, I pushed the one friend I ever cared about away. I was antisocial in a small class where making connections was everything, and I was drowning.

My mother's funeral was a blur, I don't remember much, except there was a lot of food that no one really ate. And Jonas. I'm still not sure to this day how he found out about my mother or the funeral because I definitely didn't tell him, in fact, I had been a real dick to him a few weeks before, more so than usual. But he showed up. He showed up for me when I needed someone more than I knew. He embraced me in a silent hug, and we've been best friends ever since.

So I close my laptop and recount the story of what happened last weekend. From Sam finding out the next day to how I conned Camila into thinking this was for her benefit.

And since I was laying it all out there already, I told him about last night too. I don't know why, maybe I was hoping he would be able to give me some clarity, or a pep talk. But instead, he blew out a long breath, sank back into the couch putting his arms behind his head and with the biggest smile his face could handle, he said, "Oh. You are *so* fucked."

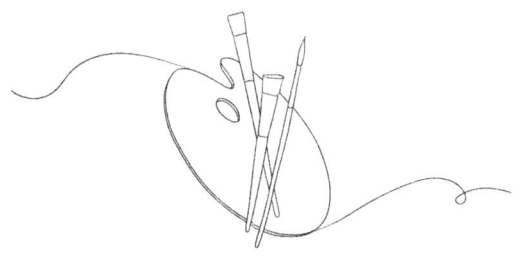

Camila

My first night here was...weird. I'm not necessarily uncomfortable, which is surprising but the whole situation is just not normal. I don't think either of us was quite prepared for how to act. The past few nights I've had dinner with Rosa —although she doesn't actually eat with me. So really I've been eating alone and I've been in bed before Miles gets home. Tonight I'm determined to stay up as late as I need to in order to see him. I have to believe that if we can just find some common ground, maybe we could build some kind of friendship and it will make everything less awkward.

I can't even use his house as a way to learn anything about him, aside from the fact that he has palm frond paintings in every room even though he seems to not care for them very much. He either doesn't have any personal items or he keeps them all in his room or his home office. I've made a mental note of the intense coffee setup he has in the kitchen and judging by the pair of sneakers I've seen by the door I'm assuming he does some kind of workout in the mornings before he goes into the office. Other than that, everything about him is still a complete mystery to me.

While Miles is at work, *being successful,* I've spent the last few days staring at my computer, willing it to show me a job worthy of telling my parents about. But also one that I won't completely hate. And every day it's the same routine—after a few hours of staring, I always find myself giving up and scrolling through some of my favorite artists' social media.

Tonight I'm curled up on the couch, scrolling through some local street artist page I just found, when I look up to find Miles coming out of the elevator.

"Oh. Hey..." I look at the time. "You're home kind of early."

"Sorry to interrupt your alone time."

I can't tell if he's annoyed with me or maybe it has something to do with work, but between trying to fight my attraction to him and trying to figure out his mood swings, it's too much for me. I had planned on staying up to have dinner with him, but I didn't think that maybe he wouldn't want to have dinner with me. Instead of waiting around to find out, I chicken out, gather my things, and start heading towards the stairs to my room.

"Did you eat?" His voice surprises me.

"Yes," I lie.

"And then did you spit it back out and put it perfectly on this plate?" He holds out the two plates of food Rosa left for us.

I roll my eyes so hard I can hear my mom telling me *'They're going to get stuck like that"*. "You just seemed like maybe you weren't in the mood for company tonight, so I was just going to head back to my room."

The crease between his eyebrow deepens but the corner of his lip pulls up ever so slightly as he starts reheating both plates. "You're not company, Camila. Have a seat."

Sitting across from Miles while we eat our dinner in silence together might actually kill me. Next time I will gladly choose to starve to death in my room before I choose to listen to the sounds of our silverware hitting the plates and our silent chewing. I can't take it anymore.

"Tell me something," I blurt out.

I'm met with a blank stare.

"I mean, I know you're apparently some kind of big shot lawyer, you prefer a minimalist design aesthetic, and I think you might be a runner." I squint, pointing my fork at him. "But other than that, I don't really know anything about you. Tell me something about yourself." When he hesitates, I'm about to give up and excuse myself from this awful dinner.

"I'm thirty-six, I went to Stanford Law School, the design *aesthetic* is called Japandi and I hate cats."

With my eyebrows practically in my hairline, but somehow unable to keep the smile off my face, I say, "Wow. You really dug deep there, Mr. Cameron."

He tilts his head and his face is a mix between confusion and annoyance.

I hold my hands up in mock surrender, shaking my head. "I don't know if I can handle that kind of info dump. You're getting a little *too* personal for me here."

I swear I can see a smile start to crack.

"Alright, smartass. Let's talk about you."

I fold my arms on the table in front of me, as if to challenge him. "Unlike you, I can tell you about myself without sounding like I'm at a job interview."

He swipes his hand out as if to say *please, enlighten me.*

"Well, where do I even begin?" I smile. "I'm twenty-seven, an Aries, I grew up in Miami, I have a younger brother, I like art…" I'm ticking things off each of my fingers now.

"So you're an artist? What do you do, finger painting?"

"*No,*" I say, dramatically. "I didn't say I liked to create my own art. Not that I didn't try when I was younger," I admit. "But a few too many flower vases that came out looking like bongs told me to just stick to appreciating art and stop trying myself."

Ever the talkative one he just nods and motions for me to continue.

"Let's see, I'm an enneagram two, my three items if I'm stuck on a deserted island are sunscreen, a knife, and a hammock. Oh, and my favorite foods are breakfast pastries."

"Breakfast pastries?"

"Yeah, you know? Croissants, scones, muffins…pain au chocolat?" I sound like the evil French villain in a kids movie. "I could eat any and all kinds for breakfast, lunch, and dinner, and be happy."

Miles puts his fork down and leans on his forearms across the table to match me. "Well, as *insightful* as this has been…"

"Knowing my sign alone gives you more information than you gave me," I interrupt.

"Knowing your enema or whatever," he waves his hand around, "and your sign means nothing to me. I don't even know my own sign," he says.

I rear back shaking my head, because I'm sure I heard him wrong. "*One,* it's ennea*GRAM,* and two, how do you not know your own sign?" I practically shout at him.

He shrugs and picks up his fork to continue eating. Between bites, he says, "I'm sure someone has told me before, but I forgot. I don't believe in any of it."

I roll my eyes so hard they might actually get stuck. "Well, you give off major Leo vibes. Maybe Scorpio because of the whole grumpy act you've got going on, but if I had to put money on it I'd say you are a Leo. When is your birthday?"

"August 1st."

I smile.

"What?"

"Nothing." I shake my head.

"What does that mean?"

"It doesn't matter, you don't believe in it anyway. Right?"

"You know I can google this right?" He goes to reach for his phone but I'm quick to place my hand on top of his, and what I meant to be a silly little game of keeping him guessing has instantly turned into something else. I go to move my hand but he catches my wrist in his, and I can't take my eyes off where his thumb starts rubbing with a feather-light touch at the most sensitive part of my inner wrist. I can hear my heartbeat in my ears and when I look up, his eyes are watching where his finger moves too.

Slowly Milles pulls his hand back. To try and ease some of the tension I inhale deeply. "Next we'll have to figure out what enneagram number you are."

I stand to bring my plate to the kitchen. As I pass him, his eyes connect to mine and I'm silently begging him to say something. To tell me this isn't in my head, that I'm not the only one confused by this situation and what I'm feeling.

Instead, he says, "There's a fundraiser I have to attend next weekend, and we're both expected to be there."

And even though he doesn't say it, I know this is only for show for his colleagues. And for some reason, I'm upset when I remember it isn't for anything more.

So I nod my acceptance and head off to my room.

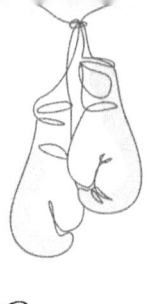

Miles

"Do you know if you'll be looking for silver or gold today, sir?"

I open the text thread to make sure I haven't missed a message from Camila.

ME

> We need to pick out a wedding ring. Can you meet me at the jeweler's on 31st later?

CAMILA

> I have some rings, I can just throw one on.

ME

> Unfortunately, if anyone sees you walking around with a mood ring on it's going to blow our cover.

CAMILA

> Ok, first of all, it's an amethyst, not a mood ring. And second, yes 🙄 I guess I'll meet you there.

ME

> Wills will be waiting downstairs for you at 3, we have a 3:30 appointment

It's 3:45 and I wouldn't be surprised if Camila decided not to show up. Jonas is always complaining, telling me I could stand to be a little nicer over text, and in general.

"I'm not sure, let's pull out both. I want her to have all the options," I say to the sales manager.

He goes into a back office and I look around the dimly lit shop. I pass rows of cases, making my way up to the front of the store and I'm surprised to find Camila standing outside my car talking with Wills through the driver's window. Her hair flows softly down her back and she's wearing jeans with a flannel button-up wrapped around her waist and a tank top that hugs her body like it's painted on. My eyes scan every inch of her. I've come to the conclusion that Camila could wear a paper bag and I would still be attracted to her.

When I came home last night and found her curled up on the couch—hair up in a messy bun and her oversized t-shirt covering her tiny shorts, giving the illusion that she wasn't wearing anything under it—I completely forgot about asking her to come with me to the jeweler today.

She's still talking to Wills as if we don't have an appointment to get to, so I stalk over to the front door and push it open a little harder than necessary. She smiles and waves to Wills. My eyes narrow on her, "What?" she asks.

"You're late."

"I was here at 3:30, the door was locked." She throws a pointed stare at me. Making me feel like a fucking idiot because she's right, the door *was* locked. I called the shop yesterday and paid extra for a private appointment. I told myself it was to be cautious. In the event that we run into anyone who thinks she should have already had this ring and that's what I'll tell Camila if she asks. But really I think it's just that I don't want to be bothered by other people when I'm with her. "Plus, Wills and I were in the middle of an interesting conversation." I'm not jealous that she's having conversations with my driver but I'm sure as fuck annoyed. I hold the door open for her as she walks in and I brush her comment off as if I wasn't aware.

The sales manager is still in the back, so we walk around the store peering in all the cases on the floor.

"So…how was your day?" she tilts her head, batting her eyelashes at me with faux sweetness. I can tell she's annoyed with my shortness and no doubt the pissed off face I've been wearing all day isn't very appealing either. I shake off the swarming thoughts and try to regroup.

"I'd bore you to tears if I told you. Plus, I'd rather hear about your day."

She scoffs, waving a hand. "My day was filled with looking at a lot of really awful job search websites."

"No luck on the hunt then?"

"I hated everything."

"Maybe you're not looking at the right places."

A sad sound escapes her lips, "Yeah, maybe."

I feel my eyebrows draw together as concern crosses my mind. Concern that she isn't happy and concerned with the feeling in my chest of wanting to erase the sad look on her face.

"Ah, Mrs. Cameron. Welcome. I've pulled quite the assortment for you, today. I hope you will both be very pleased." The sales attendant lays out a black box filled with silver and gold bands and diamonds of every shape and size. "Do you know if you prefer gold or silver?" he asks.

"Gold. I don't have the skin tone for silver."

"I can't imagine you look bad in anything." When her head snaps to me I realize I've said that out loud.

"Wonderful, well let's try some of these then, and we'll go from there."

Camila picks up one of the smaller oval cut diamonds on a thin gold band with two small round diamonds on either side of the center stone. She gasps. "This is insane."

I'm confused. "You don't like it?"

"It's stunning, but it's so big."

"Is this two carats?" I ask the man. He nods with a smile. "It's only two carats, Camila."

"What do you mean *only*?"

I hold up a four carat emerald cut on a diamond-encrusted band.

Her nose scrunches up and she shakes her head, "If I just won the Superbowl, that would definitely be the one for me."

The salesman rolls his lips between his teeth, trying to hide his smile.

"Okay. I wasn't aware I bought a ticket to your comedy show today," I say, setting the ring back down.

Her melodic laugh eases any tension that was in the room before.

"So you like this one?" I wrap my fingers around her small hand holding the first ring. She purses her lips as she thinks. "It's a far cry from your *amethyst,*" I whisper in her ear.

"It's for my anxiety!" She playfully shoves her shoulder into me.

This is the second time she's mentioned having anxiety. I assumed before she was just stressed about our situation but maybe it's something more. Since I don't understand, and now doesn't feel like the appropriate time to ask, I just place my hand on the small of her back. "Well if that's the one you like, that's the one we'll get."

"Miles, it's too much."

"Nothing is too much for you." Her eyes meet mine and I can almost feel my own pupils dilating. What the fuck am I saying and why do I keep saying it out loud? Still, I don't take my eyes off her. Never let them see you sweat, right? "We'll need a band as well."

"I have a moonstone band too, that could look nice together," she teases me.

"What kind of stone don't you have?"

We share a smile and I look at the sales manager who is now fighting a look of amusement and confusion as I realize all of this is the trivial stuff people who are actually married would already know about each other.

Thankfully I'm paying him enough that he doesn't question anything and instead heads to the back to grab the matching wedding band.

"What about you?" she asks.

"What about me?"

"What kind of ring are we getting you?"

"I picked mine out almost quicker than you."

She gives me a smile and I realize I would do anything to be on the receiving end of her smile.

"I DIDN'T ANTICIPATE THAT BEING SO QUICK. I'LL HAVE TO call Wills. It might take him some time to get back since I sent him out for the afternoon."

"Okay. Do you want me to wait with you?"

My brows tug together. "Were you planning on going somewhere else?"

Her mouth twists in a sheepish smile, "Well... I saw a

dog adoption event going on about two blocks down on my way here."

"A dog adoption…"

"Yeah. Do you want to come?"

"Why would I want to go to a dog adoption?"

"To see all the sweet babies, and give them some love. Who knows, maybe you'll fall in love."

Something about the excitement on her face doesn't allow me to tell her that will never happen.

"I don't even like dogs."

Her mouth falls open and her eyes widen. "What? What do you mean you don't like dogs?"

I shrug and hold out my arm for her to lead the way. I might not care for animals but I'm finding I'll do anything to spend time with Camila.

"Oh my god," Camila squeals, bending over a short wire fence to pick up some kind of small brown dog with wavy hair. "Oh my god Miles, look at her! Have you ever seen anything so cute in your life?" She holds the dog close to her chest like a newborn baby in one arm and rubs the top of her head with the tips of her fingers.

I heave a sigh and look around the park, there's about eight pens set up all with different dogs in each one. And all of this is from the same rescue. How can this be? How are there so many dogs out here without a home?

"Oh my gosh, you are the sweetest thing. You're going to go to a wonderful home so soon. I just know it. Yes, you are." She nuzzles the dog before putting her back down on the other side of the waist-high fence.

"Okay, seriously, how can you not like dogs?" Camila walks beside me through the rest of the park.

"I mean I'm not a serial killer, it's not like if I saw one in the street I would kick it or anything, but I also wouldn't pet it, and I've never had a desire to have one either."

She gives a disbelieving shake of her head. "I always wanted a dog when I was growing up."

"Of course you did." I smile and she scowls at me. "But?"

"But my parents worked a lot, they said it wouldn't be fair or responsible to get a dog if we couldn't give it the love and attention it deserved. I guess looking back, they were right but at the time I was always so pissed at them."

"And since you've moved out? Why have you not gotten one since?"

"I guess the same reason," she says as her eyes trail off into the distance. "Taylor and I lived in a dorm room when we first moved here and from there we moved into that small one-bedroom. I've been working ten-hour days and her schedule is all over the place. It's never been the right time. But one day."

"One day huh?"

Camila smiles up at me, "Yeah. One day."

CAMILA

As if someone just threw a blanket over the sun, the clouds roll in, dark and heavy. The sounds of puppies whining and jumping on crates intensify as volunteers begin packing up the park.

"Looks like it's going to rain." I wrap my arms around myself as thunder booms overhead. I follow Miles as we walk at a clipped pace out of the park.

We're about two blocks away from the jeweler when thunder booms overhead and it begins to pour. Long fingers interlock with mine as Miles pulls me behind him and starts to run.

His strong arms pull me under an awning and the abrupt stop has me slamming into the side of his body. My hands wrap around his chest and back to steady myself. And even though we've both been running out in the cold rain his body somehow radiates heat. The solid ridges of his muscles flex beneath my fingertips and before I can embarrass myself any further I take a step back.

His breathing has slowed. "Here," he says, starting to take off his jacket.

"No. I'm fine, really," I say, shaking my head.

"Then come here." He opens the flap suggesting I stand *in* his jacket.

At my hesitation, he raises his brows and jerks his head. "Please. Before you freeze to death."

My teeth chatter as I step into his side again and embrace his warmth. With my head a good six inches below him he can't see my eyes close as I inhale a deep pull of his fresh woodsy scent. It's quickly become my new favorite smell. It's inviting, calming even. But also so sexy at the same time. At this point, I must be huffing him because I'm completely lost in my own thoughts when his voice rumbles through his chest against the side of my face.

"I'm going out of town tomorrow."

That pulls me from my weird sniffing trance. I tilt my body so I can look up at him but this puts me right in front of him and just this slight angle change feels way more intimate than it should.

The column of his neck works as his eyes focus down on me and he swallows. "Just a few days, I need a signature from a client. I'll be back Tuesday."

"Oh. Okay." I'm aware of how disappointed I sound. So I quickly change to a more lighthearted tune. "That's a lot of work for one little signature."

His eyes break contact with mine and land on my lips. We're so close if I just popped up on my toes our mouths would meet. But I stay firmly planted on the ground and his eyes come back up to find mine again. "Well, we both know how important one little signature can be," he says.

The sounds of water rush behind me and it could very well all be in my head, but it feels like he begrudgingly pulls his eyes away. I twist in his jacket to see Wills has pulled up. Our eyes connect once more before he pulls my hand into his and we walk out into the rain together again.

Miles

The crisp air feels cooler on my sweat-soaked body. There isn't usually anything a 6 a.m. boxing session can't help me forget about, but as I take the elevator back up to my apartment, I'm still drowning in thoughts of Camila. I was itching to get back home to see her, to just be near her. I spent the first night in my hotel wondering what she was doing, thinking about her padding around the apartment in her silk shorts. The next night I was pissed off that I couldn't get her out of my head. I went over each of our conversations like some kind of lunatic trying to remember every one of her words. By the third night I gave up on trying to forget about her and I let myself think the one thought that wouldn't escape me no matter how hard I tried. I got in bed that night drowning in thoughts of what it would be like to have her body under mine.

I try shaking my thoughts as I exit the elevator and kick my shoes off by the door. Pulling the velvet box out of my gym shorts I roll it around between my fingers before setting it on the counter. I'm trying to be glad that I was able to pay to have her rings made, sized, and cleaned in such a short amount of time, but having to pick them up this morning cuts into my morning routine.

The forty-five minutes I carve out to make and drink my coffee before getting ready for work have always been the most and often only peaceful moments of my day. This morning, although my mind is wandering, it's no different.

Until a loud crash echoes from down the hall followed by Camila screaming.

My legs move faster than my brain can keep up. Adrenaline pumps through me as I start thinking of worst-case scenarios. My legs almost fall out from under me when my socks slide on the floor as I run down the hall towards her room. "Camila!" I yell, standing outside her door. No answer. I try the handle and thankfully it's unlocked. I push the door open calling for her again. She's not in here but she screams again, this time less afraid and more of a whimper or whine. I follow the sounds coming from the other side of her bathroom door. "Camila!" She doesn't respond, and this time the door is locked when I try it.

I'm getting impatient. I don't think before I Hulk out and throw the full force of my body into the door. A wide-eyed Camila stands shivering in the back corner of the shower. She quickly uses one forearm to cover her chest and the other to cover that tight little spot between her legs. My brain cannot keep up.

"You're naked!" I shout.

"I'm in the shower, what kind of psycho showers with clothes on?"

I motion for her to turn the shower off. "Okay, well can you shut those off so we don't flood the place."

"I can't!"

A heavy sigh escapes me when I take in the fact that I'm going to have to get in the shower. The ice-cold water crashes down on me as I reach my arm out, turning the handle down. "What happened?" My voice comes out rougher than I intended.

"I don't know. The water just turned freezing mid-way through my shower!"

Without the roar of the water crashing down, the mood in the room takes a dramatic shift. It's gone from loud and over-stimulating to so quiet I can hear my own heartbeat. And on top of that, I have to fight every instinct to keep my eyes on her face.

"When did you get back?"

"Late last night." If I wasn't so focused on her face I would have missed the slight nod of her head.

"Where's your shirt?" she asks as if she's not standing in front of me completely naked.

"I just got back from a workout."

"A run?" Her lips curve slightly but her eyes are daring. And not even the freezing cold water could shrink my dick right now.

"Boxing."

"Hmm." She trails my body slowly but pauses just below my hips before her eyes snap to mine again. "You have a tattoo?"

I can't think. I can't focus. I'm unable to stay in this shower with her a second longer. My legs stay firmly in place as I reach my arm over the glass wall until my fingers brush against the plush towel. I pull it down and hold it wide open, mentally preparing myself to wrap it around her and sprint like hell out of this bathroom but to my shock, she drops her hands. My eyes quickly roam over her perfect full breasts and her pointy little nipples. Her freezing fingers brush against mine where I'm strangling the towel. She covers herself at a leisurely pace, and even though the image of her nipples will be burned in my brain, I tell myself they are hard from standing in the cold shower and not for any other reason. That's the only way I'm able to pull myself away from her.

"I'll call someone to come and fix the water heater today," I say, before storming out, leaving her standing in a towel behind me as I violently scream at myself. *Don't cross the fucking line.*

I'VE READ AND RE-READ THE SAME DOCUMENT FOUR TIMES already. Four times and I couldn't tell you if it was notes on a murder trial, or another office survey asking what snacks we should provide for the junior associates' break room.

Before I attempt to read it for a fifth time, Jonas strolls in with a bagel in one hand and coffee in the other. Normally I would be annoyed with him interrupting me, but today I'm welcoming any distraction I can get.

"Do you actually work here or do they just pay you to be their eye candy?"

"Speak for yourself, I came by like an hour ago and Talan said you weren't here yet." He sits back in his usual spot on my couch.

"How did you get past Talan?" I ask, ignoring his roundabout question.

"Har har," he deadpans, setting his coffee down on the table. "Talan's running that PA training this morning. And honestly, the dude was way too stoked about it if you ask me."

Right. How could I forget? I nominated him for that job.

"So...where were you?" He smiles, biting into his bagel. "Marital problems?"

Oh, I'm definitely having some kind of problem. They start with that terrifying feeling that was coursing through every cell in my body when I heard Camila scream and they don't end after I busted the door down and found her naked. No, my problems continued to follow me as I stalked down to my bedroom to take care of myself in my own shower. Stroke after stroke I was going blind with the image of her perky nipples begging me to pull them into my mouth.

And she was definitely flirting. When she let go reaching for her towel, she knew what she was doing to me. I spilled on the shower wall imagining what would have happened if I had stayed instead of sprinting out of there like the room was on fire.

At least I remembered to leave a sticky note on her ring that I left on the kitchen counter. I know it's possibly the least romantic thing I could have done, but that's what I need right now. Zero romance. It's fine to be attracted to her, she's undeniably the most gorgeous woman I've ever laid my eyes on. But missing her while I'm away, enjoying being around her more than I should, and thinking about her while I'm at work is not what I need. Those things are going to fuck me up. In the short time that I've known Camila, it's apparent that she deserves someone who can give her the world. Unfortunately, I'll never be the guy that wants a relationship so I need to remember this is a business deal. One that is going to help keep my name on the wall. I need to regroup and refocus.

Starting with pretending to read this document for a fifth time.

"Okay if not marital problems, were you at least getting those papers I needed signed?"

"I got them last night, asshat. And next time you come into *my* office with a bagel, you better have one for me too." I dig through my bag for the manila folder when it dawns on me, in my post orgasm-induced haze, I forgot to grab the folder from my home office. "Shit!"

"No. No 'shit'. I need those papers today or I'm screwed."

"Relax, I'll just have Talan run back to my place and grab them."

"Dude," he throws his arms out. "Talan's not here! We just talked about

this. Are you okay?"

Clearly not. But with Talan gone for the day, the only thing I can think to do is text Camila.

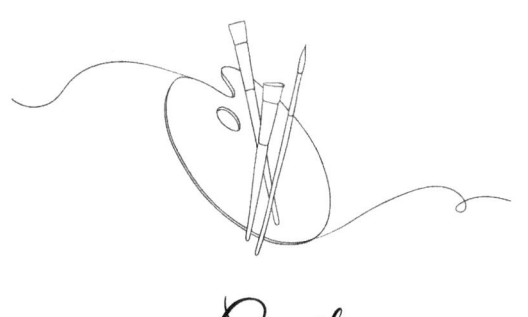

Camila

THE ELEVATOR HAS BEEN CLIMBING FOR WHAT FEELS LIKE minutes at this point and I can't stop wiping my sweaty palms on my jeans. The shiny reflection on the mirrored doors in front of me moves up and down with my hands. My breath catches in my chest when I look down at the source of the rainbow reflection. The stunning diamond and matching band were sitting so unceremoniously on the kitchen counter for me. Finding them with a sticky note placed on top was a colder bucket of water splashed on me than my actual shower this morning.

Miles breaking the door down was shocking enough but when I looked him up and down, in nothing but his borderline too-short shorts, and saw the dark ink sticking out from below them I couldn't help myself. Of course, he would have a thigh tattoo. There isn't anything about Miles that isn't sexy.

He had only been gone a couple of days, but my body sparked with excitement at the sight of him before me. Thankfully he couldn't have run out of there fast enough, or I would have made myself look like an even bigger fool. I all but sat my ass on a silver platter for him, and the man ran.

Actually ran. No words needed to be exchanged to tell me that I needed to inform my body her desires were not aligning with my brain right now.

Finally, the elevator comes to a stop. The doors slowly open to find Smith & Mitchell in bold brass letters anchored to the wall. An older woman sits at a desk smiling at me as I make my way over to her. "Hi, good morning. I'm looking for Miles Cameron's office."

She says nothing but keeps the same strange smile plastered to her face and points me in the direction of his office. My stomach churns and I wonder if she knows my fake husband saw me naked this morning. *Oh my god, you're losing your mind. She clearly doesn't know that, she just has a weird non-moving smile. You're fine. Relax. Inhala exhala.* "Thank you." I turn on my heel and make my way to his office door. The hallway is long, with offices lining only the right side and I might very well wear the skin right off my finger from twisting this ring so much.

I've seen Miles under club lights, sitting across from me at dinner with a sullen face, and half naked in my shower, but seeing him in his suit sitting at his desk, looking every bit as powerful as I know his body is under said suit, I forget the very reason I'm here in the first place.

"Mila! Nice to see you again!" I'm shaken from my lack of thoughts when I notice Jonas flying across the room towards me. By *you,* I'm sure he means the folder I'm carrying but I smile at him anyway as he pulls me into a hug. From over his shoulder, my eyes connect with Miles, who stands and rounds the edge of his desk.

I turn my attention back to Jonas. "This is for you then, I'm assuming?" I say as I hand him the folder.

Jonas all but melts to a puddle on the floor, "Ugh, yes! Thank you. You're the best!" He grips both my shoulders and plants a big kiss on my cheek before running out the door. "I'll see you Saturday," he yells over his shoulder waving the file around in the air. I shake my head and let out a small laugh, before turning my attention back to Miles who is now leaning against his desk with his arms crossed and a vein in his forehead becomes very prominent.

We stand staring at each other for a few moments. I want to apologize for this morning, so we can move on and not have any awkwardness between us, but standing in his office with glass walls doesn't seem like a good place to have this conversation. "I should get going." I point over my shoulder.

He pushes off his desk before walking over to me and placing his arm on the door behind me. That incredibly strong arm now a mere inch from my face, I have to tilt my neck all the way back to look up at him. "I'll walk you out."

I stand a good arm's length away from Miles while we wait for the elevator to make its way up to the 34th floor. I am physically crawling inside with all the things I want to say to him.

Staring at my feet I start to say, "I wanted—"

"Shit," he says at the same time.

My mind starts racing when I look up at him but his eyes are locked on a tall striking woman heading down the hall with her eyes dead set on us. Faster than I can comprehend, he grabs my elbow with one hand and pulls me to him, his other hand cradles the back of my neck, "Just go with it," he whispers.

Before I can blink his lips are on mine. I'm stiff as a board in his arms as I try to process what's happening. *Miles is kissing me.* His fingers tighten their grip at the nape of my neck and his scent fills my lungs. I vaguely register that everything about this is fake, but at this moment I don't care. I want to know what it feels like to be wanted, to be desired and he is making me feel that and then some, so I give in. The moment his soft lips part on mine, I melt into him. The world is spinning around me like I'm on one of those gravitational pull rides at a county fair. I bring one hand to his chest digging my fingers into his suit. My other arm wraps around his neck as I pull my body into his. As if I'm physically trying to melt into him. As if even crushed together with only our clothes between us is too much space between us. His hand slides out from beneath my hair as his thumb begins rubbing at the trembling pressure point in my neck. When he pulls away his eyes are dark and his breathing uneven. As if some force has pulled him back to me, his lips press to my forehead. The touch is so gentle and sweet that I have to close my eyes and will my breath to even out before I cause a real scene by passing out. My skin chills when his lips leave me but his hand finds my lower back before turning to face the woman who I now remember was heading towards us.

"Miles." She greets him with a smile before looking at me. She's an elegant woman with long dark hair and beautiful deep brown skin and she's almost as tall as Miles in her Louboutins.

"Samantha," he beams, before gesturing to me with his other arm. "I'm glad we ran into you. Camila was just dropping off some papers I left at home this morning." Gesturing between the two of us, "Camila, this is my boss, Samantha. Sam, this is Camila, my wife."

Something about the way he says "my wife" has a bite to it and it very quickly brings me back down to reality.

I'm instantly reminded of what it feels like to take that first step off the Gravitron ride.

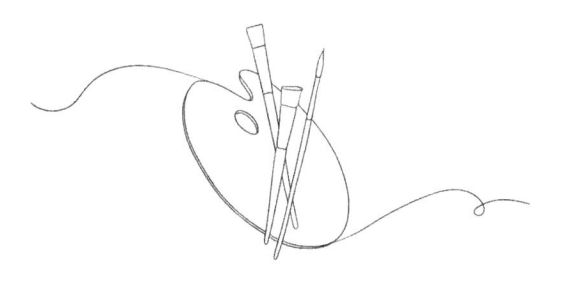

Camila

My back is pressed up against a hard body. Forearms that I would recognize anywhere wrap around me. One large hand slides between my breasts, past my stomach, and down to my shorts. *Oh god.* Long fingers slide just past my waistband before pulling out and my breath turns ragged at the loss. *Miles.* I can smell him, I can feel his stubbled jaw rub against my bare shoulder. His lips twitch, the closest thing to a smile that he can do but it's enough to send butterflies wild in my stomach and heat up my spine. *We shouldn't be doing this. But how could I stop when it feels this good?* He pushes my legs open with his knee, slipping his thigh between my legs. I rub my hips side to side desperate to relieve some of the pressure building. I'm already completely soaked through the thin fabric covering me and my clit is pulsing as if she has her own heartbeat down there. The pressure is so intense but no matter how hard I rub against his leg I can not find the relief I so desperately need. I bear down on him, my hips pumping harder and harder. My chest tightens as my breathing kicks up. This is the edging session from hell. The weight between my legs is physically painful at this point. I rock as hard as I can until I let out a loud scream.

Loud enough that it wakes me up.

I'm left sweating and panting. I can't do anything but roll over and stare up at the ceiling.

I'm not surprised. But I am disappointed. I've never been the most in tune with my sexual needs. I didn't even have my first orgasm until I was twenty-four and it was from a vibrator that I got as a gag gift in a birthday basket from Taylor when I told her about *no orgasm Jesse*—her name for him, not mine. And then when I told her he could start a club with Nate and Colin, she just about fell over dead. She told me I should try a casual hook-up with a hot guy from a bar, but as much as I wish I could be, I've just never been the one-night stand kind of girl. Something I've always admired about Taylor is even though she might be a little commitment-phobic, she at least knows what she wants, and knows how to ask for it. I, on the other hand, have always made sure every guy I've been with has been satisfied while I've always been left very unsatisfied.

I've always made excuses for the men I've been with, saying it was my fault. I was distracted with studying or coursework. I was stressed from my job. All things that were true, but still excuses. Excuses because after a while I gave up on trying to figure out what it was that *I* needed.

I'm not surprised I'm having dreams about Miles now, after that kiss in his office the other day. A kiss I should not have thought about as much as I did once I left. A kiss that even though I knew was fake, still had me desperate for more. He kisses like it's his last one to give. And as it turns out one fake kiss with Miles was filled with more heat and more passion than any real kiss I've had before. But he's made it very clear, this is a business arrangement and nothing more.

I'll scold my vagina later for thinking it was anything else.

After a quick, cold shower, I'm still on edge but head downstairs and drink in the delicious scents of hazelnut and fresh coffee beans.

Miles stands at the counter in the same lack of clothing that he was in when he smashed my bathroom door in. There's no denying his body is an absolute work of art. His abs are thick. Not the kind some men have from eating like a bird and starving until their abs are showing. No, his body is the result of hard work. His boxers peek out the top of another pair of those same black shorts that have my eyes wandering to the cut in his hips. The perfect V shape is like a flashing neon sign begging my eyes to search lower. I give him one last look as I pass him and hone in on his legs. Boxing, he said. If boxing gives you tree trunks for legs and sculpted abs, then yeah, I believe him.

"Good morning." I try to sound pleasant but it comes out rough. It's amazing how not going into my old office for two weeks has almost hindered my ability to put on a convincing smile.

Even though I know he must have been up for hours already, his voice is gruff when he replies. "Good morning. How do you take your coffee?"

"Umm, however," I shrug.

One thick eyebrow raises. "What's your preference?"

"Whatever is easiest, I'm not picky. Black is fine."

He studies me briefly before he turns back around and begins using some kind of frother.

I lean against the island behind him and even though I feel like a complete creep I can't help but take in his corded back muscles as he maneuvers around the kitchen. He confidently makes an elaborate cup of coffee and my eyes narrow in on the matte black band sitting on his ring finger. I'm not sure when he started wearing that. I'm also not sure why I like the image so much.

"Try this." He turns around handing me a ceramic mug with an intricate lotus flower made from the milk. I take a small sip and wonder what the stuff I've been drinking for the last ten years has been because it pales in comparison to this.

"This is incredible," I moan around the cup.

"It's important to know what you like, Camila."

I stare into my cup feeling slightly embarrassed that I've spent so much of my life trying not to be difficult for others or trying to make other people's lives easier because I thought that was better. And now here I am, twenty-seven years old and I don't even know how to ask for a cup of coffee.

I offer him a weak smile and nod my thanks.

"So, I wanted to say," he clears his throat. "About the other day—"

I pray he can't see the heat that hits my face. I go into panic mode and wave my hand while trying to swallow the sip of coffee I just took.

"Don't," I say, setting the cup down on the counter. "Seriously, I'm just glad I was able to catch on quickly. Hopefully, we were convincing enough." I try to wink, but it doesn't feel quite right.

His movements still and his focus on me becomes so intense that I squeeze my hands into tight fists to stop myself from fidgeting. With a small shake of his head, he breaks our eye contact and I exhale a deep breath, hoping up on the counter—the picture of casualness.

"So, did you just get back from boxing?" I ask, pointing at his lack of clothing. He nods and begins pouring water over his coffee grounds. "I've never tried boxing before, is it like a group class?"

"I have a standing private session with my coach and Jonas."

"How long have you been friends with Jonas?"

"A while." I swear it's like pulling teeth trying to get him to talk sometimes. The few times he does engage in conversation I never want them to end because I don't know when the next one will come. I keep trying until I find something he wants to engage with.

"Did you always know you wanted to be a lawyer?"

"Yes."

"What's your tattoo?"

He sets the kettle of hot water down. "What are you doing?"

"What do you mean?"

"Are we playing twenty-one questions here?"

"Just wondering if I can get you to hit your daily word count goal before 9 a.m." I'm not surprised by my boldness. Not that these kinds of remarks are unusual for me, but they typically stay in my head or if they do come out it's only when I'm around someone I'm comfortable with, which is basically just Taylor. To my surprise though the world's smallest smile flutters over his face before he hides it by running his fingers across his chin.

"It's a Japanese dragon."

"What does it mean?" I ask, taking a sip of my coffee. He moves to stand next to me while scratching his eyebrow with the back of his finger—a move that shouldn't be as sexy as it is but yet, here we are.

"I guess, if you looked it up online you would find it to be an ancient symbol considered to protect and guard families and homes." He braces his hands on the counter next to me.

"And is that what it means to you?" Sitting up on the island puts us at eye-level and I take in the darkness of his eyes that not even the morning sun flooding the room can pierce the depth of. His eyebrows furrow as he watches me, his fingers idly tap on the counter while the sound of water dripping from his last pour, continues behind him.

I'm snapped out of my daze when his finger brushes against my thigh and a shiver runs through me. I'm not sure if it's from the dream I had or the way we're dancing around each other right now, but being in this space with him has my lungs working overtime trying to take in air.

"I better get going," I whisper. "I'm meeting Taylor for breakfast soon."

He pushes off the island and leans on the counter behind him, crossing his arms. I take in a deep breath, my nose filling with a mix of the fresh brewed coffee and the spicy warm scent of the man in front of me. When I hop off the counter I open my mouth to say something but all the words escape me. The intensity of his gaze on me has me feeling like I'm laid out bare for his viewing pleasure. The drip of his coffee finally comes to a stop causing the silence in the room to only expand. When he turns his back to me reaching up for another ceramic mug, I take the opportunity of not being frozen under his stare to sneak away.

Miles

> **ME**
> I left a file on my desk, any chance you're still in the office?

> **JONAS**
> It's 9:30 you fucking weirdo. No. I'm not still in the office.

Shit. I'm typically one of the last people to leave the office but I stayed late tonight, even by my standards. I've been distracted by a certain dark-haired beauty the last few days and today was no different. I spent the first half of the morning thinking about the way her skin pebbled when my finger brushed against her and the second half thinking about the look on her face when I brought up the kiss. *That kiss.*

When I saw Sam heading towards us in the lobby, I meant to give Camila what would appear to be a quick kiss and thank you for dropping off my papers. But as soon as the weight of her body fell into my arms, everything changed. I was no longer focused on putting on a show for my boss. I was wrapped up in Camila's soft lips. The way my skin heated when she dug her fingers into the nape of my neck. It would be so easy for a man to grow addicted to kissing her. It took everything in me to break that kiss. To not back her into the elevator and pull the emergency stop button. I wanted to do things to her that would have Cindy at the front desk calling HR.

But despite the way her face heated, Camila blew the whole thing off as if it was no different than kissing her grandmother goodbye after Thanksgiving dinner. And hell, if that wasn't a punch to the gut. But I should be thankful I guess because I was only a second away from telling her how much I liked it.

I pocket my phone as the elevator doors open. It takes three steps for me to spot that messy knot of hair on top of Camila's head and stop dead in my tracks. The glow emanating from her phone lights her face as she sits in the otherwise dark room.

"Hey." Her voice is raspy and I realize I'm still just standing here staring at her because I'm still not used to someone being here when I get home. "How was your day?"

I drop my things off in my home office before moving to the kitchen and turning some soft lighting on. "Fine."

She twists around, putting an elbow on the back of the couch and her head in her hand. "What exactly do you do?"

"I'm a corporate lawyer."

"Yeah, I know. But what does that mean? What do you actually do all day?"

"It would bore you."

"You said something like that, the last time I asked. You don't like talking about work?"

I really wouldn't know how I feel about talking about my

work with someone. The few times Jonas and I get a drink after, the last thing we want to talk about is work. "Today I met with two clients and did a lot of reading." Her lips form a tight line when she nods her head. Well, looks like I've found something I'm not the best at. Safe to say even if I wanted to talk to someone about my day, I do a shit job at it. "What were you doing sitting in the dark?"

"I spent the afternoon looking at job listings. I found one that didn't look completely awful." She stretches her arms up before pulling the band out of her hair, sending the wavy strands free down her back. "I applied for it, so we'll see," she says, shrugging her shoulders. "Anyway, I ended up falling asleep and I just woke up, so now I'm wide awake." I move around the kitchen, grabbing the glass decanter and pouring myself a drink. "So, what do you usually do after work?"

I fit the stopper and turn back around to face her. "What do you mean?"

"Like when you come home at night? I know you work out in the morning and then you go to work,*"* she answers, putting 'go to work' in air quotes. "But then you come home and, what?" I take a drink from my glass and close my eyes briefly while swallowing the smoky liquid.

"Typically I go through more emails while I eat dinner and then I shower, change, and go to bed." Her head tilts down but her eyebrows shoot up.

"You don't ever just like, hang out?"

"Hang out?"

"Yeah, you know, like watch movies, read a book, bake cookies?"

"I think you know the answer to that." I finish the rest of my drink in one gulp before setting it in the sink. I thankfully ate a late lunch today and I'm not in the mood for dinner. I cross the kitchen, ready to head to my room for the night before stopping and pointing at the TV. "That should be fully loaded, if you wanted to watch a movie or something."

"Do you want to watch one with me?" I stop walking and turn to face her. A barely there blush spreads across her cheeks but her chest hardly moves, as if she's holding her breath. Something tells me she has a harder time asking for things than she lets on. Although every logical part of me knows I shouldn't be tempted to spend any extra time with her, the reality is that I'm not very logical when it comes to Camila. Before I can question what I'm doing, I nod my head once and slip my jacket off before sitting down next to her.

"What do you want to watch?" she asks.

"I haven't seen anything so…" I don't finish my sentence because she's looking at me with wide eyes and her mouth has fallen open. She thinks I'm crazy but I'm amused. I find that I like putting that expression on her face.

After scrolling for nearly fifteen minutes, she settles on something she deems a classic and I settle into the couch. It's deep enough that I'm able to lean back and spread out comfortably. Camila sits to my left with her legs crossed under her, and there is still more space. I forgot how comfortable this couch is. I could probably count on one hand the amount of times I've sat on it.

"I can't believe you've never seen *10 Things I Hate About You* before."

"Really? That's shocking to you?"

A soft laugh bubbles from her and she looks at me. "I guess not. Taylor and I used to stay up all night on the weekends watching shows and movies. There were times we wouldn't go to bed until my brother was getting up in the morning for one of his soccer games."

"Did Taylor live with you?"

"Practically. Her parents were gone a lot so she stayed with us most of the time."

"And your parents were fine with that?" I don't know why I'm asking.

"My mom would never object to Taylor because she's the only one my mom could get to cook with her. Which ended up working out great for me because, by the time we moved, Taylor could recreate any of my mom's recipes. Even in our college dorm room, she could whip up a gourmet meal with just a travel blender and an easy bake oven."

I untuck my shirt, trying to process how different we are. Here I've been actively avoiding getting close to anyone my entire adult life. It started with my parents. How could two people claim to love each other and end up like they did? But it didn't stop there, the harder I worked and the more cases I saw, the more I knew I never wanted to be close to someone like that. I've seen people be destroyed in every type of relationship. Marriages, partnerships, and friendships. People are selfish as fuck. I want no part of that.

"I'm assuming since you haven't seen any of the classics, you didn't do a lot of movie nights with your bestie growing up?" Her comment pulls me from my spiraling thoughts and I answer her with a blank stare. "I'll take that as a no." *Good girl.*

Her eyes follow where my fingers brush along the edge of my jaw. When I catch her staring she blinks twice before turning back towards the TV. "I was thinking about the fundraiser this weekend," she says. "Should we come up with a story? I mean about how we met?"

"Most people aren't bold enough to ask." She bites her lip, nods her head, and avoids looking at me. She almost looks defeated and now I feel like an asshole. I didn't realize how used to not talking to people I was until someone worked so hard to talk to me. "But sure, what do you want to say?" Her eyes sweep to me now, brighter than before.

"Maybe we could say we met at a coffee shop. That's an easy enough story."

"I don't go to coffee shops."

"Oh right. Maybe we could say we met through friends."

"Well since Jonas is my only friend..." She gives me a thin smile and I know I'm being difficult so I run my hand through my hair and say, "We'll say we met at a bar." She smiles at me, relieved. "Don't sweat it anyway, the fundraiser is just going to be a lot of people who think they're important. Something that's supposed to be for a good cause but is really just an excuse for these people to network. I'm convinced they think there's a correlation between how much money they put up and how big their dicks are," I say. "Anyway, good causes get the money at the expense of a lot of ass-kissing."

"Mmm. So it sounds like something you might enjoy very much."

A ghost of a smile crosses my face when I catch the amusement in her eyes. "Yeah, I try to avoid them when possible by just sending a check with Jonas, however, as you know..." The amusement in her eyes dies quickly and she turns her focus back to the movie.

An hour later the main character somehow gets the entire band to play "Can't Take My Eyes Off Of You" while he serenades a girl, asking her to go to prom with him. In any other situation, this would be my personal version of hell. Camila stretches and yawns a few times before grabbing a pillow and setting it on the cushion between us. Her long hair drapes over the other side of the pillow and the ends brush against my leg. My fist clenches under my jaw, and only now that I'm tense again do I realize how relaxed I had been.

After a few minutes, her eyes begin to close softly. She pulls them open again briefly before her lashes fall once more. One of my arms drapes casually against the back of the couch even though I'm feeling anything but casual. I try to ignore her and focus on the movie but I catch her lips part as her chest steadily rises and falls, and now I can't help staring at those pouty lips.

When the credits begin to roll, Camila is thoroughly asleep and I don't want to wake her but I also don't want to leave her on the couch all night. For a brief moment, I contemplate carrying her to her bed.

Fuck it. The couch is comfortable enough. I walk over to a hidden cabinet and pull out a blanket. She doesn't so much as stir when I drape the blanket over her and a few strands of hair fall on her face. *Fuck, she's pretty.* This isn't a new discovery, obviously. But there aren't a lot of opportunities to just fully take her in. I don't know what prompts me to but I lightly brush the hairs out of her face, my fingertips graze across her cheek, sending a light shock through my hand. I stand upright and before I allow myself to wonder what this feeling that keeps coursing through me when I'm with her is, I turn and make my way down the hall to my room.

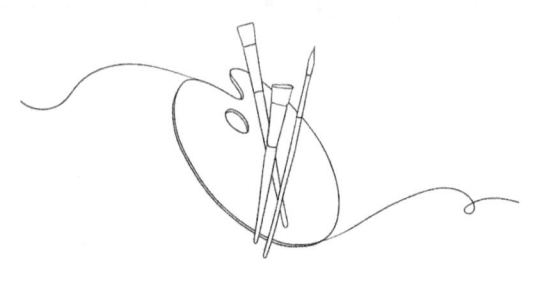

Camila

It takes me a moment to figure out my surroundings but I've definitely woken up on the couch. A warm heavy blanket drapes over my body, and the room is dark despite being morning. The large living room windows are coated in rain droplets as hazy gray light tries to trickle through. I push myself to sit up, looking around and the house is eerily quiet. Miles must already be at his morning workout. I should go change so when he gets home this morning he doesn't find me still sleeping on the couch so I quickly fold the blanket and dig my hands between the cushions searching for my phone. The floor is chilly under my bare feet as I walk through the room. I almost miss the paper sitting on the kitchen island but do a double take and notice the sophisticated script with my name on top.

> Camila,
> Rosa called, she isn't feeling well and won't be coming in today. I'll send Wills to pick you up at 7 and meet you for dinner.

-MC

P.S. Take this card and find yourself something to wear for the gala tomorrow night.

I pick up the black card sitting on top of the heavy paper, flipping and tapping it on the counter while I read over his note again. The thought of going out to dinner with Miles shouldn't leave me feeling breathless, but every day I find myself feeling something new when it comes to him. I wonder briefly if I should feel weird about using his money to buy myself a nice dress but then I realize he would likely be mortified if I showed up on his arm in anything less than something extravagant. I take both the note and the card with me up to my room and read it a few more times before I finish getting ready.

A CABLE CAR CRAWLS PAST ME AS TOURISTS HANG OUT THE windows taking pictures of the colorful buildings that line the street. This street is every small business owner's dream. It's full of clothing boutiques, flower shops, and bakeries. An overwhelming scent of jasmine fills my nose as I enter the first store, searching for the perfect dress to wear for the fundraiser. I'm looking but I'm not really paying attention. I haven't been able to focus on anything. I can still feel his words as if they are burned into the side of my head.

It takes me a few more stores before I find what I'm looking for but when I do, it all but jumps off the hanger and begs me to take it home. I immediately grab it and find a dressing room to try it on. The black dress with one thick shoulder strap hugs my chest and curves tightly before the flowing fabric drapes down to the floor. My leg peeks out of the slit that goes all the way up my thigh and I snap a quick picture in the mirror to send to Taylor.

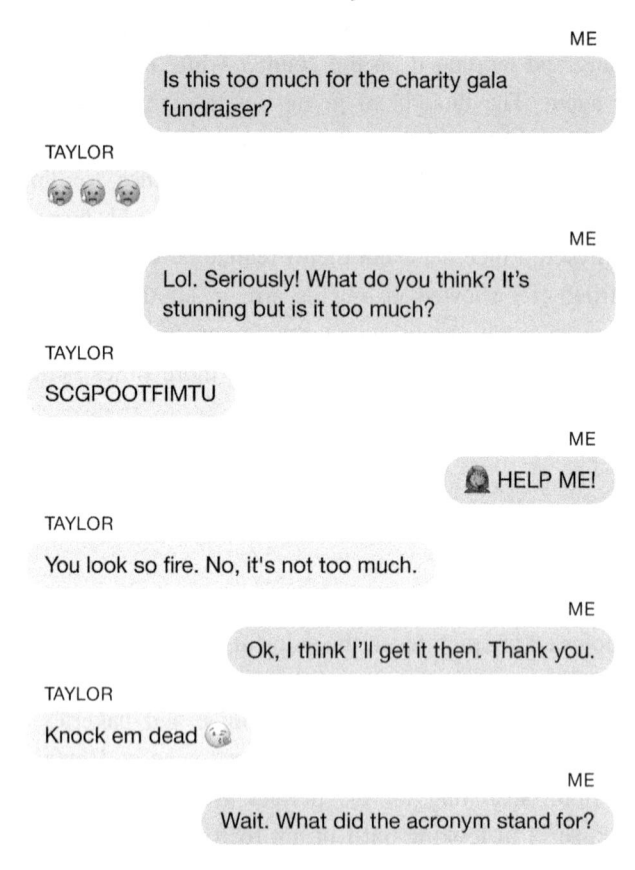

> **ME**
> Is this too much for the charity gala fundraiser?

TAYLOR
😭 😭 😭

> **ME**
> Lol. Seriously! What do you think? It's stunning but is it too much?

TAYLOR
SCGPOOTFIMTU

> **ME**
> 🙆 HELP ME!

TAYLOR
You look so fire. No, it's not too much.

> **ME**
> Ok, I think I'll get it then. Thank you.

TAYLOR
Knock em dead 😘

> **ME**
> Wait. What did the acronym stand for?

"How is everything going in there?" The saleswoman knocks on the door and I set my phone down in my bag.

"Good. Great! I think I'm going to get it," I call back.

"Oh, wonderful! I'll meet you up at the front once you're all changed."

"Great. Thank you."

I DEBATE CALLING A CAR TO TAKE ME BACK BECAUSE FINDING a dress took longer than I anticipated and I still need to get ready for dinner. I decide to walk another two blocks to a less crowded street before calling for a car. I move to step around a man taking a picture of a woman holding up a giant pretzel. I squeeze between him and a building with a For Sale sign in the window. For whatever reason, I stop. I press my face into my cupped hand and look inside. The large windows give enough light that I can make out a large open space with high ceilings and a few beams. The perfect space for an art gallery.

My whole life art has been the one thing able to help me cope when I feel my anxiety starting to creep in. Some people use meditation to keep anxiety at bay, for others it can be medication. I've tried the 3 3 3 rule, I've also tried movement and music. Nothing is able to calm my mind and body the way trying to decipher art can. I'm aware it might just be a distraction, a mask. But it also brings me joy. I love finding new art, whether it be in painting, sculpture, or even film. When deciding on a degree and career choice I chose business over medicine for the sole reason that I knew I would be able to double major in fine arts along with business.

I don't know what prompts me to take a picture of the phone number on the sign, but I do it anyway and then quickly open the missed text from Taylor before I can think about it.

> TAYLOR
>
> Screaming crying gagging passed out on the floor in my throw-up.

I close my eyes and smile as I tap my phone to my chin.

For the first time in a long time, the fog is light enough that the setting sun creates a vibrant cascade of pinks and purple across the sky. A weightless feeling floats through my body as I call a car to pick me up.

Miles

The low cushioned chair should be buckling under my weight but I guess the tiny hair-pin legs on it aren't just for show. When I had Talan research the best restaurant in the city today, I was surprised it was a place I'd never been. The glass dome is nice in theory as it offers a 360-degree view of the city. People are pressed up against the windowed walls, phones in hand, snapping the same low-quality pictures over and over again. The last of the sunset dips below the horizon and the restaurant now glows with mood lighting.

Looking out into the now crowded restaurant, everyone quickly goes out of focus as Camila enters the room. I'm having flashbacks of being a child and playing with a kaleidoscope. A blur of color acts as a background image while my sole focus is on Camila. She is the center, taking up the whole picture. Her teeth dig into her bottom lip as she searches for me from across the room. The slit in her tight black skirt trails up to her mid-thigh. *Fuck me. Those legs.* The rest of her outfit is casual with a cropped vintage t-shirt and sneakers. Her eyes squint towards me in the dim corner before she reaches an arm up to wave. My fist digs into my jaw when a little sliver of skin peeks out from under her shirt.

I stand from my chair as she approaches the table. She brushes an invisible strand of hair from her face, pats her skirt that's already completely flat, and then cracks her knuckles. I take her elbow, and I don't know if it will help or hurt her nerves but I can't stop myself when I lean down and place a small kiss on her temple. I fight the groan that tries to escape when I get a whiff of her rich, deep scent. Patchouli with a hint of something citrusy. I pull away, motioning for her to sit, and the lightest shade of pink touches her cheeks.

"Camila," I greet her

"Miles," she mockingly responds.

One of the things I've come to enjoy most about Camila is her ability to be sarcastic with me. There's a very comforting feeling about it.

"I ordered you a Vodka Red Bull," I say tilting my head towards the bar.

"No, you did not!" Her eyes widen and she pauses mid-air before sitting fully in her chair.

"What's wrong? Scared you're going to wake up in my bed again?" She sucks her cheeks trying to hide her smile and the waiter arrives. He places my whisky on a black and gold napkin in front of me, and the glass of wine I ordered in front of Camila. She thanks the waiter before tilting her head at me.

She can't hide her smile, as she laughs picking up her glass. I'm momentarily distracted by the sparkle emanating from her ring finger. Even though I know it doesn't mean what the people around us think it does, it sparks some primal feeling in me to see it on her finger anyway. I'm unable to have her in a way that I might want, but I like knowing that no one else is going to go after her either with that ring on. It isn't fair for me to want her all to myself when I can't even give myself to her for real. But the thought of her with anyone else makes my blood boil.

"So, tell me something," Camila swirls her glass around, giving me one of her playful smiles that I've grown a soft spot for.

"What would you like to know tonight, mi esposa?" That throws her off. Her hand strikes her chest as she works hard to swallow her drink. Her mouth parts but I think I've shocked whatever witty one-liner she was going to say. "Why don't you tell me something first this time?" I ask, lifting my glass to her.

Her chest puffs out as she sits up a little taller. "Okay, let's see. I went to yoga this morning. And then I went out and found a dress for tomorrow...."

"Now who's the one getting too personal?"

Her eyes narrow as she tries her damnedest to look angry but the corners of her lips give her away. "Okay well, I also took down the number of an empty studio space that's for sale." She pins me with raised brows.

That piques my interest. I want to know everything but I nod and wait for her to continue. Almost instantaneously her mood shifts. Her shoulders hunch over and she's looking at her drink as if it holds the secrets to the world.

"I don't know… I…" I casually sip my drink, giving her the time. "Okay, it's stupid. But I think somewhere in the furthest part of my mind, I've always had a dream of opening my own art gallery. A place for new and up-and-coming artists to have space to showcase their work."

"I don't think it's stupid. Why is it not at the forefront of your mind?"

She lets out a long tense breath reaching for the pendant on her necklace. "My parents mostly. My mom is from Spain and my dad is from Mexico. They met in Miami while in medical school together and they've both just done absolutely everything in their power to be successful to build a better life for themselves, but they've really done all of it for me and my younger brother." She pauses before looking at me for my reaction. But again, I only wait for her to continue. "Business was never my dream, but I knew it was something that could land me a successful job and make my parents proud. And knowing everything they went through, to be able to provide the life they did for us, making something of myself and being successful has been my only focus for as long as I can remember."

She's mentioned her parents and their expectations of her before but I didn't realize it was to this extent. I wonder how much of these expectations are actually from her parents versus Camila self-inflicting them on herself.

"Sounds like you have a little bit of a people-pleasing problem."

"*Little?*" she forces a small laugh.

"Why?"

"Why what?"

"Why do you do it?"

Her eyebrows knit in confusion as she takes a minute to think about it. "I don't know. I guess…I guess I just think if I make everyone happy, things will be better. And people like people who make them happy."

"So you want people to like you?"

"Who doesn't want to be liked?"

"I don't give a fuck if someone likes me or not."

"How nice for you." Her eyes roll back as she takes a sip of her drink.

"What I mean is, what's the point of someone liking me if it's contingent? If you don't like me and I do x, y, and z, and all of a sudden you like me now? What did I gain? I want people in my corner who will be there when I fuck up. Not people that show up because I can provide something for them. Especially if it's going to cost me what I want." Her eyes stay trained on me like she's really trying to process what I'm saying. "Look, at the end of the day, even if every single person in the world likes you, it's not going to fix whatever it is you think it's going to. I can promise you that."

"Huh." Her face has turned unreadable and she takes another small sip from her drink. "What about your brother? Does he share the same need to uphold the family's success?"

"Sebastian? No." The mention of her brother lights up her face. "No, Seb's been off traveling the world for a while. I love my baby brother, and I'm happy that he doesn't seem to have a care in the world, or at least feel the same pressures I do. I admire that about him. It does sometimes feel like I have to carry more of the load, to make up for him. But he's happy, so I'm happy for him."

Camila is showing me her cards right now, but all I can think about is this bright, beautiful woman, who feels the weight of the world on her shoulders but is constantly putting her wants and needs on the back burner. She's doing what she believes will make everyone else happy at the expense of her own happiness and as I look at her my only concern at this moment is who's taking care of Camila?

"Anyway," she drains the rest of her wine, "I guess that's why it's never been at the forefront of my mind. Art is risky. And I need to do something safe, stable."

I wasn't expecting Camila to open up to me the way she has. Most of what I know about her is based on reading her facial expressions and her body language. But the more she opens up to me, I can't help but want more and I know that isn't fair considering our situation. Even though I didn't technically lie to her, I did trick her into thinking this marriage was more of a convenience for her. But when it comes to her, I want to know everything about her.

"Wow. I'm sorry, I didn't mean to get so serious on you there." She shakes her head apologetically.

Not wanting to leave her out here hanging with all her wounds exposed, I throw the rest of my drink back, welcoming the burn. When I set the glass down I lean back in my fun-house size chair and crack open the surface of my own wounds with her.

"My father was a professional baseball player." Her head snaps to me with a hint of surprise, but just as I did for her, she doesn't push me. She eagerly waits for me to continue. "My mother was actually an artist." I lean forward, setting my empty glass down on the table between us. "The paintings you're so fond of in the dining room, and in your room, are some of her work." Camila's eyes glow but she bites down on her smile. "Actually she called herself 'A Palm Artist'. She really enjoyed painting landscapes, but she found any time she painted any kind of palm leaf it stood out amongst the rest of her pictures. So after a while, she gave up on the backdrops and focused solely on the leaves. She used to say 'Why paint the bullshit sunset when I can just paint the leaf?'" I smile now at the memory of her voice. "When I was in high school, I found out my father had been cheating on her." My mouth goes dry as I realize the shit I'm divulging and I look around for our waiter desperate to order another drink. "Anyway, we had already moved out and they had filed for divorce by this time, but it was still new information for me. I can relate to growing up with the pressure of needing to be successful. But what started as trying to get my father's attention and praise turned into me wanting to shove it in his face. I wanted him to know that I could be great on my own. That I didn't need him."

I expect to feel immediate regret sharing this with Camila but when I look over at her, it's not pity in her eyes, it's understanding.

"And your mother?" Her voice is quiet.

"She passed away when I was in law school."

Camila reaches across the low table and puts her hand on mine, where it rests on my leg. She gives one little squeeze, and I turn my hand over to hold hers in mine because it still doesn't feel like pity, it feels like comfort.

"You're the only person I've shared that with besides Jonas," I say.

"Thank you for sharing that with me, Miles."

"To be honest the only thing I hate more than cats is pity, so I appreciate you not being the pitying kind." I play with her fingers between mine.

She playfully slaps at my chest but I grab her hand again and hold her there.

CAMILA

Miles and I finish our dinner and move to more light-hearted topics. He tells me about the time he and Jonas were living together in the middle of a prank war. He claims Jonas started it by wrapping his entire bedroom in cat-covered wrapping paper.

"It's not funny, everything was wrapped. The walls, my furniture, computer, my bed, the pillows, literally everything." I'm doing that laugh where you have to cover your face because your mouth is so big it's ugly.

"Okay okay," I get out between breaths. "So did you declare a truce after that?"

Miles hits me with the most mischievous smile. I didn't even know his lips could curve that high.

"Oh no...what did you do?"

"Have you ever saran-wrapped someone's toilet?"

"I have, actually," I nod. "My brother's, but as soon as he couldn't get the lid up he just walked down the hall and used mine. And his aim is trash so it kind of backfired on me."

"I'll let you in on a secret, Camila, you have to wrap it under the lid." I hold out my palms, confused. "I saran-warped Jonas's toilet and then put the seat down to cover it. I took him out for a *long* night of drinking, when he woke the next morning he lifted the lid to pee and it sprayed back all over him and the bathroom."

"Oh. My. God. Are you an evil genius?" I can't stop the laugh that rips out of me.

The restaurant is filling up now even though it's getting late. We've been talking for hours and I only just noticed the view outside now. The city is alive beneath us. Miles stands, holding out his hand and I take it as he walks me over to the glass wall not far from our table; the view overlooks all of downtown. I place my hands on the wall and my body hums when he stands directly behind me. His powerful arms press to the wall on either side of my head, encompassing me in his heat.

Lights twinkle all over, the Golden Gate Bridge glows in the distance and I'm taken aback for a moment. Everywhere I look I'm mesmerized. "Incredible, isn't it?"

"Yes." His voice drops. And when I look up over my shoulder his smoldering eyes are staring right at me.

I slowly turn my body around to face him. The hairs on my neck stand straight up as I lean against the glass wall. I'm burning with an intense desire to touch him. To *be* touched by him. He stands noticeably still and I don't know what propels me to do so, but my hand lifts and falls to a spot on his chest. As if in answer his heartbeat knocks against me.

"Tell me something," I breathe.

He looks down to where my hand is pressed to his chest, his lips twist to the side as if he's trying to decide something. Slowly he brings one hand off the wall and places it on my hip and I fight the urge to lean into that touch even more. His mouth drops down to my neck and I draw in a deep breath. "I haven't been able to stop thinking about you since I saw you in the shower." His whisper caresses my skin like a feather.

My heartbeat is erratic. I shouldn't entertain this. I knew what I was doing when I grabbed that towel. Only Miles couldn't have gotten out of there fast enough, so I assumed that was his way of telling me to remember our arrangement. "And what have you been thinking?"

A sound somewhere between a hum and a groan vibrates against my neck. "Well, when I jerk myself off every night, I imagine my hand is your warm, wet mouth with those soft lips wrapped tightly around my cock. And when I come, it's your body, your nipples, your face, your sweet little cunt that I'm thinking about."

It's as if I've stabbed a socket with a metal fork. My body is short circuiting at his words. My breath is caught somewhere in my throat but even if I knew how to respond I couldn't. I'm thankful he is holding me up right now because without his arm around my hip, I'm positive my knees would buckle and I would go straight to the ground.

His arm moves from the wall behind me and his finger traces a light trail down my face, along my collarbone, and over my nipples. My gaze settles on his lips as he continues to slide the back of his fingers down further towards the aching spot between my legs. At this moment, I would sell my soul to the devil to have him touch me. Never mind the fact that we're in a dark corner of a public restaurant. I can feel his solid fingers through my skirt and my soaking wet underwear and I shamelessly arch my hips into his touch.

"Are you wet for me, Camila?" Since I still can't form the words, I dig my fingers a little deeper into his chest and nod my head. "Good."

Is this why I haven't had positive sexual experiences? Do I have a praise kink? Am I so detached from myself that I can't even think of things that I might enjoy? No man has ever talked to me like this before. We're not even naked and I'm pretty sure I could orgasm from his words and his touch alone. I want to tell him I need more. I need him.

"Miles, I—" My voice is embarrassingly breathy.

His eyebrows knit together as I register a coughing sound. We both straighten and look back towards the middle of the restaurant where people hover in a crowd and I spot a waiter on the phone. One man is choking as another is giving him the Heimlich, and it's silent for a moment before the man succeeds in vomiting his food all over the floor. People all around let out a sigh of relief and waiters frantically run around to help clean up and tend to the man.

Miles looks back at me and extends his hand, the moment is gone now and he's clearly ready to go.

Eyes wide, I take his hand and wonder, *what the fuck just happened?*

Miles

After dinner last night, I walked Camila back to her room and left her there with a quick goodnight. I could feel her eyes burning into my back as I started back to my own room. The whole drive home, the tension in the car was suffocating and I couldn't stop thinking about how grateful I was that that man almost choked to death.

I'm aware of how terrible that sounds. But when Camila's hips shifted further into my touch, and that sweet little moan escaped her lips, I almost took her right there.

I blame it on a combination of her consuming all my waking thoughts and my fist being the only thing to give me release in a long ass time. However, what started out as a sexual attraction has started shifting into something I don't recognize. No one has ever held my attention the way she does. I appreciate her witty remarks even if they seem to surprise her when they sneak out. It's like getting a glimpse into who she really is behind that meticulous appearance she puts on.

What really gets me though, is the way she so easily opened up to me. She might have hesitated a few times but I waited, trusting, that she would continue, and when she did it made me comfortable enough to do the same with her. I mean, I told her about my parents for Christ's sake. While she might not be afraid to tell me about her struggles and the pressure she feels to make her parents proud, it's obvious she's never expressed this to them.

So yeah, maybe I'm terrible. But if that man hadn't almost choked to death, I'm sure I would have done something that I couldn't come back from. Tonight, Camila and I have to play the part of a happily married couple for everyone, but most importantly the name partners. Now is not the time to blur the line.

I stretch my neck from side to side while taking an aggravated breath. I can't get this last cuff link on my sleeve and when I contemplate chucking it across the room, I know my annoyance has more to do with being on edge about seeing Camila and less about the way the toggle keeps falling out of my sleeve. When I left this morning for my workout, I came home to a note that said she would be out most of the day, *'prepping for tonight.'* I wasn't sure what that meant, but I knew she would be here and be ready when it was time to go so I didn't question it.

High heels clip down the hallway and my fingers continue to fumble with the cuff link. Out of the corner of my eye, I see her perfectly polished toes peeking out from under the long slit of her black dress. My eyes trail up her leg, to her waist that's pulled in tight by the fabric. My gaze continues up to her breasts, and then her face. She's wearing light makeup that only accentuates her already stunning features. Her hair is pinned back away from her face but still flowing freely down her back. Nervously twisting her ring around her finger she mumbles, "Do I look okay?"

I wonder if she's questioning herself because I must look

insane right now. The cuff link I've been wrestling for the last ten minutes slips out of my fingers and falls to the floor with an echo. But I still can't take my eyes off her. Her lips purse to the side as she floats over to me. Her wine-red fingernails lace around my tie as she straightens it before sinking down to the floor in front of me.

I all but come in my pants at the sight of her kneeling before me.

She braces one hand on my thigh while the other reaches between my legs, retrieving the gold and black onyx cuff link. Her alluring eyes look up to me through a fan of thick lashes and she fastens the link to my sleeve without even looking at it.

She loosens her grip on my wrist but doesn't move when I bring my hand up to caress the side of her face. Her soft skin is such a stark difference under the rough calluses of my fingers. My eyes drill into her when I run the pad of my thumb along her bottom lip and her chest rises a full inch.

"Okay isn't the word to describe how you look, Camila."

"So, other than Samantha, is there anyone else I should be trying to impress at this gala?" She shifts nervously in her seat, ducking her head around trying to get a glimpse outside.

"I doubt you'll have to try very hard to impress anyone," I say, running a hand over my tie.

"We're not all like you, Miles." The car slows to a stop and she huffs a breath as if she's trying to hype herself up. She rests back against the seat and her smooth leg slips out of the slit in her dress.

My teeth clamp down as I try to ignore it and look into her eyes. "Meaning?"

"Meaning, people love you."

"People are around waiting for me to get caught up and fail."

"Why would you think that?"

Because it's true. I have the reputation I have because I will do *anything* to win. The thought of Camila seeing me any differently though causes a battle in me that I'm not reading to acknowledge yet.

"Let's just say there's a reason I don't spend time with anyone that I don't have to," I say, pulling her dress over to cover her bare leg.

"You spend time with me," she shakes her head giving me a beaming smile.

"Yeah, I do." All too quickly the air hums around us as the realization that not only do I enjoy being around her, but I crave it. I move my hand from her leg and brush my fingers across my jaw, clearing my throat. "Anyway, like I said, the charity part is just used as an excuse for a bunch of rich lawyers and business people alike, to swing their dicks around and lick some ass."

"Which you will not be doing," she says.

I open the door, welcoming the evening breeze. After being in the back of a limo with her for thirty minutes, I definitely need it. Her hand effortlessly slides into mine as I help her out. My other hand finds the small of her back as I guide her to the entrance. I drop my voice to barely more than a whisper so only she can hear me, "When I saw you in that dress tonight, I wanted to do a lot more than that." Her eyes widen and her mouth falls open somewhere between pure shock and a smile. I can't help but tip my head back and bark out a real genuine laugh at her expression.

The hotel is one of the largest in the city. Everything is gold save for the abundance of flowers everywhere—tables and chairs, the many pillars and chandeliers hanging from the ceiling; everything down to the carpet is gold.

Camila's steps slow as her head spins around taking everything in. "This might be the most exquisite place I've ever seen," she whispers. Amazing how she can't decide what to focus on, because I hardly notice anything in the room with her here.

We've been trying for thirty minutes to make our way over to the bar but I'm stopped left and right by people I know and people I should know. Some stick to nods and curious glances at the woman on my arm. Some go through the full hassle of pretending to run into me to introduce themself and find out who she is. Only a small minority of them have the common sense to not act surprised, rather just offer a "So nice to meet you" and move along.

Thankfully Talan comes over and rescues us from a particularly inquisitive partner.

"Oh. Mr. Cameron, I'm sorry to interrupt but I wanted to make sure we got all your bids in," he interjects.

I smile at him and excuse myself from the previous conversation. "Thank you, Talan."

"Of course." He bows his head and gives a beaming smile towards Camila.

"Talan, I'd like to introduce you to Camila."

"We've actually talked on the phone, but it's nice to meet you in person," she says, reaching her hand out with a warm smile.

Everything about Camila is so opposite of who I am. Where I can be cold and unapproachable, she is warm and inviting. Both my exterior and interior are hard and often perceived as cruel, but she is nothing but soft and kind. I find myself shocked no one has questioned our relationship. I don't deserve a wife like her, even as a fake wife.

"Incoming, incoming," Talan squeals out the side of his mouth as he rushes past me. I pay him no attention because once again my eyes are glued on the woman beside me. She places her arm around my waist and looks up at me with a twinkle in her eyes.

"Ah, the Camerons. So nice to see you both."

Camila is still smiling up at me but it's turned into more of a panicked smile, with all of her brilliant white teeth showing. Her hand grips tighter around my waist and she gives me a bump with her hip. Her mouth barely moves but I swear it says, *'Are you going to say something, idiot?'* The words rattle around in my head and I look up to find Samantha standing with a wolfish grin spread across her face.

"Sorry, Sam, I didn't see you there. You look lovely tonight."

"Flattery will get you nowhere, I'm afraid," she quips.

I step out of our uncomfortable little triangle and grab three glasses of champagne from someone walking by with a tray. I extend one to Samantha and one to Camila, raise my glass—and my eyebrows—and throw the flute back in one gulp before dropping it back on the same tray. I slide one hand into my pocket and wrap my other around Camila, pulling her closer to my side.

I've known Sam since I was in law school, I was her personal junior associate when I first started at Smith & Mitchell. I have a certain loyalty to her, but the way she's looking at Camila like she wants to chew her up and spit her out has a protectiveness surging through me.

"It's nice to see you again, Ms. Mitchell," Camila says, ever so sweetly.

Yeah. I definitely don't deserve her—real or fake.

Samantha, still in shark mode turns towards her, "I don't think I ever heard the details of your wedding, besides that no one was there..." I know she's trying to catch me in a lie but fuck her for trying to use Camila to do it. And double fuck me for actually putting her in this position in the first place. I'm racking my brain for a quick response so I can get her out of this woman's presence as soon as possible.

"Oh, it was beautiful," Camila blurts out. "It was really special for us to be able to share such an intimate moment with just the two of us. We both spend so much time on other things; friends, family, *work."* She adds an extra bite to the word work as if all this time that I've spent in the office this last year has been a real damper for her. "We talked about doing something at a later time with…everyone," she motions to Sam. "It just hasn't been a high priority for us. Maybe for an anniversary or something, huh, babe?" She looks up at me now and not for the first time has this woman completely stunned me. I pull her in close, close my eyes, and kiss the top of her head.

"Yes. Anything you want."

"Mhmm, and what's next for you two? Shall we be expecting some babies anytime soon?"

Thank fuck I wasn't sipping any champagne or Samantha would be wearing it right now, but it doesn't stop me from choking all the same.

"Samantha!" Camila playful scolds her. "I'm no lawyer but if I could offer you any advice, it would be to not ask other women about their plans to procreate." Her smile is forced but still so beautiful. Camila has left me slack-jawed and I have to force myself to swallow. "But if you must know, I think we're going to start small. We just went to a dog adoption event last weekend, so we may potentially start with a fur baby," she says in a sing-song voice.

Absolutely not. But I smile anyway, because for all the money in this room right now, I couldn't not smile at Camila.

"Well, you two really are something." Samantha huffs and somehow I've forgotten she was even here. "I need to make the rounds now. Enjoy your night." She tilts her champagne to us before stalking off.

I turn to Camila wrapping both my arms around her, as I bring my forehead to hers. She closes her eyes and blows out a long breath. "How'd I do?" And for the first time all night, her bravado falls a little.

"I'd believe you," I answer before pressing a soft kiss to her forehead and locking our fingers together. "Let's go find a real drink at the bar."

The people walking around with trays of champagne aren't going to cut it anymore. I'll need something a little stronger to get through tonight.

"Uh, whisky neat, and a champagne please," Camila orders for us, and I look at her with a raised brow. "What? Your drink order isn't that hard, *honey*," she says, fluttering her eyelashes at me.

I'm aware that anybody in my office would know my drink order. I'm pretty sure the bartenders at every restaurant in the city know my drink of choice. But something about Camila knowing what I want hits me differently.

I feel a slap on my shoulder. "Ayye, look who finally decided to grace us with his presence," Jonas beams. With his arm wrapped around me, he holds up his glass and nods to Camila. "Camila, you look stunning." Before I know it, my elbow is jabbing him in his ribs and he folds over with a grunt. "I was going to say *thank you* for getting everyone's favorite asshole to show his face at one of these events for once, but now I'm thinking you should have left him at home."

To her credit, she purses her lips to the side trying to hide her smile.

"Here let's take a picture." I move to stand behind Camila as Jonas raises his phone with one hand and his glass again with the other. He snaps a quick photo of the three of us before he starts typing away.

"Who are you sending selfies to Jonas?" Camila giggles.

"Taylor," he responds without looking up from his phone.

Camila and I exchange a glance and judging by the way her eyebrows squish together I conclude she wasn't aware her friend kept in contact with Jonas either. Before either one of us can ask, Jonas is laughing, "Check this out." He hands his phone to Camila with a picture of Taylor on what I'm assuming is a couch even though it looks more like a pile of old blankets, holding up a beer bottle and a box of Chinese takeout. The text reads '*I hope you dance so much your feet blister. Call me later, I'm determined to stay up till I finish season 4 tonight."*

Camila hands him his phone and he goes right back to texting.

"Why is Taylor sending you selfies?" she asks.

"Oh apparently she's never seen *Buffy,* and I got her hooked last weekend but since I had to be *here* tonight and she wanted to keep watching, I told her she could but only if she sent pictures of her live reactions so I wouldn't miss it."

I'm glad Camila is able to carry this conversation because I'm at a loss for words. Jonas doesn't have female friends. And he doesn't work this hard to sleep with someone either so I'm left standing here scratching the back of my neck.

"What's your motive here, Jonas?" Her eyes narrow into tiny slits as she points a finger at him.

Jonas finishes typing his text before sliding his phone

back into his jacket pocket. "Relax, we're just friends." His head tilts to the side with his signature smile.

She eyes him cautiously before looking up to me for confirmation.

His eyes bounce between Camila and me and because he's skittish and likely worried about what I'll say, he foolishly blurts out, "And let's not throw stones, shall we? Considering what you two are trying to convince everyone here of."

I know he's joking because I know Jonas, but Camila doesn't and I can see her start to turn inward a bit and the thought of her being embarrassed or unsure of herself has my molars grinding. With my arm already wrapped around her shoulder I pull her in closer. "Camila, did you know our friend Jonas here is one of those *cool guys* that goes by his last name?"

"Ah fuck," he mumbles, throwing his head back. "Should have known this shit was coming."

I move to grab his shoulder, maybe digging in a little too tightly. "Herbert Preston Jonas the third, here."

Camila's eyes widen and her jaw falls slack before she quickly shuts it and covers her smile with her hand.

"You're an asshole, you know that," he says to me. I only offer him a wide smile.

"Okay boys, while you continue to do whatever weird thing you're doing, I'm going to head to the ladies room." She hands me her drink, as she squeezes between us.

"Look for any single ladies for me while you're in there," Jonas shouts after her.

She looks over her shoulder and gives a little salute, "Aye aye, Herbie."

His jaw falls like he's deeply offended but I can't help but burst into a fit of laughter.

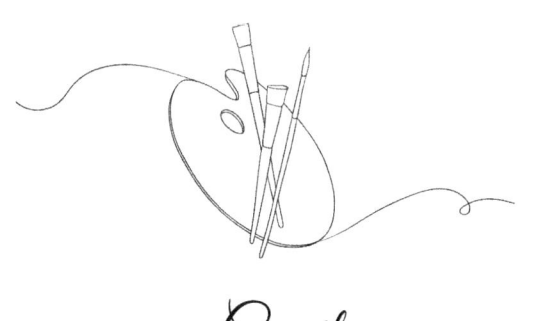

Camila

It feels like I've walked a mile through the expansive hotel but I can still feel Miles's laugh vibrating through my chest. It's a shame he's such a grump to everyone else because I swear his laughter could cure depression.

I slip into the bathroom that is no less extravagant than the rest of the hotel. There's a cushioned circle couch in the middle and a long vanity with gold-flecked mirrors behind it. My face is flush and I wish I could just douse myself in some cold water, but I settle for washing my hands and taking a few deep breaths. The heavy door swings open and the room fills with giggling women. Three of them head to the stalls in the far back to actually use the bathroom, while one sits waiting on the couch. Our eyes meet in the mirror and her eyes bulge out before she recovers.

"Oh my god. Your Miles's wife. Camila, right?"

I've met so many people tonight that I honestly don't remember who is who anymore. But I don't want to be offensive in case this is someone important, so I nod and give a polite smile.

The woman struts over to me in her short black dress, extending her hand. "I'm Nina, it's nice to meet you. I used to work with Miles."

There is nothing inherently wrong with anything she's saying, but the way she's looking me up and down has me a little on edge. I chuck it up to being an anxious Annie, dry my hands, and extend one to meet hers. "Nice to meet you, Nina. You said you used to work with Miles. Are you at another firm now?"

Her friends start filing out of the stalls as they look at her out of the corners of their eyes.

"I am, I left Smith & Mitchell about six months ago. Enjoying my new firm a lot more, that's for sure." She gives me a knowing smile. Although I'm clearly so far out of the loop.

Like a flock, they head to the door. Before Nina exits she eyes me up and down once more. "Well again, it was so nice to meet you, Camila."

What the hell is with this lady? My mouth forms a tight line and I give a small wave as they exit.

I blow out a deep breath as I throw myself onto the couch, taking another minute to myself since my first few were ruined.

ME

> So like…what's up with you and Jonas? You left out the part where you've still been talking to him?..

TAYLOR

> Lmao. Did I?

ME

> Taylor!

TAYLOR

😂 Chill. I'm just joking. We've hung out a few times, he's cool. That's it. You know me. No relationships going on over here.

ME

*raises a skeptic brow

TAYLOR

I love it when you talk dirty to me

Me

Really? My eyebrows do it for you?

TAYLOR

😊😊😊

ME

You're insane.

TAYLOR

Love you too.

I smile to myself as I slip my phone back into my extra tiny bag, straighten myself out in the mirror, and head back out.

Looking around the crowded room, it shouldn't be difficult to find Miles, I seem to have some kind of magnetic attraction to him. But I might be too focused on finding him and less focused on what's right in front of me. I get knocked back when I accidentally bump into a man who I don't recognize. His hand quickly grabs ahold of my elbow so I don't go down.

"Oh! I'm so sorry," I say, my cheeks heating in embarrassment.

"No. No." His hand moves to my shoulder as he searches my eyes, likely wondering if I've had too much to drink and need to be put in a cab. I run a hand down my dress and shake the nerves away. He grabs two glasses of champagne from a tray nearby, and hands one to me. "My fault, I should watch where I'm standing."

I take the glass and smile at this man who is clearly trying to make me feel better.

"I'm Steven," he says with a handsome smile. "And I know for a fact I haven't met you before because I would have remembered you." His handsome smile looks a little more creepy now.

For the second time in five minutes, I'm having to force myself to be polite. The worst thing I could do is be rude to someone who is important to Miles. I never want to make him look bad, so I paint a smile on my face and make small talk.

Steven is hammering on about his multi-million dollar company that he supposedly built all on his own, while I struggle to look engaged and search for Miles. I'm about to excuse myself when I feel a familiar heat burning into my neck. Discreetly, I dip my chin to my shoulder and peek behind me. I'm not surprised at all to find Miles leaning against the bar staring me down. We lock eyes in a familiar way and it takes me a minute to register that someone is saying my name.

I quickly turn my head back toward Steven. "I'm sorry. What?"

"I said, what do you do?"

"Um, well, I'm actually between jobs right now. I used to work for an investment banking company, but it didn't work out, and now I'm just looking for the right fit for me."

I'm waiting for the right moment to excuse myself when Steven puts his hand on my lower back. His cologne overwhelms me—he smells like insect repellent and not a natural one either. The pressure on my back tightens when he pulls me into him, and a slimy smirk spreads across his face. "Well, if I had any sense I would take you outside to finish this conversation."

"If you had any sense you would take your hands off my wife."

Miles's deep voice is rough behind me, I can feel his hard body pressed flush to my back and I fall into it with instant relief.

Steven takes a step back, tilting his head up to look at Miles and he extends his hand. "Miles Cameron, haven't seen you at one of these events in a while. So long, in fact, I guess I wasn't aware you were married."

Miles leaves Steven's hand outstretched. He wraps one hand around my waist and the other rests on my bare shoulder. The weight of it seeps all the way down to the bottom of my stomach and it's a good thing he left him hanging. I have no doubt that would have been a bone-crushing handshake.

Steven thankfully takes the hint. "Okay, well this has been wonderful," he snips before turning on his heels and charging off.

When I turn in Miles's arms to face him, a muscle in his jaw twitches, and his eyes are so dark they're borderline animalist. I bring my hand up to cup his jaw, feeling his stubble beneath my hands, "Hey, are you okay?" I ask gently.

Still eyeing the path that Steven headed down, Miles fumes, "I should follow him and tear that little shit apart for touching you."

"It's okay." I'm not sure if it's from the immediate relief I felt when he showed up, the way his scruffy face feels under my touch, or the way his dark eyes are now burning into me but I feel a shift in him.

"Let's go, Camila," he grunts.

"Where are we going?"

"It seems you need to be reminded of who you're married to."

My heart pounds violently against my chest as Miles takes my hand and stalks out of the crowded room.

Miles

I WAS STANDING AT THE BAR WITH JONAS LISTENING TO HIM ramble on about finding someone to take home tonight when my eyes found Camila talking with Steven McCorkle. Ice rattled against the glass from how tightly I gripped my drink. Blood rushed to my ears and when he put his grimy hands on *my* Camila, something in me snapped. All I saw was red and I was across the room in seconds. It feels as if everything from my muscles to my thoughts have been tethered down by a string that's been slowly fraying. My body is practically vibrating from the tension, I'm pulled so taught right now and the only thing keeping me the slightest bit grounded was the feeling of Camila's body sinking into mine.

I can't think. I can't concentrate as the blood still roars through my ears. I'm all but sprinting down the hallway with Camila's feet close behind me. When I find the room I'm looking for I throw the door open and check the stalls before slamming the door shut and locking it.

I prowl towards Camila, taking my time as I loosen my tie. Her chest lifts slightly as she steps back into the vanity behind her. One look at her knuckles turning pale as she clutches onto the counter gives away her calm facade.

"Miles, I'm sorry if I upset you." Her breath is shaky. "I wasn't sure who was important to you or who I should be trying to impress."

And that frayed string that was holding me together snaps. This perfect woman thinks she needs to impress people because of *me.* I did this.

I clear the last inch of space between us, gripping her hips in both hands. Searching her face, waiting for her to refuse this. But when her chin lifts and her eyes burn into me with a combination of lust and anticipation, my hold on her tightens and I spin her around. Her eyes snap open wide, hands shooting up to the mirror. A flame ignites, burning hot and bright in my stomach. My left hand sinks into her hair and I tug her head back, resting it on my shoulder. I trail my nose down the column of her neck devouring her scent. When a subtle shudder racks through her, I stop and swipe my tongue at the sensitive spot of her neck. "You misunderstand me, mi esposa," I whisper against her skin. "I'm not mad at *you.* Even though I should be mad that you've been teasing my cock in this dress all night." I keep one hand locked tightly in her hair and drag the other along the front of her thigh, digging my fingers into her hips at the top. "I'm angry because some piece of shit thinks he can touch what's mine."

Her skin breaks out in tiny goosebumps. "Yours?" she shudders.

"You're *my* wife, Camila. And I don't mind reminding you of that."

"H-how?" Her eyelids begin to flutter as her ass involuntarily presses into me. Searching.

"You're going to watch as I make you come."

Her eyes snap open and meet mine in the mirror. "Miles..." she breathes.

"That's right. And the next time you say my name it will be somewhere between a cry and a scream. Now, spread your legs."

My grip on her hip tightens but to her credit, she slides her legs out wider for me. A static shock runs through the palm of my hand as I drag it through the slit of her dress, up and down her warm, smooth leg. My fingers dance along her inner thigh before trailing back up to the center of her underwear. I'm met with lace fabric. My eyes roll and I can't help the grunt that forms at the back of my throat as I drop my face to her neck. "Did you wear these for me, Camila?"

"I—" Her eyes flutter closed and I give her pussy a tight little slap causing her to jerk forward.

"If you're going to remember whose wife you are, you need to watch. Now, tell me, who did you wear this tiny scrap of fabric for?"

"You."

Her raspy voice has my fist flexing. My knuckles drag up her slit finding her underwear already soaked through. "Look how wet you are." Her teeth pierce her lip, in an effort to stifle her cries and I hook my middle finger through her underwear before sliding them to the side. "Is this all for me?" The air in the room grows thick but her head dips forward subtly nodding yes. My middle and ring fingers split her lips and I slide them up and down, catching her clit in between and giving it a little squeeze.

"Oh my God," she whimpers. I press a kiss to the dip where her neck meets her collarbone and slide my hand down to her entrance.

She's so fucking wet.

My finger slips inside her easily and I add another. I know

I shouldn't be doing this, but right now I can't think of a single clear thought as Camila pulses around me. Every squeeze has my cock twitching, straining against my pants.

She might only be my wife on paper but now isn't the time to think about why that makes my skin sweat. My breath turns ragged as I continue to pump inside her. The logical part of my brain tells me to stop, but every fiber of my being is forcing me to keep going. I bring my thumb to her pulsing clit and stroke it back and forth. The way she grips my fingers tells me she's close and fuck, do I wish it was my cock she was riding instead.

"Oh, fuck, Miles, I think... I'm—"

I pull my fingers out and she yelps, "No! What are you—?"

"Turn around." My voice is as deep as I wish I was inside her.

Her eyes stay on mine through the mirror a moment longer before she turns her body to face me. I pull her body flush with mine, my cock now pressing into her stomach through my pants. My face hovers over her and to my surprise, she doesn't shy away from the prolonged eye contact.

If there was ever a time to stop, it would be now. "Camila—"

Her lips crash into mine. It's not gentle; she's no longer exploring. Her mouth parts open and I pull her bottom lip into mine, nipping and sucking. A faint metallic taste coats my tongue. As our tongues tease each other the moment of doubt I had flies out the window. There's no going back now.

I pull back, *fuck she's so beautiful.* Her bottom lip is fuller now and a deep red color fills her cheeks. I drop to my knees in front of her and slide the bottom part of her dress out of the way. Finally, face to face with her pussy, I can't waste my time taking off the lace fabric. I slide my index fingers down her center and rip a hole in her underwear. She's glistening for me.

Her smooth ankle feels so delicate in my hand. I drag my fingers up her calf, lifting her leg before I drape it over my shoulder, and slowly begin licking my way up her thigh.

"Wait!" Her cold hands reach between her and grab the sides of my face. I pause, looking up at her. Maybe she's stronger than I am. Maybe she's going to tell me to stop. That we can't do this. I'm ready for anything, but then she says, "I—I've never done this before."

Anything but that. I swear I hear a ringing in my ear as if a bomb just went off. My insides go feral. I'm not a religious man, I don't believe in a lot of things, but at this moment I have to believe in something. Because on what planet would I get to be the first person to get to make her fall apart like this?

I feel the absolute wickedness in the smile that comes over me. "Then you better hold on tight." I begin peppering kisses along her inner thigh. "Camila..." She makes a sound somewhere between a "huh?" and a moan. "Eyes on me." I flatten my tongue and run a path all the way up to her clit, lapping up her arousal.

"Oh fuck!" she screams as her hips buck forward.

I pull her into my mouth, relishing in her taste. When her hands find my hair and her nails dig in, I wonder if she can feel me smile against her. Her body begins to wither beneath me, "It's too much," she says, shaking her head back and forth. I grip her ass with one hand to steady her, "Please!"

"Please what, Camila?" My other hand slides up to tease her entrance.

Her glossy eyes fixate on me. "I need to come."

Her words are my undoing. I thrust both fingers in,

curling them, hitting that spot hidden inside her while my tongue continues to roll over her clit. My chest goes weightless as her body trembles. She comes apart before me but I don't stop. I continue to fuck her with my tongue as she cries my name over and over while continuing to squeeze and soak my fingers.

When she's rung out the last of her orgasm, I stand making quick work of my zipper. My throbbing cock springs out of my briefs, smacking my stomach. Camila's eyes turn dark. She still hasn't caught her breath but her tongue still swipes along her bottom lip anyway. As tempting as her mouth is—and trust that I would do vile things to have the pleasure of her mouth on me, that's not why I brought her in here. And I won't let her forget why we're here.

Reaching between Camila's legs, I swipe my hand up her inner thighs, soaking up what's left of her arousal. My hand drags up until I reach her dripping pussy and she jerks at the touch. Her eyes go wide when I hold my hand out in front of her.

"Spit."

Her heavy breathing catches as her stare darts between my eyes and my hand. I'm about to do it myself when she surprises me by dipping her head to my palm, eyes on me, and in the most demure way possible, she spits in it.

A deep rumble vibrates in my chest at the sight. Her breathing slows while her chest rises and falls in a deeper rhythm now and a lighter blush paints her cheeks.

I grab a hold of my shaft, and stroke it at an unbearably slow pace because if I add any kind of pressure I'm absolutely going to be a two-pump chump.

"Hearing you beg for what you want made me so fucking hard."

Pump pump.

"It's not your job to please anyone, you understand me? Everyone else needs to get on their goddamn knees for you. None of them matter."

Stroke.

"Seeing you in that dress tonight, knowing you wore that underwear for me, feeling how wet you were..."

Her eyes go from confusion to understanding to bold and I can feel my own orgasm building. My lower back is on fire, tingling in anticipation.

"Whose wife are you, Camila?" I'm panting now, my strokes turning into uncontrolled jerky movements.

Her eyes focus intently on me as she slides the strap of her dress down her arm and pulls the front of her dress down, exposing her full breasts to me. Her dress hangs at her waist and it's my turn to be shocked when she leans back against the vanity. "Yours."

It takes two seconds and one last stroke and I blow all over her chest and stomach. Dark spots threaten the corners of my eyes but I quickly blink them away and slow my breathing down in time to watch Camila's jaw fall. She's likely in shock from the way I just fucked my hand and spilled my cum all down her chest. But my breath stalls when she brings one of those polished fingers over her breast. She slides her rock-hard nipples between her fingers, coating them in the mess I made.

I lean forward, running my tongue along her bottom lip, letting her taste herself before I drop my forehead to hers. An hour from now I'll dwell on the fact that I lost control and see this for the major fuck up it is. But right now, I'm going to ignore it and embrace this.

Camila

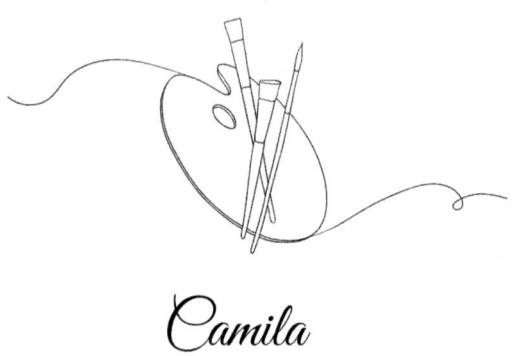

A WARM LATE-MORNING BREEZE FLOWS THROUGH THE OPEN bedroom window. When I open my eyes the sheer white curtains are blowing across the peaceful room. I focus on nothing outside, taking note of how relaxed my body is. As if I'm floating on a cloud in a dream-like state.

For approximately forty-five seconds.

My breath catches and my stomach flips at the memory of last night. I can still feel the rough heat from Miles's palm as he dragged me out of the party and into the bathroom. Every nerve in my body sparked in response to his touch. From the slow caress of his mouth on my neck to the way his fingers tugged my hair at the root. My eyes squeeze shut and I can see his black-as-night eyes as clearly as if he were in front of me right now. The hairs on my arms are alert at the memory of the way his eyes burned into mine when he got down on his knees.

I've never had a sexual experience like that before. I might not be a virgin but I'm definitely not the most experienced either. I've only been intimate with men I was in a relationship with so it's definitely been a while. I never thought sex was something that I missed but now I'm starting to think it's because I've never given a lot of thought to what I might enjoy. Likely because I know I would never be brave enough to ask for it.

I'm a people pleaser to my core, something I've known about myself for a long time. But now I'm wondering if that's something that's stopped me in more areas of my life than I realized.

Rolling over onto my back, I stroke the linen duvet cover beneath my fingers. My legs become restless and the familiar feeling of anxiety begins to work its way through my body. I'm worried about what last night meant, or worse, what it didn't mean. I've felt the tension building between us for weeks, it's almost palpable. I would be able to handle it if last night was just the cap blowing off, releasing some of that pressure. But the truth is, for whatever reason I can't explain, I like Miles. I've thought about him as more than the guy that I made some strange arrangement with. Luckily every time I've caught myself having thoughts of him, I've always been able to remind myself that he made it very clear he would never want anything more. But his actions contradict his words. And if he did want something more than our agreement, would I be able to offer him enough?

My stomach begins to turn and I'm plagued with worry around all the unanswered questions. Will this change our relationship? Will he think it was a mistake? Do I think it was a mistake? Was it a one-time thing or do I wish it were more? Will I be okay if he does think it was a mistake?

Anxiety is a weird thing because the last thing I want to do is leave this bed right now. However, staying in bed and letting the thoughts fester is just as bad, but I can't stop myself. It's a feeling I've never been able to properly voice, like dread, but heavier.

I focus on the palm frond painting above my dresser—the intricate veins of the leaves and the way the gold foil paint helps pull the eyes to the deep green colors. I trace the lines with my eyes over and over again until my tired mind finally pulls me back to sleep.

WHEN I WAKE AGAIN, IT'S DARK. THE BREEZE BLOWING through my cracked window now has a deep chill. My eyes adjust to shadows in the dark room only being lit by the full moon outside. Slowly, I peel myself off the mattress and slide to the edge of the bed. I can't tell if I'm actually feeling better or if I'm just so out of it from a full night of sleep and then sleeping the day away.

My phone lights up on the dresser and I grab it on my way to the bathroom. 8:30 p.m. *Holy shit.* I have one missed call from Taylor and one from my mom. I definitely don't have the energy for any of that right now so I set my phone down on the counter and leave it there.

The warm water plops down on my skin and then washes over me. The shampoo begins to sud in my hair and I can feel the phantom touch of Miles's fingers gripping me. My stomach flips twice before I'm able to steady myself enough to rinse off. When I get out, the rumbling of my stomach echoes off the bathroom walls. It's an effort to get dressed, but I slide into a new pair of silk pajama shorts and another oversized crewneck. Water continues to drip down from my hair onto my chest, I give it one more squeeze with the towel before I make my way downstairs.

I pause halfway down the stairs, listening for any signs that Miles is home. The hum of the refrigerator and my heartbeat are the only sounds filling the air. The recessive lighting under the cabinets in the kitchen is soft but in the dark space they light up the room enough, so I pad barefoot into the kitchen.

I search the pantry for any kind of food that would be considered 'storm shelter food'. All it takes is seeing rows of glass containers of oats, flour, and pasta to remember I'm living with a billionaire whose private chef prepares him things that, although delicious, just aren't what I'm craving now. I audibly huff my annoyance when I realize I'm not going to find a cup of noodles in here and I move on to the refrigerator.

It takes a lot of digging, but I finally find some string cheese. That and a piece of toast will have to do. I move to the island where the bread box is and drop my string cheese when I notice Miles sitting in the dark living room across from me.

"Jesus. You scared the shit out of me." My hand instinctively clutches at my chest. "What are you doing there?"

"I was going to give you another thirty minutes before I sent someone into your room to check on you."

"Someone like who?" My voice comes out louder than I intended in the otherwise silent room.

"I don't know. Animal control maybe? Let them know I have a bear hibernating in my guest room."

I cock my head at him but otherwise ignore him and go back to making my toast.

"Camila."

My tense shoulders soften with his tone. It's as if I let go of a breath that has been stuck in my chest for twenty-four hours. His hand swirls the dark amber liquid in his crystal glass and I watch the column of his neck work when he throws all the contents back in one large swallow. My chest does a somersault when I think of what else his mouth can do and I quickly try to force down the dry lump in my own throat.

I'm desperate to end the tension between us but I don't feel brave enough to ask my burning questions so I play it safe. "So who's Nina?" His full eyebrows bunch together as he tilts his head. "Nina. I ran into her in the bathroom last night," I clarify before pausing at the memory of what happened later. "She definitely knew you and her friends seemed, I don't know? Strange? I could be in my head, but I felt like they were giving me weird looks."

"They shouldn't have." He runs an aggravated hand over his jaw. "Nina used to be a paralegal at the firm, she wasn't subtle about wanting to go out or anything *else* she wanted to do with me. She used to show up at restaurants and bars that Jonas and I would frequent after work."

The idea of him with another woman shouldn't hurt me but…I shake the thoughts and quickly place my bread in the toaster. I'm counting on the fact that if I fill my stomach with food, the sad, empty feeling in it will go away. "Is she a scorned lover?" I swallow down the discomfort in my chest and force my tone to remain casual.

"Absolutely not. I don't hook up with anyone more than once, let alone people I know I'll see again. She had a going away party at a restaurant a few months back, I think she was offended that I wouldn't bring her home that night either." He shrugs. "She scored with Jonas though."

My stomach drops and I want to hide. I know he isn't looking for a relationship. I didn't expect what happened last night to lead to one, but hearing him say this practically confirms it was nothing more than a one-time thing for him.

"Come here." His head tilts, motioning for me to come sit next to him. The dread is heavy in my legs as I walk over to the chair across from him. His hand snakes around my wrist in a silent ask to sit next to him. A metallic taste fills my mouth and only then do I realize the small hole I've chewed off from the inside of my cheek. Curling my legs up under me I take a seat beside him on the couch.

"Do you want to talk about it?" His voice is like gravel.

Yes. No. Fuck, I don't know. I wasn't expecting him to be so bold and just bring it up like that. The sound of the toaster pops in the distance but I've completely lost my appetite now so I ignore it.

"Not yet," I whisper.

He nods his head and bends forward towards the coffee table, the hem of his shirt rises, revealing a sliver of his lower back and my mouth goes dry as images of last night, tornado around my mind.

I twist my wet hair into a low bun as he sets my computer in my lap. "What's this for?"

"I figured now would be a good time to find out my enneagram."

A grateful smile spreads across my face because I know he's doing anything he can to make me feel comfortable. And if he's trying so hard, then maybe he doesn't think last night was a mistake. I let my body relax a little more as I sink further into the couch and fire up my laptop.

"I HAVE A VIVID IMAGINATION."

Miles throws his head back pretending to be annoyed. "Oh my god. All these questions are the same, I don't know."

"Okay, I'll say neither agree nor disagree *again*." I throw a pointed glance at him. "Next question. I show two different sides of myself to different people."

"Strongly agree." His eyes fixate on mine causing my entire body to feel like I'm being engulfed in flames. I don't need to ask to know that he's referring to me. It's obvious to anyone with eyes that he's different around me than he is with anyone else. I should have come out of my room a lot sooner because just being around Miles relaxes me in a way I've never felt before.

"You know what? I don't need this test to tell me, you're an eight," I say closing my laptop.

"What about you? What does the test say about you?"

I fill my cheeks with air before blowing it out with a heavy sigh. "The condensed version I guess would be gentle and nurturing. A 'yes' person, someone who will take care of everyone else before themselves and at the core, my basic desire is to be loved." The second the words are out of my mouth I wish I could take them back. It feels too vulnerable.

"Hmm," his eyes narrow in deep thought. "And do you agree with all of it?"

"There's definitely a lot more that goes into it than just that." I turn to face him. "But for the most part, yeah, I think so."

"And what type are you most compatible with?" *Eight.* I stare at him unmoving, my swallow audible.

"I'm not sure," I lie. His tongue swipes at his bottom lip before he pulls it between his teeth and my chest lifts on a shaky inhale. His long legs are sprawled out comfortable in front of him with an arm casually draped over the back of the couch. I set my laptop down and scoot closer to him. I place my hand on his knee and he drops our eye contact, concentrating heavily where my hand sits. When his body stiffens I hesitate, losing some of my nerve. "Tell me something," I say.

A long silent pause fills the room. His eyes remain on my hand and I've gone back and forth one hundred times on if I should move it, but I hold my breath and keep it there. Waiting.

"I really fucked up last night."

I've never actually been hit, but I imagine this is what it feels like. I pull my hand away as if I've been burned and violently rear my body back.

His head falls back with a grunt before looking at me. "Camila, I—"

I hold up a hand to stop him, "No. You know what, I shouldn't have said anything." I untangle my legs from under me and hastily move to get off the couch.

"You didn't say anything."

I don't remember what I said or didn't say. All I can hear is a ringing surrounded by *I really fucked up last night.* I walk around the coffee table trying like hell not to fall because I'm not even sure my brain is connected to my muscles anymore.

"Camila, wait. That's not what I meant."

"Please. Let's not do this. We have a few weeks left before we can do anything about our situation," I wave a hand between us. "And you were right before, we shouldn't complicate it. It's not a secret we might have had a little attraction to each other in the beginning but I've definitely worked that out of my system now. So, we're good. Let's just leave it at that. Please?"

His lips pull slightly down and his intense stare is too much for me to bear. He opens his mouth once and I look away.

"Okay..." His voice is dull and my eyes close for a brief moment before I hurry to the stairs. I don't need to look back to know his eyes are following me.

Staying in bed this morning and worrying about this exact outcome couldn't have prepared me for how terrible it would actually feel. I'm crushed and embarrassed. Mostly I'm annoyed that I even let myself believe last night would have changed anything. I've slowly been allowing myself to search for the things I didn't know I wanted, and the first thing I decide I want tells me a night with me was a mistake. But he did tell me from the very beginning this would never be anything more than a business deal and I would be better off remembering that from now on.

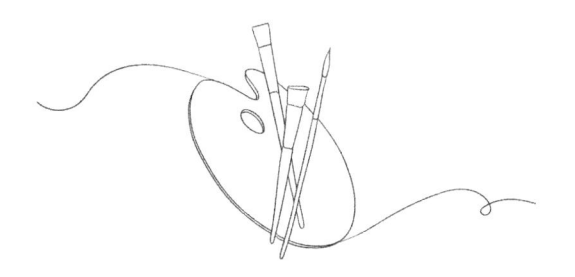

Camila

"It says here you were at your last company for five years?"

"Yes. That's correct." I'm lucky my bones haven't snapped from how hard I am twisting my fingers in my lap.

"Okay great." Mr. Moris flips over his stapled stack of papers while simultaneously grabbing a pen. "And Camila, what would you say your greatest weakness is?"

I should have canceled this interview the minute I woke up this morning. I was mentally drained. Instead, I laid in bed for twenty minutes, imagining a life where I was the type of person who could cancel anything last minute. Specifically an interview for a job that I don't want.

My face starts to heat because even though I don't care if I get this job or not I still want this man to be impressed by me, to like me. "Well," I shift around in my seat. *Fuck. Calm down.* The stale air is making it difficult to breathe. The moment I recognize the panic building inside my chest I start sweating and my voice comes out shaky. "I have a hard time saying no," I manage to get out. "But it's something I recognize about myself and I've been working on it."

"Great. And what are some steps you've taken to begin working on that? Because I'll be honest, we're a fast-moving ship here at LG & Co. and we tend to just pile on the work and it's up to each individual employee to know their limits. Especially before they get to that breaking point, you know?" His carefree chuckle has my nails digging tiny crescent moons into my palms. The sound of my thrumming heart battles the buzz of the fluorescent lights overhead and I have approximately two minutes left in me before I run out of here in tears.

I can't even tell *myself* no, let alone others and it's a bullshit lie that I've been working on that at all.

"Well let's just say it's an ongoing learning experience for me."

His lips press together in a straight line before looking down at his papers and shuffling them around. "Well, I think that's all I have on my end, do you have any questions for me?"

I shake my head harder than necessary, desperate to get out of here. I've made a complete fool of myself. I know it and Mr. Moris knows it. He moves to stand, reaching his hand across his desk. "It was a pleasure to meet you, Ms. Sanchez. We'll be in touch." I give an embarrassingly weak shake and force a smile before I turn to leave.

My heels clack on the marble floors as I dash through the lobby. Desperate to get outside. I can't get through the revolving door quickly enough. As soon as my feet hit the concrete outside, my shoulders rise on a massive inhale. But not even the fresh air is enough to get the oxygen needed to my lungs. *It's over. Breathe. You'll likely never have to see that stranger again. The job wasn't for you so who cares what he thinks. 'I don't give a fuck if someone likes me or not.'* Miles's words ring in my head. It was a bad interview for a job I didn't want. The strain on my chest is still present but not as painful as I let those words sink in.

When I decided to take the long way home I didn't take into account that I was wearing my interview heels and not my sneakers. The pinching pain digging into my toes is a sick distraction until my phone vibrates against my side.

Hobbling a few steps I make it over to an outdoor bistro and sit at an empty table before digging through my bag. I've taken so long that when I finally find my phone I answer it without even looking to see who's calling.

"Mija!" My stomach churns and my only saving grace is that I'm sitting down. "Hello?"

"H-hi mom," I answer, clutching my purse in a death grip to my chest.

"Hi honey, how are you?"

"I'm…" I'm having a difficult time breathing. "I'm good. How are you?"

"Busy, busy as usual." A waiter comes over to my table and I feel guilty for sitting here, not ordering anything so I cover the speaker of my phone and mouth 'coffee, black' and when she doesn't reply with an over-the-top smile, a cartwheel, or a 'great', I assume she hates me and I begin picking at a notch in the table. "Are you there, mija?"

Moisture begins to burn behind my eyelids. I haven't talked to my mom other than a few texts here and there over the last few weeks. I tried a few times. The least I could have done was let her know I left my job and I'm looking for a new one. Every time I picked up the phone to make that call I saw the disappointment across her face. I heard her asking a million questions that I either didn't have the answers to or *did* and couldn't stomach telling her the truth. The nausea rolled so heavily that it was enough to make me put the phone down every time.

"Yeah." The high pitch of my voice trying to fight back the cry is threatening to give me away. "I'm actually out to lunch with Taylor right now, and it's just kind of hard to hear."

"Okay, honey. Give me a call later then, yeah?"

"I will."

"Tell Taylor, I said hi. I love you, both."

"Love you too, Mom."

I drop my phone in my purse and put my head in my hands, focusing on my breath. The clink of my coffee hitting the table forces me to look up in time to see my waitress already heading back inside. I pull out cash to cover my drink and a tip and leave it next to the full cup.

Between the interview from hell and a phone call from my mom, caffeine is the last thing my anxiety needs right now.

Miles

"One, one two, five two!"

Sweat is dripping into and burning my eyes as our coach, Ray, calls out combinations.

"One one two! Five two three!"

We've been at this for almost an hour, but I'm so full of pent-up energy that even now when I should be exhausted and have nothing left in the tank I'm still throwing out punches at full force and unfortunately for Jonas, he's taking the brunt of it.

"One two one two! Good. Nice job today, boys." Ray gives us both a fist bump from the side of his palm as he leaves Jonas and me to cool down.

"So…what's up? You want to talk about why you're so on edge today?"

"No."

"Cool. How about why you've blown off our sessions the last two days and have had your ass parked in your office with Talan out front like a member of the secret service?"

I continue to untie my wraps as quickly as I can so I can get the fuck out of here. I don't bother responding to him.

Through the corner of my eye I make out the little smirk that hits his face and I know he's not going to let any of this go.

"Okay, then let's talk about where you and the Misses vanished off to the other night. I saw you drag her away from McCorkle and didn't see either of you the rest of the night. What happened?"

What happened was I lost my shit. I dragged her to the bathroom, where I demolished the line between a business relationship and something else. And not only that, but I wanted to. I wanted to cross that line. I wanted her and fuck, if I'm being honest with myself, I've *been* wanting her. The problem is I thought I could get her out of my system. I thought my desire to have her body under me, my hands and mouth roaming every inch of her would be enough. But it's not. It's like somehow she's worked her way into every part of me, filling my thoughts in ways I'm not used to. And now I want her in ways I never thought I would want someone.

When I told her I fucked up, I meant that I should have had a conversation with her. I should have made sure we were on the same page. I could have taken her home and fucked her right. Instead, I waited until the pressure got too heavy, and I popped off like a lion let out of a cage.

"Dude..." Jonas says waving his hand in front of my face.

Just thinking about Camila calms me down and spins me out all at the same time. "I don't know what you want me to tell you. We left early. And I've been busy."

He scoffs at my vague answer. "Bullshit."

Our session might be over but I give him the look that tells him I'll go another round. Unfortunately for me, he's like a dog with a bone and I know he's not going to drop this.

"Alright look, I didn't want to say anything the other night, but if your piss poor mood has anything to do with Camila, I've gotta say it now…" I shove my wraps in my bag while he continues to stand there with his hands on his hips trying to hide his dumb-ass smile. "You like her."

I wish he would let that smile rip so I could knock it off his face.

"I know the almighty, anti-feelings, no relationship having, Miles Cameron might not know what it feels like to *have* feelings, so if you're confused bro, it's alright." He slaps my shoulder and I actually snarl at him. "But seriously, I think it's good. Camila's great, and you're...alright. If you like her, I think you should see where it could go."

"It's not going to go anywhere," I snap at him.

Jonas hangs his head and comes to sit by me on the bench, his face serious now. "Miles, I know you never wanted to be in a relationship because of your parents—"

My back goes rigid at his words, and not because we've never talked about my parents before, but I guess out of habit.

"But not every relationship is a mirror of another one. If it was, nobody would be happy." When I don't respond he lets out a breath. "I'm just saying you could have something real with her if you wanted."

"Even if I wanted to, she doesn't. She told me so last weekend, and she's been avoiding me since, so drop it."

"If she said that, and you believed her, then you haven't been paying attention to the way that girl looks at you."

I want to believe him. I want to ask him how she looks at me. But I know all it will do will make me more interested in someone who told me to forget about it. So instead I throw my bag over my shoulder and storm out into the foggy morning chill.

"First, I want to say thank you to everyone who attended the fundraiser this past weekend. I'm aware it's not a competition but if it were, I would be proud to say that our firm put up the most money out of any other firm in attendance."

All twenty people sitting around the massive conference room table smile and clap. I on the other hand only notice that Smith is back in attendance for this mid-week senior partner meeting. It goes without saying that if I convinced Samantha that my marriage is legitimate, I could be walking out of here as the new name partner. If I didn't, all eyes will be on me because the rumor mill hasn't let up over the weeks. Whispers about my title have been spreading like wildfire according to Talan.

"Second, we have some very exciting news today." Sam's smiling but all her teeth are showing which tells me it's forced. And since she hasn't bothered to look at me, for the first time, I'm nervous. "After many meetings and careful consideration, we are happy to announce our new name partner, Miles Cameron."

Internally, I let out a huge sigh of relief and brace my elbows on my knees, but outwardly I barely give anything more than a nod, and at that, all eyes in the room are on me. Some genuinely happy, some skeptical or confused, but everyone claps anyway and shakes my hand in congratulations.

"Smith & Mitchell is officially Smith, Mitchell, & Cameron as of today, and it is our hope that the transition goes smoothly for everyone." She finally looks at me but her eyes are more threatening than congratulating. So I lean back in my seat, the picture of unaffected, and give her a winning smile.

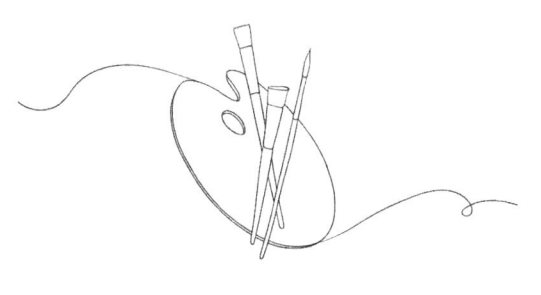

Camila

"Wills is kind of hot, in like a *who's your daddy* kind of way, no?" Taylor leans over, whispering to me in the back seat.

I roll my lips between my teeth, bringing my hand to my forehead. "Please don't."

She backs up to her side of the car. She shrugs. "What?"

I've been in hermit mode since the interview from hell. And I haven't seen Miles in two days. When he texted me to meet him out tonight, he neglected to mention that it was a celebration for such a huge accomplishment. I only found out from Taylor who found out from Jonas.

As the car pulls up outside the bar, I look out the window and my fingers twist my ring back and forth. I've been telling myself I've been avoiding Miles since my interview but truthfully I would have avoided him after that night anyway. I let myself catch feelings for him and the rejection stung more than I anticipated. I shouldn't be avoiding him though. It's not his fault. He told me from the beginning that he doesn't do relationships. And I don't need any more confirmation that I need to keep my feelings in check. So I've played it safe the last few days by avoiding him. I think the close proximity and the tension have just been playing tricks on me. I didn't plan to avoid him forever just long enough to get my mind—and libido—in check.

There's no avoiding him now though. As soon as we walk into the bar my eyes find him. I'd like to think it's because of his sheer size he sticks out, or because he looks sexy as fuck in his massive 6-foot-something frame wearing a three-piece suit and standing at a tabletop next to the bar, but I know it's not. I would be able to find Miles in a packed stadium. I'm attracted to him like a moth to a flame. His eyes find mine and my legs still. I try to swallow the dry lump in my throat with only a second to normalize my breathing before Taylor's arm loops through mine and she points in his direction. "Ah! There they are."

My eyes never leave his as Taylor pulls us through the crowd towards the table. "Hey! Congratulations, big guy!" She slaps his shoulder as she passes him to head towards the bar where Jonas is standing.

Before I've even set my clutch down, Miles's hand splays across my lower back as he pulls me flush against his body and his mouth finds mine. His lips are soft. Questioning. As if in answer, my lips part on their own and invite him in. He gets the message because a heartbeat later, his other hand cups my cheek, and his tongue glides along my bottom lip, causing a soft moan to escape my mouth. One which he quickly soaks up with a more forceful kiss. I immediately miss his touch when he pulls back and looks at me. "I've missed you."

My eyes go wide and bounce back and forth between his eyes and lips. "I—"

"Hey, congratulations Cameron!" A man in a suit claps him on the shoulder interrupting my thoughts. He shakes the man's hand while keeping his other hand firmly planted on my back.

"Thanks, Dom. Did you get a drink?"

"Not yet, but I heard they were on you tonight."

"The rumors are true."

"Alright alright." Dom smiles and shakes his hand again. "I'll be at the bar then. Camila, it's nice to see you again." He reaches his hand out and I give it a small shake confused about where I would have seen this man before but I smile anyway and he turns to leave.

As I watch him head off, I look around for the first time and notice the room is full of people I vaguely recognize.

A waiter arrives with a tray full of shots filled with a brown liquid. "These are from that table over there." She points to a table surrounded by people sitting in a booth behind Miles. He picks up one of the glasses and holds it up to them in thanks before turning back towards me.

"Shot?"

"No thank you, I only do clear alcohol." He doesn't drink his either, but instead puts it back down on the tray with the others "Who are those people? They look familiar."

"Some colleagues from the office. They were all at the fundraiser."

Of course. This room is filled with people from the fundraiser. Meaning we're surrounded by people he works with and the reason behind that kiss was nothing more than for show. Disappointment floods my body but I recover quickly, throwing a pinched smile on my face.

Jonas and Taylor return with drinks but don't set them down. "Let's go, the dart boards are open," Taylor says, motioning her head towards the back.

Miles leads the way and to play up my part I slip my hand

into his. He looks back at me and for some reason, his face seems relieved.

"Boys against girls?" Jonas shouts.

"What do I get when I win?" Taylor asks.

I look at Miles who's only trying to hold in his laughter. He seems so relaxed tonight. Like the Miles that I know when it's just us alone together.

"How about a thousand bucks?" Jonas asks, and my jaw drops but Taylor's eyes narrow into tiny slits.

"You're on," she says.

"Um, we don't have a thousand bucks to bet, Tay."

"We don't need it. We kill it at darts," she says. "Alright, five minutes of practice, and then you're going down, Jo-Bro."

I step back, bumping into Miles's hard body. His arms wrap around me, steadying me and his head dips to my shoulders. "You've been avoiding me, mi esposa." My knees threaten to buckle under me at the combination of the name and his touch.

"I've just been busy," I lie.

"Busy avoiding me?"

He turns me around to face him. "What do you want me to say? It's weird. I don't know where we stand and I don't know how to act now," I mumble, mortified that I'm one, admitting this and two, doing it here in a crowded bar. He cracks a smile and tugs me against him in a tight hug. My body melts into his and even though he hasn't said anything, the tightness in my chest eases tremendously with the feeling of his body pressed to mine, holding me, he's like my own personal weighted blanket.

"I'm sorry if you've felt uncomfortable and I never want you to feel like you need to *act* any certain way." He pulls back just enough to search my face. "What do you want,

Camila? What will make you happy?" What I want is to go back in time. To whenever I started having these weird feelings for him and tell myself it's not going to go anywhere. I want to tell him that this awkward place we've been in since the fundraiser is killing me and I want to stop being confused, trying to differentiate between what's real and what's not between us.

But since I'll never say any of that out loud— "I want us to get back to whatever our version of normal is," I mumble without looking at him.

"Okay done," he shrugs. And my head snaps up to look at him.

"No, Miles."

"What?"

"You can't just say *done* and it's fixed."

"Then tell me what you want me to do and I'll do it." I might not know what I want, but I'm not sure he knows what he wants either. He's constantly contradicting himself—one minute he's starting to open up, and the next he's telling me that night was a mistake. The fact is, I *have* been avoiding him. And I might be setting myself up for failure here but I like being around him too much. I'd rather stuff my feelings for him down to the deepest parts of myself, than avoid him anymore in hopes that those feelings go away.

"I just want you to talk to me. Or at least do that annoying one-word answer to avoid my questions thing that you do when I talk to you. Just something," I say.

"Okay, let's talk." I eye him suspiciously as we sit down on a pair of stools nearby. A minute passes and the corners of his lips start to twitch, like he's working overtime to hide his smile. "So," he begins. "What do you want to talk about?" I roll my eyes and shove his broad shoulder getting up from the stool.

"Wait, I'm sorry. Come here," he says, reaching for my arm. "Let's talk." The combination of the warmth from his hand wrapping around me and the way his eyes are pleading with me causes me to melt. So once more I sit back down on my stool. "Why don't you tell me about the job interview you went to the other day."

I'm caught off guard at the mention of that interview or how he even knows about it but at least my stomach doesn't sink at the memory like I expected it to. "Who said I had an interview?"

"Well, it's been a week since you said you applied." My head tilts knowing there's more. "And I saw your little black heels on the floor the other day."

I shake my head, not surprised by his attention to detail. But even though I've moved on from that particularly unpleasant day, I still don't want to talk about it. "Alright, well it doesn't matter because that would be me talking to you, *again.*"

"It's just so much more enjoyable for me to hear you talk, though." His hand rests on my lap and I instinctively scoot closer to him. I've never been so attracted or wanted to understand and be let in by someone so infuriating. He's saying all the right things now but it doesn't negate all the wrong things he's already said.

"Well, it doesn't seem like we're getting anywhere or that we'll figure anything out tonight, so instead, why don't you tell me what your tattoo means now?"

"I already told you what it means," he whispers against my cheek.

"You told me the textbook definition." His lips twist in thought as his thumb brushes lightly over my thigh.

"You're up, Mila." Taylor's arm slings over my shoulders and she holds a handful of darts in front of me.

I take them, hopping off the bar stool and Miles follows close behind me as I make my way to the battered old line of tape on the floor. I pull my arm back, squinting out of one eye, aiming for the board. I feel the weight of Miles's hands rest on my hips as he whispers in my ear. "We'll figure it out, Camila. Together." I let the dart fly.

"Bullseye!" Taylor shouts, running to give me a high five. "And that's how it's done, boys." She turns to Jonas who's standing there slack-jawed, and fires off finger guns. "Pew Pew," she sounds off before holstering her fingers.

"Alright relax, Annie Oakley. It's only the first round and you haven't seen what I can do yet," Jonas drawls.

"Well if you're so confident, let's double the bet."

Jonas's eyes narrow before he sticks out his hand for her to shake. "You're on."

When I turn around Miles is already sitting back down on his stool. My chest is still sparking like a live wire at his words. *Together.* None of this has felt like it was for show. No one could hear us, if he wanted to be performative, he could have been whispering dad jokes in my ear for all these people would know. I hand my remaining darts to Jonas and make my way over to where Miles is sitting. I stand between his legs and his hands clasp together behind my back. Heat radiates through my shirt and I can feel his touch down to my bones. My fingers dig into his thighs as he leans forward and brings his lips to the corner of my mouth, leaving a trail of soft kisses from my nose, to my forehead, and back down to my neck. "Let's go home," he whispers.

The car ride home is so quiet I wonder if Miles can hear my thoughts. I don't know if it's the one watered-down drink I had almost three hours ago, or my own stupidity that propels me to reach for his hand. But before I have time to question it, his big rough hand is sandwiched between my cold, smaller ones.

"Do you always have these callouses?" I ask, running my finger over the thick pads on his palm.

"Mostly."

"From what?"

"You'd be surprised how many hours a week I'm spinning that damn jump rope before a boxing session," he says, resting his head on the seat behind him.

We drive the next few blocks in a more comfortable silence. The dancing lights outside reflect off the windows casting shadows across his sharp jawline. I watch Miles stare aimlessly outside but after a moment I feel his hand tighten around mine. "Jonas hustled me at poker one night," he says. I frown at him confused but he stays focused on the city outside. "We were in college and I won six games back to back. During the last game, he lost all his money and I had the hand of a lifetime so we made a bet." His thumb brushes over the top of my hand where it still holds him in my lap. I squeeze his hand back, waiting to find out where this story is going. "A tattoo of the other person's choosing." My eyes blink rapidly and Miles finally looks at me. "Needless to say, I lost. We went out that night because there was no way I could be sober while getting a tattoo Jonas picked out. When we got to the tattoo shop at 3 a.m. he fell asleep looking through the book. I could tell the artist was getting annoyed and instead of leaving and coming back the next day—I chose the dragon. I told him to make it different from the one in the book but other than that he could do what he wanted with it. It wasn't until later that I found out what a Japanese dragon tattoo symbolized."

Considered to protect and guard families and homes. I remember what Miles told me about his parents. I've often thought about how he's told me from the beginning he never wanted a relationship. Knowing a little bit about what he witnessed growing up, it doesn't surprise me that he would have an aversion to relationships. His choice could have very well been a fluke. A random chance accident. But I'd like to believe it was something more.

Our car pulls up outside his building, and Miles gets out, extending his hand to mine. When my hand slips into his, his grip tightens. His body towers over mine when he reaches behind me to close the door. His head drops to the crook of my neck and I inhale his homey smell while his lips graze across my ear. Every hair on my body stands straight up as I hold my breath.

"No more avoiding me, Camila." His fingers lock with mine and I stare at his retreating back as we make our way inside.

Miles

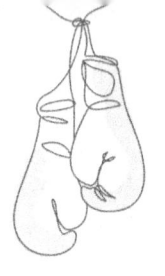

"What—what is all this?"

Even with my back to her, I can hear the smile in Camila's soft voice. I turn from my espresso maker to see her hand covering her mouth, which has fallen open with a disbelieving smile. I look around the kitchen as Rosa pulls out a tray of hot muffins with a mixture of blueberry and crumble on top. They really do look like something out of a magazine. I can tell she's just as concerned with where she's going to put them as I am. I look across the expansive kitchen island and I can not see a single square inch of the marble underneath. Everywhere I look there is some kind of breakfast pastry. Hot butter, chocolate, and almond croissants. Coffee cake, scones, cinnamon sticky buns, french apple turnovers, and some kind of strawberry jam biscuits.

"Rosa… She got on one of her baking kicks again, I guess."

"Ah, yes. It's concerning how often I wake up with the urge to turn your kitchen into a pastry shop." She whips her hand towel at me and rolls her eyes. "I'm going to put these in the wash and then I'm going home." She fixes me with a stare as if to tell me she won't be back tonight. I don't blame her, I texted her late last night asking her to come over and bake any and every kind of pastry she knew how. But when I look at Camila with that ear-to-ear smile on her face, it's completely worth it.

I hand her the hazelnut latte I've made her while she grabs a blueberry scone and sits down at the island. I finish making my own coffee before I come around to sit on the stool beside her. "So, how are you feeling today?" she asks, breaking off a piece of her scone. "After the promotion. I mean name partner. That's a big deal, right?"

Guilt sinks in my stomach like a boulder holding me down. Of course, I should be excited about this. Her excitement for me would be contagious if I hadn't known about this for weeks. I don't mention that the officialness of it has been dependent on whether or not I could convince my boss that this marriage was legitimate.

"I mean my job is still the same, it's more so the prestige that comes with it, I guess."

"So are you happy?"

Her question catches me off guard. "What?"

"I mean, at the end of the day, and by *day* I mean, your life. In fifty years are you going to point and say *The day I got my name on the door was the peak highlight of my life. That's what made me happy* or is there more?"

If yesterday was supposed to be the peak of my life, then I've been doing it wrong. Because after holding Camila in my arms at the bar last night, the partners meeting with the official announcement wasn't even the peak of my day. And goddamnit, that thought alone is alarming.

"I used to think it would be." I drink from my steaming mug before turning in my stool to face her. "I'm not sure anymore though." She gives me a smile that doesn't quite reach her eyes. "Like I said, a lot of my goals in life have been slightly misguided and lately it feels like maybe I've focused and given my attention to things that actually aren't that important." I don't know why I'm saying any of this. Especially because it's not so much my job that isn't as important as this never-ending grudge that causes me to do things I never would have thought I would do. But when I look at Camila her expression is thoughtful when she nods her head in understanding. "What about you? What's the moment you're going to point to knowing that was your highlight?"

Her middle finger idly runs along the rim of her mug, "I don't know."

"That seems to be your go-to answer." Her finger stops as she audibly swallows. "Okay then, where do you see yourself in fifty years?"

"Well, first of all, I've got at least sixty left in me. You're the elderly one in this house." She playfully bumps my knee with hers. "I guess, if I really think about what would make me happy, I see myself as a happy little abuela. My kids and their kids come over for Christmas dinner and I look over at my husband in our matching pajamas and know that someone can be happy with me. And I'm not pretending to be happy for someone else, I want to know in my bones that we're genuinely happy together."

"You want your future husband to wear tiny silk pajama shorts?"

Her head falls forward when she laughs and I'm positive there's never been a more beautiful sound.

"Who knows, maybe in fifty years I'll be the gray sweatpant-wearing kind of girl." Her eyes dip to my sweatpant covered legs and the feelings of jealousy I have at the thought of her life with someone else quickly turn into a feeling I can't for the life of me figure out.

"I'd like to see that," I say.

Her lips push into a small smile before she takes another small sip. "So, this isn't your usual coffee time."

"No. It's not. Jonas bailed on me this morning."

"Ah. And I'm assuming you don't like to box with others?"

"Not particularly, no."

She nods her head in understanding. "Well, maybe you could come to yoga with me. I think you'd really like Mira."

The way her eyebrows wiggle tells me as beautiful as she is, she's full of shit.

"You need to work on your tell, Camila."

"My tell?"

"Yeah, the thing that gives you away."

"And what gives me away?" she puffs her chest out.

"Every facial expression you've ever made."

Her eyes narrow in on me but I remain stoic. A few seconds later she gives up. "Ugh." She rolls her eyes. "Fine, you know everything."

I smile as she hops off the chair and starts heading back towards her room. "I'm leaving in fifteen to go see Mira if you want to come."

I watch her walk away. Realization dawns on me and I almost fall out of my chair.

Fuck. Hope. That feeling is hope.

"Let's begin."

The brick room is surprisingly warm with dim lighting.

Camila sits an arm's length away from me with her legs crossed under her and her eyes closed. Two other women sit directly behind me and the instructor keeps motioning at me to close my eyes.

She rings a bell and for the next thirty minutes, I twist and stretch my body in ways I'm not entirely sure it's supposed to move. But the smile it brings Camila to watch me struggle is worth it.

"Lower your body one vertebra at a time to take your final savasana."

At the risk of Mira holding her hands over my eyes to force them shut, I take one last peek at the woman lying to my right.

"Relax your mind."

"Relax your forehead."

"Your cheeks, your jaw."

I watch the muscles in Camila's face physically drop as she does what she's told.

And I close my eyes and listen to Mira's calming voice guide us through more relaxation techniques.

"Relax your chest and your heart."

My mind has been running wild and I've been blaming that confusion on what happened between us last weekend. But the truth is, I've caught feelings for Camila and it happened before the fundraiser.

"Take as long as you need here."

I know she wants to pretend like it didn't happen but I can't forget it and I don't want to. I'm done playing games. If I want her to be bold and go after things she wants, I need to do the same.

"When you're ready, slowly roll onto your side and move to sit."

Now I just need to help her figure out what she wants and hope like hell it's me.

"So Mira is...something."

Camila's hand covers her mouth but I don't miss the little snort she lets out. "I'm sorry," she says. "How was that downward-facing dog?"

"Oh, you mean when she came up behind me and pulled my hips into her like she was trying to fuck me from behind?" The laugh that rolls out of her is better than anything I've ever heard. People all around the pier turn their heads in our direction, searching for the source of the melodic sound.

Camila's feet stop moving and one hand grabs my bicep while the other wipes under her eyes. "When I saw…" her legs cross and she folds over with laughter still holding on to my arm for balance. "When I saw her come up behind you I had to look away."

"Yeah well, she just went right in. No foreplay necessary for Mira." Her laughter turns soft as we move out of the way and stroll over to the pier railing.

The sun is warm on my back as we silently watch the boats sail across the bay. Camila's fingers pick at the wood grain railing and I instinctively cover her hands with my own. Her shoulders rise and fall before turning to face me. I know Camila will never be the one to say something first. Not after she let her guard down and tried to talk to me the day after the fundraiser. I've been fuming for days knowing it was just stupid miscommunication on my part, but if I want us to figure something out moving forward, that's got to be on me. I also know she's not written me off yet. I could feel it last night—

there's something there—and no matter what brave face she puts on, I know she's not oblivious to it. But I need to be the one to do this because I'm done fighting it. I reach one hand up and rub my thumb between her furrowed brows, trying to erase the crease that formed. My eyes briefly dip to her lips that I so desperately want to pull onto my own. Her eyes are swirling with questions and I take a deep pull of that citrusy patchouli scent that is her and find myself annoyed with the wind and the Pacific Ocean that it dares try to mix with her scent.

"You're vibrating," her voice trembles.

I mentally shake my head. When she takes a step out of my grasp I realize it was my phone. I open my mouth to say something but she's already shifted her gaze back towards the water. I close my mouth, pulling out my phone.

> UNKNOWN NUMBER
>
> Miles, I saw the big news of your promotion. Congratulations, son.

All the blood quickly drains from my body. My hands go cold, and the black band that usually sits firmly on my finger loosens. I stopped answering calls from Paul Cameron in high school but he's continued to reach out. I've heard updates on him as well, enough to know he travels to the city often. But San Francisco is one of the most populated cities in the United States. And even though I don't answer his calls or texts, I'm aware that he still checks up on me in other ways. It's been one of my driving forces to work as hard as I have all these years later. As a teenager, during my parents' divorce, I worked hard for their attention. As an adult, I worked hard as a *fuck you* to my dad.

And when I look at my phone once more, the sole reason I never wanted a relationship stares right back at me.

When Camila looks at me again, her eyes are bright. I pocket my phone and clear my throat. "Ready?"

Her eyelashes flutter as she blinks rapidly and I don't miss the way she drags her palms along her leggings. "Umm, ye-yeah."

"I'll walk you up the street where Wills is waiting. I have some things to take care of."

"Oh. Okay." Her eyes look everywhere but mine and the most forced smile graces her face.

And I hate myself for putting it there.

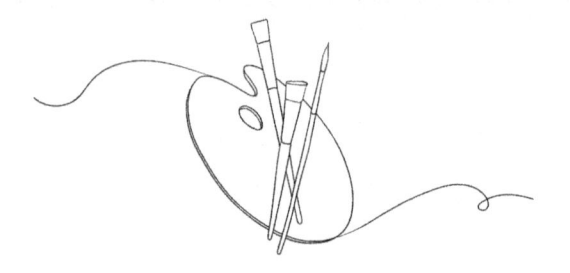

Camila

> **ME**
> Can I use a regular skillet to cook my tortillas? Miles doesn't have a comal.

> **TAYLOR**
> What is he? An animal. Who doesn't have a comal?!

> **ME**
> Someone who doesn't cook a lot of tortillas I guess.

> **TAYLOR**
> 🙄 But to answer your question, yes you can. Look for a cast iron skillet first though!

After searching for ten minutes I finally find a rolling pin and cast iron skillet. I pull my little dough balls out and lightly flour the surface. "Hotel California", the Gypsy Kings version, plays through my earbuds and I begin rolling out my tortillas.

A dark shadow appears out of my peripheral and I yelp before smacking the counter. "What are you doing here?" I ask, pulling my headphones out.

"I live here," Miles says, looking at me like I'm crazy. "And you startle easily." I take a deep breath trying to tell my body we're okay. He's not wrong, I do get scared by anything and everything. But it's 4:30 on a Thursday afternoon. I wasn't expecting him home for another three hours. "What are *you* doing?" he shoots back, eyeing the mess I've made.

"I'm sorry about the mess. I really wanted homemade tortillas and I didn't want to be a bother and ask Rosa so I waited until she left for the day to start them."

"I thought Taylor was the chef in your little duo," he says, sitting down across from me at the island.

"Oh, she is," I hold up my floured hands. "But tortillas are the one thing I know how to make. The only thing I forced my mom to teach me because I couldn't live without them."

"Aren't tortillas supposed to be round?" he points to the first tortilla I rolled.

I bite my cheek and feign annoyance. "They are," I give him a pointed look and begin rolling my next dough ball. "But along with not having a comal, you also don't have a tortilla press. So forgive me if some of my tortillas come out looking more like the state of Hawaii."

His full lips purse together and he nods as he sits casually on the stool, losing his tie. His deft fingers tug on the silk fabric and when his lips turn up into a smirk I know I've been caught staring. I clear my throat and reach for a decanter on the counter. I hold it up in a silent offer. "Please," he says.

I wipe my hands on a tea towel before grabbing one of the crystal scotch glasses and sit it in front of him. As I pour his drink I'm surprised to notice my steady heartbeat. I went back to my early morning yoga class this morning so I wouldn't have to be here when Miles got back for his morning coffee. With the weird way he ran off on me at the pier the other day,

I didn't want to get into it. I knew it would end up being another round-about conversation of how I want him to let me in, and just when I think we're getting somewhere, he'll shut down again.

I go back to rolling out my tortillas and out of habit I ask about his day. "It was no less eventful than any other day. I had to go to a client's office and strong-arm them into taking a deal they thought they never would, but to everyone's surprise—but my own—they did." I drop the rolling pin, staring unblinkingly at him. "What?" he asks.

"I'm—I'm just surprised."

"That I was able to close the deal? I don't know if anyone's told you this yet, but you're married to the best closer in the city, Camila."

I feel my smile take over my face as I shake my head, focusing back on rolling out my dough. "No, I mean...I'm surprised you told me about your day." When he doesn't respond I peer up at him, the column of his throat bobs up and down as takes a drink. I probably shouldn't have said anything. I've likely spooked him and ruined this nice moment. With my dough rolled out, I move to turn on the stove, letting it heat up before I cook the tortillas.

"When I was a kid my mom used to listen to a lot of Laura Pausini," he says. "She would start a pasta sauce at eight in the morning and let it cook all day. If I focus hard enough I can still see her walking back and forth from the kitchen to her art studio, stirring the sauce with a wooden spoon in one hand and holding her paintbrush like a cigarette in the other." Miles points to the stove where my tortilla has turned into a tostada.

"Shit," I say, pulling it off the pan. I lower the heat, adding another one and then turn my attention back to him.

His forearms rest on the island and he spins the near empty glass around.

"You say I never tell you anything. And maybe you're right. But typically when people meet with the intention of dating they show a glamourized bullshit version of themselves. Maybe it's because our situation is different—but I've never felt like I needed to pretend to be someone I'm not with you."

There's a lightness in my chest when it hits me how much Miles actually says without having to say anything at all. He could tell me a hundred and one stories about his childhood and although I would welcome them, they don't tell me what I already know. I know that he's a workaholic who's made sure to be home early every night to have dinner with me. I know that when he saw me talking to Steven Whats-his-name at the fundraiser gala he was jealous. And I know that he doesn't talk about work—or anything really—very freely. He keeps most things bottled inside him and doesn't seem to trust easily, but any conversation that begins to get the even tiniest bit difficult, he pauses waiting for me—trusting that I'll continue. So while he might not say things out loud, he's still saying them all the same.

I'm pulled from my thoughts by a blistering pain burning up my arm. "FUCK!" I scream, pulling my hand away from where my fingers were just sizzling on the pan. Before I get the chance to assess what's happened, Miles is up and in front of me.

"Let me see," he says, reaching behind me, turning off the stove.

"It's okay. I'm fine." I say, holding my hand unable to even look at it.

"Camila." I take a deep breath and hold my hand out towards him. My eyes water as I try to hold back my tears but the pain is still so hot. He holds my wrist gently inspecting and I notice the tips of my first two fingers are red and blistered. "Let's go take care of this." His voice is thick and heavy.

"Really, I'm okay," I say.

"Please." My heart melts quicker than my skin on the skillet at his pleading eyes. I nod my head and let him guide me down the hall towards his room.

Miles's room is so completely him in every way. It smells like him, spicy and warm, but also clean. His large bed faces more floor-to-ceiling windows and hanging above his bed is another palm leaf painting. I'd bet my measly life savings it's another one of his mother's paintings. He pushes open the door to his bathroom, going straight for a cabinet under the sink, and motions for me to sit up on the counter. The burning sensation is still there but my racing heart begins to slow when Miles's fingers fumble around a first aid kid. I place my good hand on his chest and his movements still. He closes his eyes, pulling in a deep breath, and his heart beats frantic beneath my palm. It's the first time I've ever seen him flustered.

"This won't feel good but I'll try to be gentle," he says, turning on the water.

He holds my palm firmly but gently at the same time as he sticks my fingers under the running water. He's right, it doesn't feel good but I let the water run over me while I focus on him. The deep crease between his brows, the pained expression on his face, the tightness in his jaw. I stare at him for so long when I look back at the counter, he's cleaning up the trash from putting ointment and some band-aids on.

"Thank you," I whisper.

"You don't have to thank me for covering up a burn."

"I meant thank you for letting me in." He braces the weight of himself on the counter next to me.

"You think I let you in?"

I bring my hand up to his back, where his shoulders are hunched over. "You don't do it in a very common way—but yeah, in your way, I think you do."

His lips twitch slightly in a way that tells me he'll either say something to surprise me or he'll shut down on me again. And even though I've decided it's easier to hide my feelings for him and be around him than it is to avoid him, I can't stand the thought of him pulling away again right now. So I run my fingers across his hair, combing away the piece that's fallen down his forehead, and slide off the counter. I exit his room and he doesn't follow.

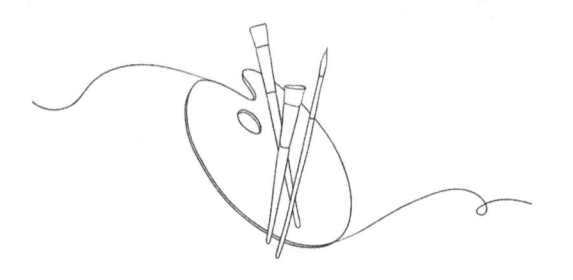

Camila

I'M PULLING A FLOWY OVERSIZED T-SHIRT OVER MY HEAD when my phone vibrates on the dresser, lighting up with a picture of me and Taylor in cowboy hats from a trip we took to Banff two summers ago.

"What are you doing?" I squint my face at the phone screen as if it would help me see her better.

"I'm…h-heading…up…Br-B-Bradford," she pants, completely out of breath and although her face is in front of the camera behind her, all I see is the sky. "Oh fuck. I gotta sit down."

"Taylor, what the hell are you doing?"

I wait for her to catch her breath. "I signed up to pick up those scooters around the city, it pays some good change but fuck, these hills, man."

"Tay, you know I'll never push you, but just throwing it out there…do you think maybe you'd like to try and find maybe one career you could stick to? I know that would require a little commitment, but it's gotta sound better than multiple jobs, especially when one of them now requires you to crawl up the steepest street in the city." I hesitate because I know all too well what it feels like to have pressure put on me about a career and I never want to put that on Taylor but her situation is different than mine.

"Yeah, I think I'll just stick to my other gigs for now, this scooter shit is for the birds."

I laugh and look at the time. "Hey, I gotta get going. I'm meeting the realtor soon to check out that space I was telling you about."

"Mila, I'm so proud of you, this is a huge first step."

"Simmer down, I'm not doing anything. I'm just going to look fun funsies. Just like when we would go look at multi-million dollar beach homes, pretending we could afford them." The truth is, even though I know nothing will come of this visit, I couldn't stop myself from taking the number down and I couldn't stop myself from calling for a viewing appointment. I don't know why I did it. There's absolutely zero security in owning and managing an art gallery. So until I'm ready to give my parents the middle finger—which I don't see myself ever doing—there really is nothing that can come from this.

"Nah. I feel it in the air, it's something," she says, waving her hand in front of her face.

"I think you're feeling your sweat." We both laugh and I quickly check the time again. "Alright for real, I have to leave now, I'll call you later. And please be careful on that hill."

She blows a kiss into the phone screen before hanging up. I take one more look at myself in the mirror, tuck my shirt into my cutoff black denim skirt, and smile at my reflection. I'm feeling good about myself. I think a piece of my confidence comes from the fact that Miles and I are in a good space. I'm no longer tiptoeing around him and that's one stress off my back.

I'm double-checking my bag to ensure I have all my

things, and I'm momentarily confused when I hear the elevator doors open. Miles steps out of the elevator strutting over to me with one hand in his pocket, looking sexier than usual in his suit.

"H-hey," I stammer. I pause, one hand holding my bag, the other digging around in it.

"Hey yourself. Where are you off to?"

He stops just in front of me with a smile seductive enough to bring me to my knees. But I can't even look him in the eyes. "I'm uh...I'm going to meet with a realtor to look at that studio space I was telling you about."

"I'll come with you." My eyebrows bunch together, but he ignores it and reaches his arm out toward the elevator for me to lead the way.

"What are you doing home in the middle of the day, anyway?"

"I just wanted to see you." My chest cracks open and a million butterflies begin fluttering throughout my entire body. *He wanted to see me?* "Camila." His husky voice pulls me from my thoughts. His searing eyes lock on mine when we reach the elevator and my heart pounds rapidly against my chest. Something about the way he's looking at me right now has my body melting with a mixture of nerves and excitement. His face is calm but somehow still intense and he's the picture of seduction with one hand in his pocket while the other reaches behind me to press the call button. His face hovers an inch above mine and I have to fight my eyes from dropping to his lips. "Say it."

I don't know...Say what?

His eyes are searching mine and between him coming home to see me, wanting to come to the studio with me, and his attention on me now, I need to know what's going on. "Tell me something," I whisper.

The corners of his mouth pull up into a satisfied grin and his eyes bore so deep into mine, I think he sees through them. His free hand finds the back of my neck in a tight grip as he lowers his mouth to my ear. "I don't regret what happened the other night." I audibly inhale as my eyes go wide. "I regret not making sure we were on the same page beforehand. I regret not bringing you back to our home so I could worship your sweet little pussy properly. And I regret allowing you to brush it off the next day. But I don't regret what happened, and I don't think you do either."

Oh my god. His words bleed into every thought trying to bounce around in my mind. I had a feeling—it was more like a fleeting thought. But after that night I suppressed any more thoughts deep in my gut but to hear him say the words out loud. *He doesn't regret what happened.* "What?"

"It took me some time to wrap my head around it. To voice what I was thinking, and what I was *feeling*, and for that I'm sorry."

"What does this mean?" I ask.

"If you're asking what it means for us moving forward, I don't know. But I do know that I haven't stopped thinking about you. Not just that night, but you. Every minute I'm not with you, I'm thinking about when I get to be with you again. I'm thinking about that night. About you." His hand lifts from his pocket dipping below my skirt and his thumb swipes smoothly across my thigh. If he moves half an inch higher he'll feel how embarrassingly wet I am through my underwear. "Tell me you want this, too." My hips involuntarily inch forward. His long thick middle finger runs up my seam, and my legs tremble at the touch. "Tell me it's not all in my head and that you want this, Camila."

"Don't you think this would complicate things?" I don't

recognize my own breathless voice. I can barely register my own thoughts over his admission.

"That's not what I asked you."

My sweaty palms tighten on my bag, searching to get a grip on anything tangible. "I—"

Ding.

The elevator door opens behind me and Miles slides his hand out from under my skirt. My body protests at the loss of his touch but I follow him into the waiting elevator on shaky legs.

The door is unlocked when we arrive. The realtor is on her phone by a door in the back. She smiles at us and waves around the room, telling us to look around before she steps back inside the office, closing the door to finish her call. I'm filled with wonder as I step into the studio for the first time. The space is so much larger than it appears from the outside. It's unfinished, the floors are solid concrete beneath my feet but the bones are perfect. Light pours in from the large front windows, while a partition wall in the middle of the room gives way to a more private backspace. There aren't any other windows so custom hanging lights could be used to spotlight wall art, and there is plenty of space for a projector as well. The place is empty with the exception of a wood workbench, a card table, some discarded paint cans, and a few sheets of rolled-up canvas tarps.

My fingers trace the wood grain patterns on the workbench and excitement bubbles inside me at all the possibilities available in a place like this.

"What do you think?" Miles asks, stepping over some scattered paintbrushes.

"I think—" *I think I love it and that breaks my heart.* "It's a great space."

"I agree."

I look away clearing my throat. "This backspace has so many possibilities."

Miles tilts his head. "What's your perfect case scenario here, Camila?"

I hope my eyes aren't betraying me with the way I'm looking at the room around me. "I guess, in a perfect world, I would use some of my investment banking contacts and potentially find someone interested in owning and opening an art studio. And I would work here, in this space with them."

"Is that really your perfect world? Or is it a safe bet?"

I start to feel warm. Exposed. He knows I want this place for myself. I pick up a paintbrush and run the bristles along my palm, trying to slow my heartbeat. And all too quickly I'm reminded of the time I told my parents I was moving to California.

"And this is what you really want?" My mom's intense eye contact had me shriveling back.

"Yes," I squeaked.

She looked at my father with furrowed brows waiting for him to say something. He only stood there, with his hand under his chin, finger tapping his lip.

I twisted my hair so tightly around my finger, that the tip had started to turn blue. I spent months, YEARS, working hard in school so I could get into a good college. Every accolade, award, and achievement I brought home had my parents beaming. But the look on their faces when I told them I was moving across the country with my best friend, for school, had my stomach churning.

"I've told you. It's too risky." I throw the paintbrush down on the table and head towards the front door.

It takes two steps for Miles to catch up to me with his long legs and I can feel my throat tightening as I try to shove down the tears threatening to escape.

His hand loops in the crook of my elbow but he doesn't make a move. "Hey." His voice echoes in my ear. I close my eyes, swallowing up the tears before I turn to face him. "I'm sorry. I can just see how excited you are about this space. And it fucking guts me to watch you want *anything* and not get it. But I'm sorry if I pushed you before you were ready."

I do want it. Fuck, more than anything I wish I could just be able to voice all the things I want. When I look into his soft eyes I can see him battling something. And the realization steamrolls into me. I don't feel exposed by him at all. I feel seen. I hesitate momentarily because I know he's referring to my desire for this studio and he's right. I do want this space. But I also want him. And for the first time, the fear of not getting the things I want feels far worse than failing to go after them.

"Miles, I—"

"Ah! Ms. Sanchez, sorry about that. Were you able to get a look around?" I'm in a complete daze as I stare at the realtor whose name I've now forgotten. Thankfully, Miles extends his hand and introduces himself. And just like I am, the woman is completely captivated by him.

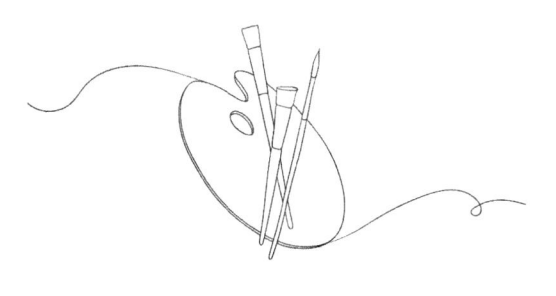

Camila

"Thank you again, Mandy, I'll be in touch." I wave to the real estate agent as she heads off down the street, leaving us outside the studio space.

I zone out looking at my shoes as if they are the most exciting thing in the world. "Should we um, call a car?" I ask.

"Wills is on his way, he should be here any minute."

I kick an invisible rock and finally bring myself to look at him. His lazy smile is such a far cry from the grumpy scowl he usually wears. But it's his hungry eyes that cause my breath to hitch. "Good. Yeah, that's, that's good," I stutter and go back to kicking invisible rocks.

I twist the diamond around my finger, giving my nervous energy somewhere to go. Miles sits casually next to me in the back of the car, scrolling through emails on his phone.

"What are you thinking about?" His head drops back on the seat behind him. My eyes flicker from where his muscular legs are spread out in front of him to where the partition separates us from the front seat. "It's soundproof, he can't hear you."

His hand covers mine where it was twisting my ring and I relax slightly at the touch. "I guess I'm thinking about what you said earlier. I'm trying to figure out what it all means. And maybe how I feel too," I confess.

He waits for me to continue like he always does. The weight of his hand moves to my thigh as his finger spreads across my exposed skin.

"It's not all in your head," I whisper. "I don't regret what happened, either." His grip on my thigh tightens as he audibly inhales. "But that doesn't change the fact that we could really complicate our situation. So, what does this mean?"

"That'll be something we'll have to figure out together." There's that word again. *Together.* Like he's thought about us more than he's let on. "What I can tell you, is I'm not going to let you get away with hiding what you want anymore. You've been so busy trying to please everyone around you, and it's cost you. I don't think I need to tell you that I don't care what anyone else thinks or wants. But you, Camila. What do you want?"

It's not his words that surprise me. This is something I've known about myself for most of my adult life. It's that he's paid enough attention to know this too, that gets to me. I've been running around with a cloudy haze over my thoughts, and as if the skies have parted I've never seen anything more clearly than I do right now. I'm the best, most bold version of myself when I'm with Miles. And it's never been more evident than right now. My hips sink down to one side as I reach across and slowly stroke my hand up his massive thigh.

"Is this what you want?" His voice is like gravel.

I nod my head and lower my lips to his jaw, pressing lightly over his stubble. My fingers drag slowly up his length where he's already straining against his zipper. One of my fingers runs over the button of his pants before his hand covers mine to stop me. When I pull back to look at him, his jaw is clenched tight and his dark eyes penetrate me.

"On your knees, Camila."

Something in my chest flips at his words. But I've never wanted to please anyone as badly as I want to please Miles right now, so I slide out of my seat and nestle myself between his legs on the floor of the car.

At a painfully slow pace, I unzip him. His substantial bulge is straining to get free of his briefs. When I finally pull them down I'm met with his throbbing cock that is already dripping with his arousal. My mouth waters at the sight of him. I lower my mouth, desperate to lick that salty bead at his tip, but Miles grips my jaw between his thumb and index finger. The rest of his fingers splay down my neck. With a shocked breath, I look into his eyes which are now borderline black and his hand squeezes just a little tighter. "Beg."

If he wasn't holding my jaw right now, I swear it would drop and hit the floor. *Beg?* I've never begged for anything in my life. Let alone anything from a man.

"I want to know that you want this, Camila. Beg for my cock and maybe I'll give it to you."

I've never experienced a sexual desire for anyone the way I have with Miles. Of course, I want this with him. I want this, and I could want so much more with him. My eyes narrow on him. "I think you want my mouth on you more than anything else you want."

"Do I want to fuck that sweet mouth of yours? Yes. But if you think I want *anything* more than I want you to admit you want this, then you haven't been paying attention."

"And if I refuse?"

He lets go of my jaw and grabs the base of his cock,

giving it long strokes. My mouth is salivating and my underwear is soaked.

"Then I'll bend you over that seat, take care of myself, and blow my load on your back. It wouldn't be my first choice but I've done it before."

He's serious. And the memory of the last time he did that has me rubbing my thighs together. But I want more now.

His strokes are slow but his tip is full of precum now. "What's it going to be, Camila? It wouldn't be the first time I've used my fist pretending it was your mouth."

His confession lights something inside me. I want Miles. Even if he's using this as some kind of fucked up teaching moment. I want him and I won't be scared to admit it. I grip his wrist where he's still wrapped around himself, "Please. I want you, I want this." My eyes narrow. "I'm begging."

"That's my girl."

My nipples somehow turn even harder at his words. There's something about knowing that this man, who doesn't care about anything outside of his office, could potentially care about me. It could very well be my undoing.

I lower my mouth over him. My tongue glides along the underside of his length, he's warm and veiny. My tongue swirls around his tip and the hiss that escapes him makes me sweat. His rough hands gather all the hair that was covering my face like a curtain and he pulls it back, giving himself an unobstructed view. I should feel embarrassed but the way his hips are inching forward, silently begging for more, and the moans he's trying to suppress have me feeling empowered. My fingers gently roll his balls while my other hand works in tandem with my mouth.

"Oh fuck," he grunts, digging both of his hands into my scalp. "I've been dreaming of fucking this sweet mouth for weeks." His hips jolt forward and he hits the back of my throat causing my eyes to water.

I'm working him at a sloppy pace now. Every time I pull my mouth back, his length shines with a mixture of pre-cum and my saliva. The flat carpeted floor of the car bites my knees as my thighs rub together trying to get any friction to my throbbing clit. It's painful how turned on I am right now. As if he can sense it Miles gives my hair a tug, causing goosebumps to flare over my skin and my eyes snap to him.

"Touch yourself."

My pace on him doesn't let up as I drag one hand to reach between my legs. My palm grazes against my swollen clit and the touch sends an embarrassingly loud moan through me.

"That's it, Camila. Put a finger in."

Oh God. How am I already so close? I can feel his cock pulsing in my mouth, so I know he must be close too.

"Add another," he says through clenched teeth.

I do as he says. Pumping my fingers inside myself while I rub the heel of my hand against my most sensitive spot. Thank god the back of his car is soundproof because the noises we're making are completely obscene.

"Sucking my cock turns you on?"

My eyes roll back and something between a cry and moan is my only response.

"Jesus, Camila. You feel so good." His hips thrust harder now as he holds on to my hair like reins. "Watching you finger fuck yourself while you choke on my cock…" I squeeze my eyes shut as the pressure builds. "Fuck, I'm going to come."

His words aren't a warning, they're a detonator for his release.

I feel him shudder as he spills down my throat and that's all it takes for the fire in my core to burn white-hot and my breathing to become impossibly quick as my own orgasm rips through me. I lift my head, look Miles in the eyes, and swallow.

His knuckles turn white as he grips the leather seat underneath him. "Who knew mi querida esposa would have such a filthy mouth." He grabs ahold of my hand, bringing my fingers to his lips, gently pressing a tender kiss to each one before bringing them into his mouth and sucking them clean. My eyes are wide and I know right here and now that Miles Cameron has ruined me for any other man. I will never be sexually satisfied the way I am with him.

My body still trembles beneath me but I'm able to feel the car slowing to a stop now. I climb back up into the seat next to him and he's looking at me with an expression I've never seen. His hand cups the back of my neck as he pulls me into him. His soft lips press into mine and I'm taken aback by the tenderness. He sucks my bottom lip into his mouth and I grip his forearm, needing something to hold on to. His kiss is soft but intense at the same time. It feels like everything I've ever wanted and yet I can't get enough. His hands run up my thigh and I know he can feel my pebbled skin. This kiss feels different like I'm definitely not pretending anymore.

Miles is the one to break away first. He drops his forehead to mine before giving me a quick kiss on my nose and then sitting back in his seat. I'm trying to catch my breath while looking at the smile on his face.

"What other things do you want, Camila?"

Miles

"Yo." Jonas tosses me a wrapped bagel as he enters my office and finds his usual seat on the couch. "So…how was the little art studio thing?" he asks around a mouthful of food.

I cock my head, narrowing my eyes. A possessive feeling consumes me when I think about what happened at that studio—and the drive home—and I wonder what Jonas knows.

"What? Taylor said Mrs. Cameron was heading to look at a space and since you left early, I assumed you went with her."

I ignore the way my lungs constrict when he calls her *Mrs. Cameron.* Oblivious to my tightening chest, he continues to house his bagel as if he's never eaten before.

"What's up with you two?" I ask him.

His head lulls back, rolling his eyes with it and he's lucky he doesn't choke. "Oh my god." He shakes his head with a smile. "Can't two people just be friends anymore?"

"Two people can, yes. You, however, have never had a female friend before, so I'm just curious."

"She's cool. That's it. We hang out *platonically,* not sure if you're familiar with the word." He bites a mouthful of his bagel. "I'm not looking for anything more, plus the girl has got some serious commitment issues anyway. She actually reminds me a little of you. You know, just with a cuter face." He flashes me a sarcastic smile.

"I don't know why I put up with you."

"It's my good looks," he shrugs, "and the bagels. So, get on with it, how was the studio?"

It took me one day to come to the conclusion that I couldn't avoid Camila if I was chained to a wall. I'll admit the text I got from my father rattled me. The following day I paced my office with a raging headache before I realized I wasn't going to get shit done until I spoke to her. I had every intention of explaining why I shut down on the pier that morning but then I got home and found a sight I'd never thought I'd see. Camila was cooking in my kitchen and it felt like the most natural thing in the world. I wanted to just enjoy that moment for a little while. But then she made a comment about how I don't open up to her. I shoved the negative feelings about my father away and I told her the last happy memory I had of my mother. Opening up and sharing things with her isn't difficult. I've just operated a certain way for so long, but I shouldn't be surprised she feels that way. I can't expect her to know how I'm feeling, especially when I think about how we communicate in such different ways. It's not bad, and my knowledge on the topic is limited, but if I had to guess, that's a normal thing that people in relationships need to learn.

And the reality is, it's not something I ever gave a second thought to because when I approached Camila with this arrangement I really believed I could keep things simple between us—business. Nothing more, nothing less. And then when my attraction to her proved it couldn't be tamed I was

ART OF CONVENIENCE

willing to toe the line. But then I saw her heart and passion. When it came to her mind, I couldn't stop myself anymore. I've been falling for Camila. And I can't even blame her for being confused. I did tell her that night was a mistake but I didn't mean it the way she took it. It kills me that she thought for even a second that I regretted that.

So yesterday when I left work early—again—I couldn't hold it in any longer. I certainly didn't mean for it to come out the way it did, but I can't say I fully regret it either. When I saw her in that studio and saw her battling herself I knew it wasn't the time to bring it up. But after—my hands flex under my desk just thinking about that car ride home. When she told me she wanted something more too, that it wasn't just in my head. I squeeze my eyes shut at the memory of her giving herself so freely to me. Tonight. Tonight I'm going to tell her how real this is. That I'm all in.

"Jonas, get back to your office, your briefs aren't going to submit themselves." Samantha's voice is soft velvet and lethal poison somehow wrapped in one as she interrupts us, charging through my office.

"Awe, come on Sam," he holds out his arms to her but she continues to stare him down.

"I swear to God, you're worse than my children sometimes," she scolds him.

But not even Samantha could get Jonas down. He wads up his bagel wrapper, shooting it in the trash can with an over-extended arch, "Kobe!"

Samantha's face is unforgiving. Jonas leaves with no other words but I don't miss the peace sign he throws over his head when he's halfway down the hall.

"Why do we tolerate him?" she asks me.

And even though I joke about the same thing, it leaves a bad taste in my mouth when someone else does it. "Because his billables are the highest at the firm and they don't make people as loyal as Jonas anymore. Honestly, we don't deserve him."

She smiles but it doesn't reach her eyes. When she doesn't sit down, she unknowingly has given herself up. It's her tell. She always stands when she's about to have a conversation that requires her to feel like the most powerful person in the room. So naturally, I double down. I lean back casually in my chair, letting her have the floor.

"I know your marriage is bullshit."

The blood collectively drains from my body. I get light-headed and wonder if I'm going to slide right out of this chair, into a puddle on the floor. My fingers tap against my lap keeping the slight tremble there less noticeable. I keep my voice as bored as I can muster when I lean forward and ask, "What are you talking about?"

"I didn't become name partner," she pauses on *name partner* to remind me of one, who she is and her power here, and two, what's at stake for me, "By being a fucking idiot."

All the sweetness in her smile is gone. "Maybe you've been stuck up in this corner office so long you've forgotten the basics of a marriage license but it's public documents, Miles. I've known since the fundraiser."

Fuck. Fuck. Fuck.

"I will say you picked a good one, she can bluff the shit out of a story. She might even have you beat."

I know I should be panicking right now, but I can't help feel a little proud of Camila. I bring my folded hands to my face to both cover the smile threatening to come out and to also appear as if I'm deep in thought about what I've done. But the truth is, our relationship might have started out every bit the lie she thinks it is, but something more is definitely happening now. I keep my face neutral and let her continue her speech that I know she's planned. If I let her keep going I lessen my chances of screwing myself over.

"So here's what I know. You lied to me. *Me*, your goddamn mentor of all people. And considering when you were promoted, the date on your marriage licenses, Smith being out longer than expected, and affecting your promotion being announced, I'm assuming this was all a big fuck up and you lied to cover your ass." I might be the best lawyer on the West Coast, but she's right, she was my mentor. I won't confirm or deny what she's saying so my best bet right now is to just sit and take it. "You pull shit like this all the time and I get pissed because everything you do directly affects this firm. *My* firm. But lying to me is *personal.*"

This conversation would have been my worst nightmare at one point. For a moment, I stop and think about that, about how I'm this relaxed about potentially throwing everything I've worked for down the drain for someone who only told me the other day that maybe she wants something more with me. We haven't even decided what that something more is, or what that would look like, but just the idea of anything meaning more to me than my job is enough to shake me up a little.

"Are you going to take away my title?"

Her eyes bore into me. "I should."

Should. I've been doing this long enough that I have to fight the smile that's threatening to cross my face because the moment she utters *should*, I know she's not going to do shit.

"But *I* brought up your name to Smith, and we just bolted those letters to the wall, and I'm not going to allow *your* fuck up to make me look like a fool to the rest of the world."

My chest shakes as I force the exhale so painfully slow out of my nose.

"But here me, if you so much as look at a client the wrong

way, I'll not only take your name off the door, I'll fire your ass."

This conversation is pissing me off. This looming threat over my head. I don't have the best track record when it comes to being subtly threatened, so I know I need to get out of here now.

I take the elevator down to where Wills is already waiting outside for me. "Home, Mr. Cameron?"

"Yes. Thank you."

Normally after a shit day, I would work myself till the latest hours of the night and then find a bar where I can pay a stupid amount of money for a single glass of whiskey. Today I just want to go home.

> UNKNOWN NUMBER
>
> Miles, I'm in town for a few weeks. Was hoping we could get together.
>
> PC

My knuckles turn white around my phone as I smash it into the seat next to me. *Not again.* I'm in a good spot with Camila and I won't let another message from him psych me out and ruin this.

"Actually Wills, we need to make a pit stop."

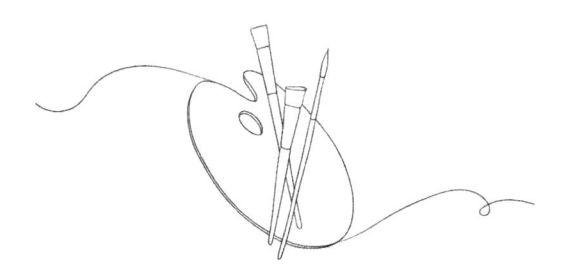

Camila

"Mila, my angel baby, I've missed you!" Taylor runs out from behind the bar and pulls me into one of her bone-crushing hugs. She leans back, keeping her arms on my shoulders, and begins scanning me. "Still as beautiful as ever."

"I just saw you last week," I say.

"Yes, but when I go from seeing you every day, a few missed days in between feels like forever."

I offer her a smile because even though I know she's somewhat joking, it is strange to go from seeing each other all the time to having a ninety percent FaceTime relationship.

"Blondie! Get back behind the bar!"

Taylor rolls her eyes as her manager, Chuck, barks at her from his dingy little office. "Hop up, since there's no one in here," she yells loud enough for her boss to hear. "I'll make you a drink."

"Chucky doll still not letting you in the kitchen?" I ask her.

She flings a towel over her shoulder and begins pouring

and mixing a strange array of liquids. Her face falls slightly, "Nah, not yet. But he did say he would give me a shot once I *prove myself* out here. Whatever that means." She shrugs, handing me the drink. "So what's going on? How much longer are you playing house for?"

I want to tell her it doesn't feel like I'm playing anymore but that will subject me to a line of questions I don't have the answers for. "Umm, just a couple more weeks, I think. I've honestly started losing count of the days."

"And then what? Do you have to get a fake divorce to cover up your real annulment?

"I'm not sure." These are definitely things I need to figure out soon though.

Condensation begins to drip from my untouched glass, I pop each individual droplet trying to make sense of how I feel about going through with the annulment right as we're possibly starting something.

"Let me ask you this, have you caught feelings for your grumpy husband, Mila?" she asks with a knowing smirk.

I thought I was careful to keep my feelings surface-level. Nothing beyond a physical attraction. But I'm so far past that now. Of course, I've caught feelings for Miles. Real feelings. The kind that makes me smile just by seeing his face. The kind that makes me nervous, excited, and relaxed all at the same time. I can cause my heart to flutter against my rib cage just dragging up an image of him in my mind.

Never mind the fact that the sexual chemistry between us is nothing like anything I've ever experienced before. And we haven't even actually had sex yet. But it's so much more than that. I haven't stopped thinking about the morning he had Rosa turn his entire kitchen into a bakery simply because he knows pastries are my favorite.

I've been confused about my feelings for Miles since the

morning I woke up married to him, but the truth is, every day things become more and more clear. His belief in me is contagious. The way he is so adamant about me fighting for what I want leaves me feeling worthy. I suppose I have always known what I wanted, somewhere deep down, but I don't think I ever felt worthy of those things. And somewhere along the way, I've masked that worry with a need to please everyone. As if by making everyone else happy they'll focus on what I've done for them, and not the things I've been too scared of wanting for myself.

I feel different around Miles. I feel like I can be the part of myself that I've forgotten. A part of myself that I've desperately missed.

"You know that goofy ass face tells me yes even if you don't say it out loud," she says.

"Yes! Okay. Yes. I have feelings for him. But don't ask me what that means because I don't know!" Her eyes don't leave the glass she's drying, but her know-it-all smile reflects off the tap handles in front of her.

"Okay, I won't ask. For now," she pauses. "What about the studio space? How was it?"

"Perfect," I confess.

"Yeah? Does this mean you're going to put in an offer and *finally* open your own art studio?"

"With the amount I would need to take out in a loan, it still just feels too risky."

"Does it seem more risky than having to work another job you hate that triggers your anxiety every day?"

That's one point for Taylor and zero points for me.

"I'm still thinking about it. I haven't written it off." It's not a lie.

"Okay good. That's all I'll ask for....for now."

The bar around me has started to fill up. Taylor continues

making drinks while I begin to feel a little overwhelmed with all the unanswered questions I have floating around my head. I need to get back to the only man who can help me answer these questions, and I'm not going to let them go unanswered anymore.

Miles

I'M STILL IN A FOUL MOOD AS I TAKE THE ELEVATOR UP TO the penthouse. I couldn't come home to Camila after I got that text. I had Wills drop me off at Villetta—a private club that I pay thousands of dollars a month for, only for Jonas and I to attend a concert once every other month. A drink at the grand bar and lounge, a walk around the grounds, and five hours later did nothing to improve my mood. But as I exit the elevator and spot Camila in her usual spot curled up on the couch, I unclench my first for the first time and the permanent crease between my eyebrows seems to relax.

Her face is deep in concentration, but when she pops up from her computer she hits me with a smile that takes up her whole face. "Hey!"

I clear my throat, "Hey."

"Everything okay?"

I loosen my tie as I pull out a chair sitting at the dining room table. "It's nothing." I begin rolling up my sleeves and then I catch myself. My short reply is what she expects from me and I don't want to give her that anymore. But I was determined to come home and have a real discussion with her, and bringing up my father would ruin this. "It's not that I don't want to talk to you about it, but I had a shit day at the office and I just don't want to deal with it right now. Is that okay?" I just want to be here with her and soak in her presence.

She sets her laptop down before slowly walking over to me. The corner of her bottom lip pulls in between her teeth like she's trying to decide something. She slides between me and the table and leans back against it as she massages my chest and shoulders.

"Yes, Mr. Cameron. Thank you for telling me."

"But I didn't tell you anything," I say, confused.

"You said enough. You don't want to talk about it right now, and that's fine. When you're ready, I will be too."

Her words mean everything to me. I'll never understand how someone as sweet as Camila could give herself to me or could be interested in me. But selfishly I want everything she's willing to give me.

My hands slide up her bare legs and rest on her hips. The silk fabric underneath rubs under my palms, sending a shiver down my spine. "I don't want to talk right now," I breathe.

She nods her understanding and brings her arms behind my neck, her fingers combing through my hair. "What should we do then?" Her smile is playful but her eyes are hungry.

My hands tighten around her hips as I guide her down to my lap to straddle me. She lowers her forehead to mine, and her hair falls forward, covering us and I soak her in. I know if I wanted to talk to Camila, I could, but I appreciate that she knows I'm not ready and she's trying to distract me in other ways.

I tuck a strand of hair behind her ear. "There isn't anything I don't want to do with you—" I don't think she was expecting that answer because her head melts into my hand.

But Camila came over here with a purpose and I'm going to deliver for her. "But right now, I want to bury my cock so deep inside you, that even if you wanted to get out of my bed in the morning, you wouldn't be able to."

"Promise?" There's no shock in her eye or blush on her cheeks. No, Camila's voice is pure seduction as she raises a challenging brow, strokes her fingers at the back of my head, and circles her hips over my now throbbing cock.

I've always thought Camila was sexy, but she's downright pornographic when she's radiating this much confidence. I can feel my own calluses as I rub my hands up and down her thighs, pausing a few times to squeeze them. My hands graze a trail over her tiny silk shorts and under her oversized shirt. As I get higher up her ribs I'm met with more bare skin. My thumbs drag along the underside of her breasts and her nipples harden to sharp little points.

"Arms up, Camila."

My eyes follow her tongue when it slips out, tracing her full bottom lip. Her arms raise and my fingers brush along her body when I pull the hem of her shirt up and over her head. That wild head of hair that I love cascades down her back and her bare breasts are now exposed to me.

The city lights beam in through the living room windows casting a soft glow against her tan skin. I take a long look at her, my eyes roam over every inch of her body. She's so beautiful. I want to worship her in a way I've never felt before. In a way she's never felt before. She deserves nothing less.

My thumb brushes over her perky nipple and her nails rake down my neck in response. I lower my mouth, replacing my finger with my tongue and lightly sweep at it before covering her with my mouth and giving it a firm suck. Her chest inches forward and the moan that escapes her only fuels me to keep going. I move to her other breast, nipping at the skin around her swollen bud, savoring her, taking my sweet time. Her hips move over me at a more rapid pace now, grinding and rubbing against my erection.

I don't need to check to know that she's wet. "So needy, mi esposa."

"Miles." Her throaty moan makes it nearly impossible for me to not strip us both down and take her right here on the kitchen table.

I take her breast in my hand and move my mouth to bite the sensitive spot at the slope of her neck.

"Miles, please."

The roaring in my ears is only muffled by the sounds of Camila's sweet voice. I hook two fingers through her shorts and run the backs of them over her underwear down the middle. She's dripping. Her hips buck forward at the touch and any restraint I had goes out the window.

In one fluid motion, I stand, sitting her ass down on the table behind her. My fingers wrap around her neck and guide her body to lay flat against the table. Her pulse flutters like a caught butterfly under my palm but I keep it at her neck. I love how responsive her body is to me. The girl that doesn't know what she wants, but goddamn does her body know what she likes. I roughly drag my other hand up her leg, taking in the feeling of her warm silky skin under me. She lies there completely exposed to me and when I look down at her gleaming wet pussy, my cock somehow swells even more. I sit back down in my chair, hook her legs over my shoulders, and grab onto her thighs before I greedily run a wide flat tongue through her lips. I'm rewarded with the sounds of her crying out my name. She's even sweeter than I remember. As my tongue slides inside her, her fingers dig into my scalp.

"Oh fuck. Yes," she breathes.

"I've thought about eating this pussy every day since that goddamn fundraiser. I'm going to fucking gorge myself on you," I say, smiling against her. Her hips move under me and my fingers trail along her hip bones before I bring them down and give her clit a little pinch. Her back arches off the table as she screams. My own spine is twitching and I drag two fingers down to her entrance. She's so wet they slide right in. I watch her squeeze my fingers before I add a third and lower my tongue back over her. I alternate between long flat strokes and the tip of my flexed tongue. Her cries become more desperate and I know she's close. I pump my fingers harder and the strokes of my tongue don't let up.

"Oh fuck. Miles, I'm going to—oh God."

There's not a single other thought in my mind right now, other than to please her. To give her what she needs. And as it turns out, pleasing Camila is what I need too.

I suck her clit just a little harder and feel her body tremble against me. A warm liquid runs down my shoulder blade where her nails dig in tightly. I brace one arm on the warm wood table beneath her and roughly drag the scruff of my beard down her thighs before pressing my lips over the red spots, soothing her skin with light kisses. Camila sits up, propping herself on her elbows. Her face is flush but her eyes still shine. I stand from my chair finally freeing my painful hard-on. I grip the base, lining up just the tip, stroking it through her lips but not yet entering.

"Oh my god!" She jerks from the touch, still sensitive from her orgasm.

"Are you ready to move to the bedroom so I can find a condom?"

"I—I'm on the pill," she breathes.

Jesus. My eyes close for a brief moment as guttural noise escapes from the back of my throat.

"You gonna let me fuck you bare, Camila?"

She looks between us at where I'm still just grazing her. "I want this. I want you, right now. And I'm not afraid to say it." Her hands cup my face and she brings me into a soul-crushing kiss. Her breasts flatten against my chest as she wraps her legs tightly around my waist. Her wet little cunt presses to my stomach and I swell even more.

Her words say she wants this, but her kiss confirms it. This woman who could barely voice how she liked her coffee is now telling me she wants all of me deep inside her. Is it weird to feel proud of someone in a moment like this? Maybe. But I can't help it. I've completely fallen for Camila.

"Turn around." My voice is husky against her lips.

"Wha—"

I bite her lip to stop her words and the sounds that leave her mouth have thrown me over the edge. I step back, unlock her legs, grip her hips, and flip her over on the table. I wrap her hair around my wrist once and then twice before pulling her back until my lips brush against her ear. "I said turn around."

I've been dreaming about Camila's hair decorating my wrist since the first night I saw her and I'm not letting go of it now. I fold her over the table and line myself at her entrance. Her fingers scratch into the table up by her face.

"What do you want?" I ask, sliding in only the thick head of my cock. "Do you want to go slow?" I begin inching my length into her at a torturously slow pace. Enjoying the view of stretching her as she takes every inch of me.

"More. I need more."

My molars grind together as I let out a deep groan. My free hand tightens on her hip, and in one deep thrust, I fill her completely.

"Oh god!"

I pull out halfway before slamming back into her. "Is this what you want?" Her fingers spread across the table as her chin lifts up over her shoulder, and her watery eyes connect with mine.

"Harder."

All the blood rushes out of my head and moves straight to my cock. I let go of her hair and my fingers dig into her sides hard enough to bruise as I lift her up onto her toes. I thrust in and out of her at a punishing pace, the sounds of my ragged breath and her cries are only muffled by the sounds of my hips slamming into her ass.

"Fuck me, you're so tight," I grind out through my clenched jaw.

I reach one hand around her and find her swollen clit. "Oh god, Miles. I'm close." She jerks beneath me and she's somehow even more wet now.

I continue pulsing my fingers over her while I lean over her and whisper in her ear. "I didn't think anything would feel better than your pretty lips wrapped tightly around my cock, but I was wrong. This pussy was made for me." I pull back almost completely before slamming back into her with full force. I'm buried so deep inside her that I don't know where she begins or I end. Her body slides up the table as her feet leave the ground. "My wife takes my cock so well."

"It's so good, Miles," she moans.

"That's it, Camila, come for me." Her pussy clenches around me, squeezing me, getting unbearably tight as she comes all over me. Every time I pull out I lose my breath when I see my cock covered in her arousal. I'm getting close to my own release when she reaches a hand between us and cups my balls, which are so tight they're practically inside me now. But she keeps moving her fingers just past my balls and lightly strokes that sensitive spot, one light press from her middle finger has the base of my spine tingling. All of my senses are heightened to the point where I feel my lungs expand and shrink with every labored breath I take. My cock hardens and I dig into her hips so hard as my own orgasm almost knocks me off my feet and I spill inside her.

My dick still twitching, I have to brace one hand on the table beside her to keep from falling over and crushing her with my weight. I've never felt an orgasm as powerful as that. I'm still trying to catch my breath and blink my vision back into place as I slowly pull out of her. She stands, turning to face me, her breathing just as erratic as mine. I kiss her once before dropping my forehead to hers. "I'm going to bring you to my shower to clean you up now, but just know, I'm not finished with you, yet."

"I'm ready when you are." She raises a challenging eyebrow with a full-on smirk.

I lift her up and wrap her legs around my waist, the feeling of her wet pussy against me has my dick twitching again.

"I'm going to fuck that smirk right off your face, mi esposa." I slap her ass and she throws her head back laughing as I carry her down the hall to my bedroom.

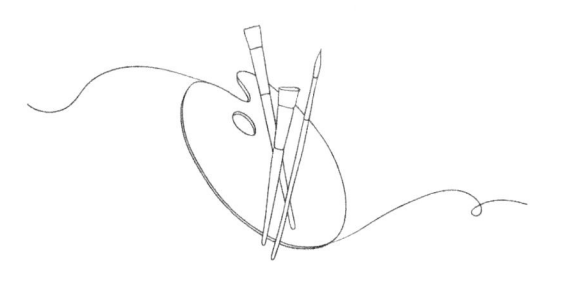

Camila

The thud of Miles's foot kicking his bedroom door open is loud enough to rattle me but I don't stop kissing him. I don't stop when we enter his room or when I feel his hand leave my ass to turn on a light somewhere. His body leans forward still not breaking our kiss and the room fills with the sounds of the running water.

Finally but very unwillingly I pull back, searching his face. His features remain hard, but his eyes are soft. I unwrap my legs and he lowers me to the ground but keeps me pulled tight to his body. The steam from the shower begins to fill the room. And a warming sensation that has little to do with the steam weaves its way through my chest. Small bursts of electricity course through me, as if my heart is telling my brain, *it's okay, we're safe here, you can finally relax.* Our bodies, completely naked and wet, are pulled flush together. The mirror fogs up behind Miles, and the shift in the mood is palpable.

My fingers brush along his hairs that have sprung free from its usual perfect placement. "Tell me something."

His chest digs into me on a deep inhale and he doesn't blink. "This is real for me." His voice is soft but confident. "None of this has been fake for a long time."

His words stop my breath, "When?"

"I think since that first night we had dinner. When you told me my facts about myself were bullshit."

I gasp at him. "I did *not* say that! I said you didn't get very *personal*."

He huffs a laugh, "Fair." He pauses and I can tell he's putting thought into what he wants to say. "I guess I didn't know how. I've never gotten really personal with anyone. But you make it easy. I want to share things with you and more than anything I want you to share things with me. It's definitely a foreign feeling for me, but for the first time in my life, my every waking thought doesn't revolve around work. I think things like *'Are beignets considered a pastry? Would Camila rather have a weekend getaway in the woods up in Oregon or down the coast to Catalina? Is she thinking about me as much as I'm thinking about her? How can I help her realize this art studio is hers? When can I taste her sweet pussy again?'*

I'm so caught off guard by his confession but at the same time, I'm not. I've known there's been something real between us for a long time now. I questioned whether it was just me while feeling deep down it wasn't. His face searches mine looking for an answer and silently asking me if I feel the same way.

I bring his face to mine and kiss his warm, soft lips. "Yes, they're elite pastries." *Kiss.*

"Definitely woods." *Kiss.*

"Only when I'm awake, or dreaming." *Kiss.*

"You being you and supportive is more than enough." *Kiss.*

"And right now." *Kiss.*

The relief in his muscled body is immediate. He pulls me into him even more, as if our bodies could somehow morph into one. I take a step back towards the shower and he follows, never breaking the contact of our bodies. Even pressed this close together I still crave more. The steam around us keeps us warm as he presses me back against the stone wall. Despite what we did not only thirty minutes ago, somehow just holding each other in the back of this shower, after those admissions feels more intimate. I don't know how long we stay like this, but the air continues to grow thick around us.

"Camila—"

"This is real for me too," I breathe.

His eyes close as he drops his forehead to mine. "Are we really doing this?" His lips drop to my jawline briefly before coming back to search my eyes. "For real?"

My chest is still heavy with a fear of excitement but I can't stop the smile that spreads across my face as I nod my head and his lips find mine.

His kiss is passionate and all-consuming. His hands grip the back of my thighs as he effortlessly lifts me. I reach between us and move him so he's at my entrance. He pauses a moment, and the eye contact is so intense but I don't look away. I welcome the way it makes my chest tighten. He brings one arm to wrap around my back and the other on the wall behind me. His lips find mine again, warm and wet. All it takes is a soft moan from my mouth to his and he slides himself in. His movements are slower this time, but I can feel every inch, every ridge, every pulse of him as he fills me up completely. Despite the heat from the shower my neck still fills with goosebumps. I can't ever imagine my body *not* reacting this way to him. The angle he's holding me at has him brushing against my clit with every thrust. Still sensitive from my earlier orgasms it doesn't take long for me to reach that peak pleasure. He finds his relief right after me, and drops his forehead to mine, our breath in sync. We don't say anything for a long moment, but we don't need to.

Miles

I wake from the most peaceful night of sleep I've ever had. A cool breeze blows through the room, and this high up, the morning fog is so thick outside, it gives the illusion we're wrapped in our own personal cloud.

Camila's body lays comfortably under my arm. Her chest rises and falls with each soft breath she takes. I run my nose along her neck and take a deep inhale of her scent. That rich but creamy smell gets me every time. I'm still riding a high from last night. I couldn't have anticipated how badly I needed to hear her say that she wanted this too. That being with me wasn't a mistake and the feelings I've had for her weren't one-sided.

Her breathing changes and she begins to stir. Her ass rubs up against me as her back arches in a small stretch. If she wasn't awake before, my rock-hard cock digging into her now would certainly wake her. She moves to sit up and I close my eyes pretending to be asleep. I feel her slide to the edge of the bed. Through the ends of my lashes, I watch her pull her hair up into one of those messy knots on the top of her head before she bends down and slides one of my T-shirts over her. As much as I love to see her naked body sitting at the end of the bed looking like a goddamn angel, I fucking *love* the sight of her in my clothes.

"Okay see, this is the second time now you've tried to sneak out on me. You're going to give me a complex."

Her spine twists as she looks over her shoulder at me. My eyes narrow in on her as my tongue wets my bottom lip and she comes crawling back up the bed. She lays her body on top of mine, with her fists propped under her chin. "I was going to attempt to make us some coffee with your fancy machine." Her sexy raspy morning voice has my dick twitching under the sheet.

"Touch the fancy coffee *machine* and this relationship might be over before we even have a chance to begin."

"What if I try it naked?"

"I would enjoy that, but you might make Rosa a little uncomfortable." Her mouth parts and a laugh bursts out of me, causing her to shake up and down on top of me.

Her eyes narrow as she points a finger at me. "Rosa doesn't come in the morning."

"She does when I text her the night before asking her to come make my wife some scones." I rub my thumb gently against her cheeks and her face tilts into the touch.

She sits up excitedly, straddling my stomach, "Well, if there's scones down there then what are we still doing up here?"

"The scones are your breakfast, Camila. Mine is up here. And after all that sex last night, I'm absolutely famished." I squeeze her thighs with my hands. "Now be a good wife and come sit on my face."

"Good morning, Rosa."

"Good morning, Miss Camila."

She grabs an eclair and sits at the counter pulling it apart.

"Oh my god, Rosa, you've outdone yourself, these are incredible."

"I'm glad, on such short notice I had to work with what I had," she says, throwing an evil eye at me.

"What do you have planned for this beautiful day?" Rosa asks.

Camila watches me as I start to prepare her coffee. "I'm not sure." She takes a bite of her pastry, then says, "I have a few more job applications I should get to. Unless you had other plans, Miles, I could put off the job hunt for another day." Her eyes light up and she flashes me a mischievous smile.

I had plans yesterday, but after my conversation with Samantha and the icing on the cake of my father texting me, I wasn't in the right headspace. And as much as I would love nothing more than to spend all day with Camila, there's something more important I need to get done right now.

"I actually have to run out for a little bit." I clear my throat and her smile dims. "But I saw there was an art fair going on one street over this morning." I hand her her coffee. "I thought you could check it out while I take care of some business."

"You have work on a Saturday? And the art fair is a dangerous place for someone like me. I have no self-control."

I smile and walk down to my office. When I come back I lean in kissing the top of her head, and set my black card on the counter in front of her. "Go wild, mi esposa." She pulls her lips between her teeth trying to hide her smile, but her leg bounces with excitement under her. "Finish your tart and add some pants to your wardrobe—"

Both women gasp at me, it seems I've offended them.

"This is not a tart!" Camila scolds me.

I blow out a long breath pretending to be annoyed but honestly, I can't get enough of her. I've known for a while, but after last night and now knowing we're on the same page, it's further confirmation that I will do anything for Camila. And that's why I need to leave her here and work on a Saturday.

Turns out pulling strings took me longer than I expected because when I step off the elevator Camila's laptop glows like a beacon in the dark living room, illuminating her face as she sleeps on the couch. I close the screen and sit down next to her head.

Her eyes remain shut but her lips curve into a small smile. "Hey."

I lean over and kiss her forehead. "Hey yourself, sorry I'm so late."

"Where were you?" She doesn't open her eyes but she scoots up so her head is resting on my lap.

"I just had to take care of some business," I say, running my fingers through her hair. "How was the art fair?"

One eye cracks open. "Don't look in your office," she winces and I breathe a laugh.

"Are you still tired?"

Her arms stretch as her body flexes under my hands. "No,

when I fell asleep I'm pretty sure it was right after noon and now," she pops her head up looking around, "It's definitely dark."

"Seems you were maybe a little tuckered out from your night last night," I say as she moves to sit up beside me. I kiss the corner of her lips and her mouth turns up in a sleepy smile. "You wanna get out of here for a bit?"

"What'd you have in mind?"

Camila's fingers dig into my arm as her feet come to a stop. I face her and jerk my head, "Come on."

"Miles, it's closed." She throws her arm forward pointing to the double doors of the museum.

I uncurl her fingers from my bicep and link our fingers together. "Not for you."

Her feet slowly shuffle behind me. When we reach the doors I give a nod to the security guard and he unlocks the museum for us. The silence is deafening.

"What. Are. We. Doing. Here?" She enunciates each word.

"I thought it would be fun to check out the Museum of Modern Art. I've never been here before."

The muscles in her neck work hard "I—you—" Her head shakes slightly as she looks around.

I step up behind her, trailing my fingers down her spine. "I called some people," I whisper against her hair. "It's all for you Camila." Her head falls back against my chest and I take the opportunity to kiss her cheek.

"Was this your *secret business* you needed to take care of today?"

"No." I move to hold her hand in mine again. "This is the apology for my secret business taking so long today. Come on."

"Huh. Well, this is…interesting."

"What the fuck is it?" I ask.

"I think it's a fountain maybe?" She tilts her head as she looks around the sculpture, eyes squinting.

"I'm pretty sure it's a urinal."

She rears back as if it's an active one. "What?" she gasps.

I cover my laugh with a cough, "Yeah, that's a toilet, babe."

Her eyes widen and her mouth opens once before closing again. "Okay well, it *is* interesting."

"You can say weird. It's just us here. I won't get offended."

"It's not *all* weird, you liked that creepy spider sculpture." She points an accusing finger at me and I feel a weightlessness in my body like I've never felt before.

A handful of sculptures later we find a dimly lit room with four large paintings, one for each wall. "Pick your favorite," she says, and her eyes sparkle.

I look at each frame carefully, knowing she's going to ask me to defend my choice.

"This one." I point to an all-black canvas with light strokes of gray slashed across it.

She presses her fingers to her lips trying to hide her smile. "Hmmm…A Moment of Death. What made you choose this one?"

"I knew what it was without reading the title. That one over there looks like a bowl of spaghetti and it's supposed to be about a farmer."

"They're meant to make you *think*."

We stand side by side in the shadow of the room. "Well, what do you think Camila? Does that look like death?"

"This might possibly be the least romantic date conversation I've ever had." She smiles. "I don't know, I guess I like to think we live multiple lives. So for me, a picture of death would have some kind of light on the other side."

"What do you mean multiple lives?"

"Just what it sounds like. I think maybe we live different lifetimes over and over again."

"Like reincarnation?"

"Kind of, but I think that one is more karma-based, and while I totally believe in karma as well, it's just kind of cool to think that maybe we meet new people in every lifetime or maybe we meet some people over and over again, you know?"

I shouldn't be surprised by how mesmerized I am by her but I find myself wanting to know her thoughts on everything. I never want these conversations with her to end. I realize I've just been staring at her when she rolls her eyes and says, "Okay, all-knowing one, what do you think happens when you die?"

I exhale a deep breath and look back at the painting. "I don't know. Black. Nothing. A deep sleep with zero dreams?"

"I'm honestly not surprised by that answer." Her face is the picture of mirth and my stomach bottoms out when I look at her. When we went into this arrangement, I told her I didn't and would never want a relationship but everything about her has taken me by surprise. Being with Camila feels like home. And not the home that I grew up in, but a home for my soul.

"Thank you, Miles. That was the best date I've ever been on. Bar none." Camila's hand holds mine as she leans against me in the back seat of the car.

"Even with the morbid death talk?"

"Surprisingly, even with the death talk." The corner of her lip twitches and she lets out a small huff.

"Sounds like you've dated some real winners," I deadpan.

"I've dated people…that I thought I should." I look at her now, and my body tenses. "In high school, this guy asked me out, and I didn't really know him, but I felt bad so I said yes." She pauses while twisting that pendant across her necklace. "We dated for about a month before he realized he was wasting his time and finally broke up with me."

"I can promise you, time with you could never be wasted, Camila." Her eyes are distant. "That was it? High school was your last boyfriend?" I ask, feeling relieved.

"No. I dated in college too. Casually." This has me clenching my fist, but I listen intently. "But just like with that high school boyfriend, I always felt like I was just *there*. None of them brought any value to my life, and I don't know, I always just felt like an accessory. Does that make sense?"

"Yes." But I wish it didn't. As much as I can't stand to think of her with anyone else, the thought of her being unhappy tears me up even more. How could anyone be with her and not worship the ground she walks on? Her heart is so big, and anyone being with her just to pass the time makes me want to shove my fist into a wall. She deserves the world and then some.

"Anyway, on a scale of one to ten, where does this rank on the most romantic thing you've done for someone you've dated?"

"I don't know, what would you rate it?" Her eyes narrow as she cocks her head to the side. I lean my head back on the headrest. "I've never dated before, Camila. I've never had someone I wanted to spend all my time with. Someone who I want to know all their waking thoughts. I've never wanted someone to confide their desires and fears with me and vice versa."

"You want that with me?" Her eyes are glassy but her smile is so beautiful my hand itches to hold her face and kiss her.

"Yeah. I want it all with you. I can't promise that I'll be great at the relationship part because I have nothing to compare it to. But I can promise that I'll give you my everything. And you'll never just be an *accessory* to me." I grab the back of her neck and kiss her forehead lightly before whispering against her skin. "I see many more dates like this in our future."

Her body sinks against mine and if I wasn't holding my breath I would have missed the soft sigh that escaped her mouth. "I would rate it a ten."

"Oh Camila, I'm just getting started with you."

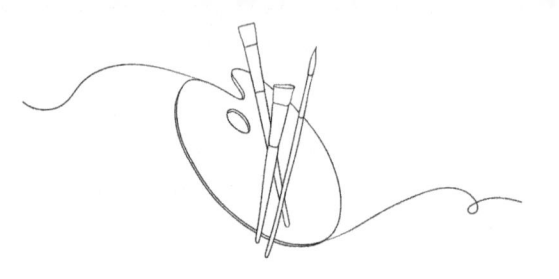

Camila

Today is the day. I feel it in my bones. My last interview would normally have been enough to break me. I mentally give myself a pat on the back for showing some serious growth in getting back at it. Physically I give myself a little shoulder rub and do some neck rotations. I've been working hard on this presentation—from renovation ideas to projected cost to income and revenue. The last couple days I've been up early and staying up late working on this, and I've finally found a potential investor for the art studio. It wouldn't be *my* studio but with some stipulations I've put in, with any luck I'll still be able to help facilitate it. This feels like an appropriate small step for me. I would be closer to a job that I love but without the risk of failing and disappointing anyone.

I've been living with Miles for a month and a half now and even though we've moved into relationship territory, I don't know what it means for us in regards to our annulment. It seems crazy to stay married when everything is still so new but does going through with it say that this is just for fun, and maybe he still never plans on being married? Either way, I still need to figure out my next move. Whether I'm able to get an investor on board today or not, I'm trying. I've missed too many calls from my parents. With only a responding text claiming to be *super busy.* I want to get back on my feet and today is the day.

My fingers hover over the keyboard of my laptop as I review my PowerPoint. The familiar ding of the elevator has me poking my head up over my laptop. Miles crosses the entryway with his shirt draped over one shoulder. My eyes instinctively go to his thigh tattoo before I trail his body. His thick ab muscles flex in and out with every deep breath he takes. When my eyes land on his face he hits me with that sexy-as-sin smirk as he closes the last bit of distance between us.

"Good morning." His wet lips kiss the side of my face and I pull back.

"Listen I love…this," I wave my hand around him, "but you're very sweaty." His rumbly laugh vibrates against me and it's almost enough to distract me from the fact that I think I almost just told Miles I love him.

"Okay well I'm going to go shower, and then I want to take you somewhere." I almost don't register his words as my thoughts swirl around my head.

"Don't you need to get into the office?"

"I let Jonas know this morning that I would be in later."

"Where are we going?"

"It's a surprise. Let's go shower." His eyebrows wiggle as he pulls me out of the chair and drags me down the hall.

I take a breath and try to process how I almost just had a Freudian slip.

MILES

"What are we doing here?"

A strong breeze blows past us on the sidewalk as I unlock the storefront. I open the door for Camila and follow her inside. As soon as the door closes behind me, the silence is deafening. Slowly, she turns around to face me, arms crossed and her eyebrows raised. "Miles?"

I have half a second to wonder if I've made a mistake or if I've overstepped. Truthfully I probably have, but that's never stopped me before. I take one look at her and I know with every fiber of my being there was no other choice. So I lift my chin and say, "I bought it."

Her eyes go wide and her mouth hangs open. "What do you mean you bought it?"

"I mean, you kept saying you wanted someone to buy this space and open an art gallery, so I bought it." I slowly begin closing the gap between us. "Now, I don't know shit about art but thankfully I know someone who does." I stop half an inch in front of her, her head tilts back and her wide eyes are a mix of panic and confusion.

"Why would—" Her breath catches as liquid forms in the corners of her eyes. She begins shaking her head and I grab hold of her face to look at me.

"Camila."

"Why would you buy this place?"

"Because I believe in you. I believe in your vision and I want you to believe in it too."

"Miles—" she closes her eyes tightly and a lone tear slips down her cheek. "This is, this is too much, not to mention it would *definitely* complicate things."

"We're already complicating things." I shrug my shoulder

and wipe away her tear. "And nothing is too much for you." The tears she was desperately trying to hold back come out in full force as she smiles, cries, and lets out a small laugh all in one. I kiss her cheeks where the salty streaks stain her face. I know just buying this studio isn't going to erase all her fears and worries, but my hope is she'll at least be on the path.

"I would do anything to help you achieve your goals. Because you deserve to be happy. Not a bullshit happy for someone else, but really, truly, genuinely, happy. Nada es demasiado para ti, mi esposa."

"How have you had time to purchase property *and* learn Spanish?" She teases me. I wipe her tears once more before turning her body around in my arms so she can take in the full space around her.

"I spend more time on the language app than I do working most days," I whisper in her ear.

Her head falls back onto my chest and I soak in the feeling of her body wrapped in my arms. "I don't know what to say," she breathes.

"Camila, this place was yours from the moment you stepped foot in here. We both knew it. You just needed a little push. And like I said, there isn't anything I wouldn't do to help you. But the truth is, you don't need me. You're the most deserving, capable, kind, and creative person I know. So if you'd let me, I'd love to be by your side and watch all the great things you come up with."

Her shoulders shake under me and tears plop onto my forearms.

"What are you thinking?" I ask against the top of her head.

"I'm just trying to wrap my head around this." She turns back around, wrapping her arms around my waist. "I don't know how to thank you. Not only for this but for believing in me enough."

I kiss her lips tenderly. And a sigh of relief passes through me.

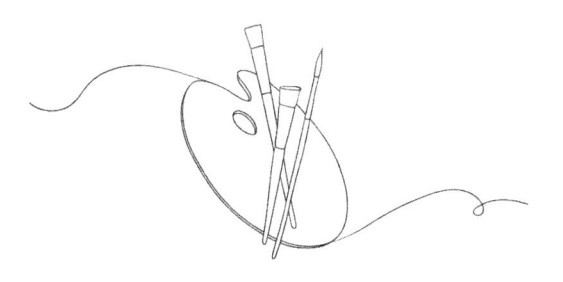

Camila

THE BATH WATER IS SILKY WITH OILS AND SLIGHTLY PINK WITH some discarded petals from a rose bath bomb. After the last few days of nonstop manual labor, this bath is calling my name. It's been a week since Miles brought me to the property he bought me and I immediately hit the ground running with ideas. I think a part of me wanted to busy myself so I couldn't focus on the slightly overwhelming feeling that he bought this space for me, and the more overwhelming feeling that I would now definitely have to talk to my parents. Some days it feels like things are moving too quickly and maybe they are. But at the same time, nothing has ever felt more right.

MILES

What are you wearing?

ME

Paint.

MILES

Mmm sexy.

> **ME**
> I think you might be the only person to think that.

> **MILES**
> Then everyone else is foolish!

> **ME**
> You're crazy.

> **MILES**
> For you? I'm out of my goddamn mind.

It's easy to get caught up in this world with him. In this world, I can go to my studio every day and feel a sense of pride in my work and in myself while I create a space worthy of the artists in this city. I can come home to Miles and we can live in this perfect little bubble together. In this world, I'm falling in love with my life and I can't imagine living it any other way. But the reality is, at some point, I'm going to have to talk to my parents and deal with the potential reality of disappointing them.

> **MILES**
> I gave Rosa the night off, I'll send Wills to pick you up and I'll meet you for dinner.

> **ME**
> I noticed she wasn't here. I wasn't joking about the paint though, I'm about to get in the bath.

> **MILES**
> Fuck the dinner. I'll be home in 15. Meet you in the bath.

> **ME**
> See you then.

It's only taken me seven weeks but I've finally figured out how to connect to the Bluetooth to play music from any speaker in the house. With the music playing softly, I didn't hear the elevator doors open so I am pleasantly surprised to hear that husky voice behind me, "I could come home to this every day and die a happy man."

I know he means it as a simple comment but hearing the way he says *every day*, has my heart longing for some kind of future with him.

He leans against the vanity. When he untucks his shirt from his pants I get a glimpse of that dusting of dark hair trailing down from below his belly button. I know realistically he's probably moving at a normal pace, but watching him it feels like he's pulling his jacket off and undoing his shirt buttons in slow motion.

"Now if you just ditch the pants you could join me in here," I say.

His head falls forward with a small laugh and he looks up at me from under his thick lashes. "Well since we've already almost flooded this place once before, I think I'll stay out here." He pulls a bench away from the wall and props it next to the tub before sitting on it. His strong hands find my shoulders and unaware of the tension I was holding there, I relax them. I look down at his bruised knuckles as he continues to knead my shoulders.

"How was your day?" I ask him.

"Boring. How was yours?"

His tone is sarcastic but I still can't help myself. "Miles," I playfully growl at him while I let my head fall back and rest against the rim behind me. The truth is, I've been busy renovating the studio, but I don't miss the way his eyes have been heavy. Like he has something on his mind. I bring my lips down to his hands and leave a kiss, silently telling him, *I'm here, you can talk to me.* As if that was the reassurance he needed he huffs out a long breath and continues.

"My dad reached out to me."

I shoot up from the bath and turn to face him. "When?"

"Last week maybe? Or the week before? I don't really remember."

"Why? Are you okay?"

His eyes stay trained where my hands clutch tightly around his. "I wanted this. I wanted him to see that I could be successful without him. I wanted it to sting. But I've been so angry at him for so long and when I hit that level of success, he was the last thing on my mind."

Understanding dawns on me. His father, who he doesn't have a relationship with, and is the sole reason he claims to work so hard. He says he wanted this as a way to hurt his dad but he doesn't seem happy with the way this situation has turned out.

"Hey—"

"I'm okay." He looks at me now. "I was mad to hear from him initially but I think that was just a programmed response at this point. After a while, I realized I'd been successful and done all the work and I hadn't thought twice about doing it to spite him. I don't really even know this man anymore. And I don't want to continue being pissed off and working for his reactions."

"Have you ever thought about reaching out to him?"

His lips purse as he shakes his head. "There's no point." He kisses the corner of my mouth. "Calling it a good thing might be a stretch, but I can see the situation better now. I don't care what someone who I don't even know anymore thinks about me. I still want to be the best at what I do but I want to be great for myself. I want to make myself proud. And you."

His words make my eyes well up, and I have to bite my cheek to stop myself from crying.

"Maybe one day. Maybe clearing that negative air between you two will help you to really let go and move on." I kiss his hand that I'm still holding. "And Miles? You *do* make me proud. Honestly, the only thing bigger than your scowl is—"

"My dick?"

I flick my wrist, spraying him with water. "Is your *heart,* jackass."

"Must be the Leo in me." He shrugs with a laugh and gets up to turn on the shower. After it's running warm he reaches his hand out to mine. "Come on, let's rinse you off," he says, unbuttoning his pants with his free hand.

I climb out and step up to him on my tip toes so I'm closer to his face. I trace his soft lips with my fingers. "I could do this every day and be happy too."

"Your mind is wandering."

We got in bed hours ago. The warmth of Miles's body seeps into me. His powerful thighs cradle me from behind, providing immense comfort. But still, I've been lying here with a thousand thoughts and not one of them is clear.

"How did you know?" I roll over to face him.

"I can just feel it. You're not sleeping. What's going on in that head of yours?"

"You can feel me not sleeping?"

He makes a small frustrating growl before dipping his head to my neck. "Camila."

"I don't know." I squirm against him and laugh when his beard tickles my cheek. "It's like, I have a lot on my mind, but at the same time I can't make out a single thought." His eyes bunch in confusion but I'm used to not being able to explain how I feel to people. I rub a reassuring thumb over the crease between his brows. "It happens. I'll be okay, I just need to relax and go to sleep."

"You shouldn't be the one comforting me right now."

My arms wrap around his back as I nuzzle in close to him. "Shh…go to sleep." I close my eyes and tell myself things are fine. *I can relax. I am safe. I take things one day at a time. This feeling is only temporary.*

"Let's get out of here."

My eyes snap open and I peel back looking at him. "Umm..it's the middle of the night?"

Even in the dark, I can see his smirk and slight eye roll. "Not right now. This weekend."

I hesitate, wondering where this is coming from and I shouldn't be surprised, if he can sense when I'm not sleeping, he can obviously sense my hesitation.

"We'll leave Saturday and come home Monday morning. Let's just get away and relax a little."

It's a gesture that tugs at my heart. I know this trip is in an attempt to help me, so I kiss his mouth and whisper against his lips, "Sounds perfect." I try to slow my breathing to mimic a deep sleep so I don't keep him up with my running thoughts. But a familiar feeling begins scraping at the corners of my mind.

Miles

My phone buzzes inside my suit pocket. Talan's desk number flashes across the screen. "Talan," I answer.

"Sorry to bother you, Mr. Cameron. But Jonas is here asking for the Bainbridge files. And I—"

"On my desk sitting on top of my computer. You can get them for him but then tell him to leave you alone. I'll be back in thirty." I don't wait for his response, I pocket my phone and my fast-paced walk comes to a halt when I see Camila pulling wood planks twice her size down from the shelves. Her beauty stuns me every time I see her. Her dark hair is pulled back into two braids that hang down her back. Her white T-shirt lifts up under her denim overalls as she reaches above her head. I shouldn't be fighting a hard-on from overalls but this is what I've become around her.

I will my feet to finally move when I see her start climbing the unstable wood planks. I step up behind her and grab the plank she's trying to reach.

"What do you think you're doing?" I ask, lowering the wood into her lumber cart.

"I could have gotten that," she scolds me. "I've gotten all

the other ones, by myself." There's no humor in her eyes. She seems on edge. Frustrated. And now I'm pissed that she's been at this home improvement store for who knows how long and no one has helped her.

"I have no doubt that you *can,* the fact is you shouldn't *have* to. Where the fuck are all the employees in this place?" I ask, looking around.

"It's fine." Her fingers squeeze the bridge of her nose and she lets out a breath of air. She shakes her head like she's trying to shake away her frustration. "Anyway, it's nice to see you, midday." Her hands clasp around my biceps and she tilts her head back to look at me. A smile that doesn't reach her eyes crosses her face and I'm painfully aware of how spoiled I've been by her real smiles.

I pull her body in close to mine, it's my way of telling her *I've got you* and she responds by allowing her body to soften into mine. Out of the corner of my eye, I see a flash of the hideous orange that is a part of the employee's uniforms. I whip my head to find a man walking past the aisle. "Excuse me!"

He stops abruptly. "Yes sir, how can I help you?"

I keep Camila tucked tightly under my arm. "My wife is renovating her art gallery. I need you to help her get anything and everything she may need or want."

I feel Camila's eyes snap to me. She's likely aware of the same thing I am. That's the first time I've said the words *my wife* to someone without any bite to them or dripping in sarcasm. I'd be lying to myself if I said I didn't like the way it sounded.

"Yes of course. I'll make sure she gets everything she needs."

Unfortunately, I have to get back to the office to wrap up

some things before we can leave tomorrow. "Will you be okay?" I ask her.

She nods her head with a reassuring smile and pats my chest. "Yes, go."

"I'll see you later," I say, pressing my lips to her forehead.

As I walk through the store I can't stop feeling like something is wrong. Did I push this on her? Is this too fast or too much for her? I need to figure something out because I'll never forgive myself if I fuck this up.

"Shouldn't you have your own personal associate now?" Jonas asks when I get back to the office.

"Why would I need one of them when I have you?"

He reaches over his head behind his back as if he's pulling out an arrow, notches it into his imaginary bow before pulling it back, and sends his middle fingers flying at me.

"Mr. Cameron, sorry to interrupt. Hi, Jonas." Talan pokes his head in the door and offers a small wave to Jonas.

"Talan! My guy, you're looking sharp today," Jonas says and I swear Talan blushes. I motion for him to continue.

"Thank you, Jonas. Mr. Cameron, you're all set for tomorrow, the plane will be ready for you to leave at 10 a.m."

"Thank you, Talan."

Jonas's smile drops and his eyes shoot to me. "What?" I bark at him.

"Where are we heading?"

"Jonas, the only place I would go with you is to a monastery in Thailand."

"Har har, dickhole. Where are you going?"

"Dickhole? Really?" I ask at his use of an insult.

"Yes really. But now I know this involves Camila since you only avoid my questions when they involve her…"

Touche, dickhole.

"I'm handing these files off to you because I'm taking Camila up to Oregon for the weekend."

"Nice. Take her out into the woods and act out a little vampire romance."

"As usual I don't know what the fuck you're talking about, but by all means keep talking to hear yourself talk."

"Who knew we would ever see the day?" I ignore him, making sure all the papers are in the file. "You're a simp daddy."

"Don't ever fucking call me that again."

"Miles Simp Daddy Cameron."

"You really do get off on annoying me don't you?"

"Is it weird?" he asks, unable to keep the smile off his face.

"Is what weird?"

"Being in love with your fake wife?"

For thirty-six years I've been content to be single. I never wanted to go through what my parents did. Even though I knew I would never be like my father—I would never cheat on anyone—I still saw the way he crushed my mom and I never wanted to be the reason someone could be so broken. I never wanted to open myself up to that kind of torture either. I always thought it was easier to not expose myself to that possibly than it would be to endure it. So I never tried or wanted a relationship and I definitely never planned on being married. But now I can't imagine a life not married to Camila. So I catch myself being honest with Jonas.

"No. It's not."

He nods his head knowing not to push it.

. . .

After my conversation with Jonas, I was desperate to get home to Camila. I completed the bare essentials that needed to be done and I packed up my stuff and met Wills downstairs. As we drive home, I'm noticing things I never noticed before. Specifically the people outside— couples, families, and groups of friends. Some heading out for dinner, some heading back to their hotels after a day of sightseeing. Every light Wills stops at feels like torture. Even though I've known I've been falling in love with Camila for some time now, acknowledging it out loud feels different. I don't know if she's there yet, but I can't go another minute without telling her how I feel.

Miles

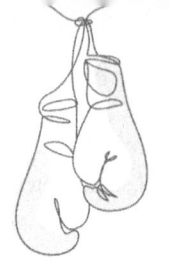

Empty silence greets me when I get home. I've gotten attached to the comforting feeling of coming home and finding Camila curled up on the couch. I head down to my room, finding it empty as well.

"Camila?" I shout into the empty space as I pull out my phone and head back towards the kitchen. No missed calls or messages. I start to call her as I walk up to her old room just to check.

The battle of relief and panic crashes into my chest at the same time when I find her curled up in a ball on the bed with her back facing me.

I set my phone on the dresser and walk around to the other side of the bed. My chest cracks open when I see the skin around her eyes, puffy and red. Careful not to disturb her I sit on the edge of the bed and place a gentle hand on her arm. "Camila," I whisper, failing to hide the concern in my voice.

"I'm sorry." She sits up, looking around confused. "I didn't realize what time it was."

"You don't need to be sorry. What's going on? Are you

hurt?" Confusion and panic duel in my brain as I try to figure out what happened and how I can fix it.

"No." She shakes her head, crossing her arms and hugging her body tightly. "I just—I have—" She's working hard to try and get a breath in and I'm on the verge of exploding. I take a deep breath through my nose and I watch my knuckles turn white where my hand grips the comforter. I slowly let go and bring her hand into mine. "I just," her inhale is shaky, "I just have a little anxiety today," she cries out.

Her shoulders fold in and I scoot up, wrapping her in my arms, and rub her back.

"What are you anxious about?" It seems like a stupid fucking question but I'm so far out of my element here, I don't know what to do or say. I just know I need to fix it for her.

She collapses, shaking, against me. "I don't know," she says through her tears. "It's not something specific, it's just this uncomfortable feeling inside."

I pull back to look at her and her face brings a sharp pain to my chest. "Is it because of the flight? Or maybe all the work you've been doing lately?" I'm looking for anything tangible that I can fix for her.

She shakes her head looking down at her lap while wiping away her tears. "No. I don't know. It's… it's hard to explain." I don't press anymore. Instead, I kick off my shoes and scoot up to sit against the headboard, trusting that the words will find her. "I'm not *anxious* about something in particular. I just have *anxiety.*" She wipes her tears with the back of her sleeve before resting her head on my shoulder. I hold her thigh under my hand and rub soothing strokes with my thumb. "It's just this feeling that consumes me sometimes. Some things can exacerbate it and make it worse, some things help, but sometimes it's just this unexplainable *feeling*. I'm uncomfortable, irritable, and restless, and sometimes I have a hard time sleeping, but I couldn't tell you why." Guilt plagues me when I think if this was something I could have spotted sooner. "Eventually, it builds and builds to a point where it becomes too much and the feelings don't have anywhere to go and I can't help it, I just cry. I'm sorry I'm doing a terrible job explaining."

I feel helpless. My heartbeat is a dull thud in my chest. I've been nervous before, sure, but never for a reason unbeknownst to me. More than anything I hate that she's apologizing. I sit up to face her, her loose hair sticking to her where tears stain her face.

Pushing her hair back from her face I pull it all up to the top of her head while grabbing the silk band from around her wrist. I stretch it around the mound of hair and it all falls right back down her back again. An appreciative smile forms on her face, and I try again. This time twisting the silk around a few times. "Please don't apologize, Camila. I wish there was something I could do, I wish I could understand better." The hair tie is holding her hair, and I wouldn't say I've mastered it but it is out of her face and I can now hold her cheeks with both hands. My thumbs brush lightly where the tears have spilled down her cheeks.

"I don't fully understand it myself so I can understand why it's difficult for you." She sniffs.

"Can I do anything?" I ask helplessly.

She shakes her head, "No, I know it sounds I don't know, stupid maybe? But sometimes watching a comfort movie or reading a book and getting lost in something else until the time passes helps."

"It doesn't sound stupid at all."

She tries to take a big breath and I can hear it shudder. I

press my lips firmly to her forehead as she slumps into the headboard, closing her eyes. "I'm actually kind of tired, it can be exhausting crying multiple times a day. I'll think I'll just try to sleep it off."

I look her over for any sign that tells me she wants my company but her eyes are already closed. I pull her blankets up to cover her and start to head towards the door.

"Miles."

I pause, turning to her.

"Can you change your clothes and come lay with me?"

It feels selfish to feel relief at this moment but I'm completely overwhelmed with the thought of her feeling safe enough to not only want me to be near her during a moment of struggle but also not be afraid to ask me. Now isn't the time, so I'll tuck this win of hers away to be admired later. "I'll be back in a minute."

My mind is trying to pull me from my dream. I'm vaguely aware of a light touch running along my bottom lip. I fight the smile and school my face to remain unphased as I realize Camila's fingers are tracing a line along my mouth. The soft caress both tickles and excites me. The moment I feel her begin to pull away I part my lips and nip at her fingertip. I don't need to see her to know she's smiling. I suck her delicate digits, rolling my tongue around until her breathy exhale kisses my ears. She slowly slides out of my mouth and my eyes finally flutter open, meeting her piercing gaze with my own.

"Good morning." Her voice is barely more than a whisper.

"Good morning." I reach under the covers and run my palm along her warm thigh.

The playful smile on her face eases a tension that has been wrapped around my chest since last night. Camila is good at hiding her feelings—shoving them away so others can't see them—and I want to make sure she isn't doing that now.

"How are you feeling?"

"I'm still a little embarrassed, but other than that, I feel much better."

"You never have to feel embarrassed with me, Camila." Her eyes soften as she scoots closer to me. Her body radiates warmth and I use my hold on her leg to wrap her around me.

"What time do we need to be ready to leave?"

"We don't have to go if you feel stressed or tired. We can cancel and go another time."

"No." She firmly shakes her head. "I'm not stressed, and I want to go. I feel much better this morning waking up with you. So, what time do we leave?" I take a deep breath, studying her face. Her eyes lock on mine. "Miles, I'm serious. If I didn't want to, I promise, I would tell you. I *want* to go." I exhale the breath I was holding and roll over on top of her.

"We've got some time," I whisper against her neck and her chin lifts, giving me better access. I lower my body, settling myself between her legs as I watch that devilish smile I've come to love spread across her face.

I slowly begin to roll up the t-shirt she's wearing, watching how its oversized fit flows down her body. I kiss a trail up her hips and stomach until her breasts are exposed to me. "You're so fucking beautiful," I say between kisses. "I don't know if I've told you recently, but even if I have, it's not enough." Her hand lifts to my face. Her thumb strokes along my jaw. "I mean it, Camila. I could tell you every day in every language and it still would never feel like enough."

"It's more than enough, Miles. *You're* more than enough."

My mouth descends on her and our bodies relax, so in tune with one another as we give ourselves to each other freely.

Miles

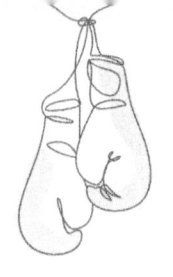

"When you said we were flying you forgot to mention it was private," Camila whisper-shouts at me.

I smile and nod to the flight crew waiting at the top of the stairs with Camila tucked in tight to my side. "I wasn't aware there was another way," I say, boarding the plane and handing our bags to a flight member. There are two beige leather couches on either side of a mahogany table, and a partition wall past them leads into the back bedroom. The flight is only an hour and a half, so we take a seat on one of the couches and order a drink before taking off.

"Have you ever been to Oregon before?" Camila asks, legs bouncing with her hands rubbing together between them.

I place my hand on her thigh, and it covers almost half of it. Her legs stop bouncing and she takes a deep breath, her shoulders moving up and down on the exhale. "I have, but only for work. I've flown in, talked to clients, and left."

"You work a lot." It's not a question, she knows my hours are long, even though I've been going in late and leaving earlier than I ever have for nearly two months.

"I never had anything worth coming home to until recently," I say, kissing her forehead.

The flight crew goes over the safety rules and we're airborne shortly after. The plane engine fills the silence between us. Camila sits curled up against me while I watch us move in and out of clouds as I absently stroke her arm.

"I'm going to see my parents on Tuesday."

My hand stills for a beat before I recover. I'm not sure if she's going home to tell them about her career change, or us. When I first proposed this plan to her, I didn't care if she told her parents about us, and I didn't care what they would think of me. But now, things are different. I clear my throat, "What did you end up telling them? About us, I mean."

She sits up, moving out of my touch, taking her warmth with her. I want to pull her back to me, but I turn to face her, waiting to hear what she'll say.

"I never actually told them anything. It never came up." Her face cringes as her shoulder lifts.

"They never asked you if you've been to Vegas lately and got so drunk you married the first man you could find? So weird. I make sure to ask everyone I know those kinds of things, often," I tease her.

She smiles and playfully shoves my shoulder. I grab her arm and pull her back into me. "I never *needed* to tell them. I've only talked to my mom once and it was after that terrible interview. The conversation was short after I lied and told her I was out with Taylor. Other than that I only know that they plan on visiting my brother in Italy for a few weeks this summer because of a group chat. I've not told them about quitting my job, or the gallery, or you..." she trails off.

"And now?" I hesitate because I'm so far gone when it comes to Camila. I know how I feel about her, hell, I was on my way home last night to lay it all out there for her. Consequences be damned.

"I'm ready. I'm ready to tell them about everything." She sits up again but this time stays close, keeping her hand on my chest. "I'm all in with you, Miles. I'm not afraid to tell you that, and I won't be afraid to tell them either." She leans in, pressing her lips into mine. It's a kiss that mimics everything she's saying.

"Do you want me to come with you?" I ask.

Her smile is soft, "No." She quickly shakes her head, "I mean yes, I do want you with me, but only for selfish reasons." She inclines her head.

"You can be as selfish as you want with me, Camila."

"I appreciate the offer, but I think it's something I should and *can* do on my own." And I don't have a single doubt that she can't. "Plus, when you *do* meet them, I want it to be under better circumstances."

I never thought I would be in a situation to be nervous about meeting someone's parents, but her confidence in the fact that I will meet them tells me she's just as serious about us as I am. And that's enough to calm me down...for now.

"Do you want to use the plane?" I ask with a knowing smile.

She rolls her eyes and lays back down on my lap. "I think I'll travel with the common people for this one." I watch her head rise and fall as I shake her with my laugh.

CAMILA

The sweet scent of rain and pine fills my lungs immediately as we step off the plane. Miles keeps his fingers intertwined with mine as we walk up to an old Jeep. My lips purse together.

"*You* know how to drive?" I ask, suspiciously. When he tilts his head with a blank stare, I put my hands up. "I'm just saying, I've never seen you drive, and there's a lot of trees and probably wildlife out here. I don't want you to plow us into anything," I say climbing in. The warmth of his body covers mine as he reaches over, buckling my seatbelt.

"Oh. I'll be plowing into *something*." His face hovers over mine for a brief moment before he closes my door. And I have to clench my thighs together while he makes his way around to the driver's side.

As we drive along the tree-lined road my mind is wandering. I was embarrassed when Miles came home and found me crying. I wasn't surprised he was so understanding, but I was surprised by how comforting I found him. I felt the anxiety creeping in for the last few days. I tried to ignore it when it presented itself as trouble sleeping, and again when I was irritable the next day. But when I woke up yesterday morning I knew I couldn't fight it off any longer. I had canceled breakfast with Taylor over text. I knew if I saw her or even called her she would know I was going through it. And I didn't want to put that on her. It's hard for her to see me struggle and not be able to do anything about it. I've always rather ride the wave out alone, so I wasn't expecting to release wave after wave of discomfort under Miles's touch. His closeness alone was enough to help me relax enough to fall asleep. I'm not sure how long he rubbed those circles on my back. But the two times I woke in the night, his hands were still moving.

I'm shaken from my thoughts—literally. As our car begins to rattle around. I squint my eyes, looking out the windshield as we make our way off the paved road and begin bouncing along a dirt path.

"Are you sure you know where we're going?"

His only response is a slight smile and a reassuring hand on my leg.

I lean closer to the dash, trying to get a better view and the crunch of gravel is loud as the car begins to slow. Through the shifting fog, I make out a stunning, large oak wood home. The way it sits on the hill, completely surrounded by trees, gives the illusion that it's built directly into the forest.

Miles grabs our bags and I follow him up the stairs. When he opens the door, I'm in awe. A large leather sectional sits in the middle of the living room on top of a beautiful plush rug. There are vaulted ceilings and a built-in bookshelf that goes on forever. While most of the walls are made of natural wood, the back wall is made entirely of glass and the view of the woods takes my breath away. "This doesn't even seem real," I whisper.

His only response is a kiss on top of my head before heading down a long hallway.

I pull my phone out of my back pocket and move to sit on the couch. The cold of the leather bites through my pants and I drape a white fur blanket over my lap.

ME

Made it.

TAYLOR

And? How is it?

ME

Incredible. It's like we're up in a little tree house. It's so cute.

TAYLOR

SCGKMF

ME

so cute get knifed mother fucker?

TAYLOR

Swooning crying giggling kicking my feet.

But close.

ME

🫠 What are you up to later?

TAYLOR

Got another hot date with Netflix.

ME

This is like the 3rd time this week. Things sound serious between you two.

TAYLOR

And they say I have commitment issues.
Please.

Heavy hands gently squeeze my shoulders and I let my head tilt to the side. I feel the knots I didn't realize were there as Miles rubs into them with his fingers. "So, I know you wanted to try out a hike. If you're up for that we should go soon, before it gets dark out. But if you're tired and want to stay in," his teeth nip at my ear, "we could do that too." My eyes fall shut as I smile against the feeling of his lips now pressing against my neck. I know if I don't get up, we'll easily get distracted so I throw the blanket off me and jump off the couch like my ass is on fire. I momentarily get whiplash from how quickly I spin around to face him.

"We're going," I say, with my hands on my hips. "Get dressed."

"I am dressed." His eyebrows bunch together.

"You're wearing *that* to go *hiking*?" I ask, pointing at his fitted tan pants and black knitted sweater.

"What's wrong with what I'm wearing?"

"It's a little fancy for hiking."

"It's a sweater, Camila."

I raise my eyebrows, giving him a bemused smile before padding down the hallway to change.

We're lost.

Not surprising since Miles has his own personal driver and prior to two months ago, I walked to the same office every day and barely had the energy to go anywhere else. When I suggested we just go back and play cards, he actually growled.

My leg bounces restlessly as I impatiently wait for him to give up and turn around. To my surprise, he pulls over to the side of the tree-lined road.

"What are we doing?" My eyes widen in confusion.

"We're hiking."

"This isn't a hiking trail."

"We'll make our own." His muscles flex under his sweater as he moves to get out of the Jeep. I make a mental note that Miles is likely not the hiking type. No one who's ever hiked a day in their life would choose to make their own path in the woods. I get out and follow him through some bushes. "I'm sure these woods are filled with trails, we just need to cut through some of these bushes and we're bound to find something."

"I'm not sure hiking works like that."

As we continue pushing through the woods, I think I feel a raindrop. "It's probably leftover water on the trees," Miles says.

Whoshu whoshu.

"What was that?" My breathing accelerates but my body freezes. Miles slowly inches his body in front of mine.

"Don't. Move," he whispers slowly.

My knuckles pale as I hold the back of his sweater in a death grip. I squeeze my eyes shut and hold so still I swear I can hear the pulsing of the trees around us. I'm fairly certain I don't have fight or flight because I always go into freeze mode, which would hopefully be best case in the event that we've just encountered a wolf or a bear.

I physically feel Miles's back muscles release under my hands as he hunches over, letting out a long sigh. "It was a rabbit." He looks over his shoulder at me with a relieved smile.

It takes some bush-whacking but we've finally found some sort of a path. The buzzing of insects and chirping of birds offers soft background noise.

"Can I ask you something?"

"Always."

"It's about your dad." If I wasn't holding his hand I might have missed how his step faltered once before quickly recovering. His eyes remain forward, a slight dip in his brows is his only indication that he heard me. And when he doesn't say anything I continue. "When he texted you last week, was that the first time he's reached out to you?"

His thumb slides back and forth across my hand. Something that he's done numerous times when I'm in need of comfort but maybe it's a gesture that's just as helpful for him.

"No. After I cut him out, he tried regularly to get in contact with me. His attempts lessened over the years but never stopped. Every year or two I would have Talan get me a new number but that was a pain in the ass. Now, I just accept that I'll hear from him from time to time." My lips twist to the side and I nod my head. "What else?"

My eyes snap to him and I playfully nudge him with my shoulder. "Why do you assume there's something else?" I ask.

"I told you. You can't hide your tell." His finger taps my nose. My eyes roll back extra dramatically and his thumb rubs against me again as he grins. "That day on the pier. I knew how I felt about you. I wanted to tell you then. But I got that text," he pauses and I vividly remember how his face had drained of color and there was a very clear shift in him. "It was from him. He congratulated me on making name partner." I nod my head in understanding. "But I wasn't thinking about work. When I looked at you, I got scared."

We stop walking and I turn to face him, wrapping my arms tightly around him. "What were you afraid of?"

"All the reasons I never wanted to be in a relationship had just come through on my phone. I was reminded of how easily everything could go to shit and I just shut down."

"What changed your mind?"

"You." His hands run along the back of my head, patting my hair down. "You made it impossible to stay away and I knew *their* relationship would never be ours."

My throat is tight with emotion. His piercing gaze makes it difficult to breathe and I know that if I could form words without fear of crying, I would tell him I'm in love with him.

A FEW TOO MANY FALLS AND ANIMAL ENCOUNTERS LATER, have us running back to the car. Without a trail to follow we have to be extra careful about heading straight back in the direction we came from, which is proving to be more difficult now that it's started raining. We finally make it out of the clearing and we're about 100 meters down the road from our car. I can't help the laugh that rips through me when Miles grabs my hand and starts jogging towards the jeep with his ass covered in dirt. I stop mid-run and bend over laughing uncontrollably.

"What are you doing?" he shouts through the rain.

"You're covered in mud." I choke on my fit of laughter.

"Yeah, hence why I'm trying to get us back to the car."

I'm wheezing and panting, out of breath from the run, and laughing so hard. Miles closes the distance between us, and his hands grab either side of my face. I stop laughing long enough for him to pull me into a deep, stomach-fluttering kiss. A kiss I can feel down to my freezing bones. His teeth rake across my bottom lip demanding entrance and I happily give it to him. One hand tangles in the back of my wet hair as he holds my head close to him. His other hand slides down my neck, over my shoulders, and grabs onto my hip.

A sigh escapes me when he pulls away, but warmth spreads across my face when he kisses the rain droplets off my nose and forehead. "Estas loca." His warm breath whispers against my cold skin before pulling me tightly against his body and walking us back to the Jeep. It dawns on me that just like our relationship, this hike started off as a half-assed plan. But also like our relationship, I'm left laughing, genuinely happy, and feeling free.

When we make it back to the car, he opens my door. "As much as I would love to stand out in the freezing rain and have a good laugh at my muddy ass—" His lips find mine again and I close my eyes, soaking in their warmth. "I would rather not die of hypothermia."

I look at him with the biggest smile I can muster and make a mental note to look up the dangers of a smile etching itself into your face permanently.

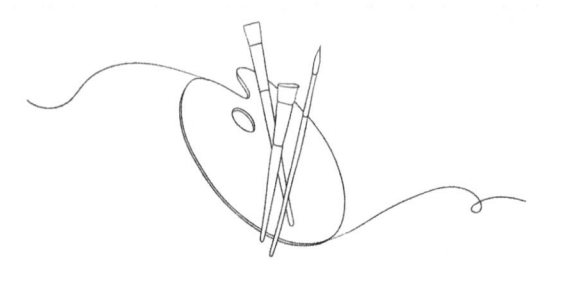

Camila

CANDLE LIGHTS FLICKER ALL AROUND, CASTING SHADOWS ON the walls against the room.

Although there is a small dining room, we've ordered takeout and when I suggested we eat outside on the deck, you would have thought I suggested we wear wet socks with the way Miles looked at me. Apparently, it's too cold outside, so we compromised by putting all the couch pillows and blankets on the floor near the sliding glass doors and we're *camping* indoors.

He sits across from me on the floor, leaning against the couch behind him. He looks so different on this trip. At home, he exudes power and dominance; always in his suits or half-naked when he's done boxing. But here, he's relaxed. His outfits are casual—jeans and sweaters. I'm not an idiot, I've felt his clothes. His T-shirts feel like they're made of some kind of witchcraft. It wouldn't surprise me if his sweater cost my share of mine and Taylor's monthly rent, but the illusion of casual is still there. And it looks so good on him. My heart still beats erratically every time he looks at me.

"Hand me that pen behind you, please." I twist, looking

behind me. There's a notepad and pen sitting on the side table, I grab it and slide it across the coffee table to him. "Thank you."

I suspiciously watch him pull out an envelope from his pocket. He opens it, sits a piece of paper on the table, and covers it with his hand when he begins writing.

"Want me to whoop your ass at Snowman?" I tease him.

"No." He doesn't look up from the paper. "But I am curious now, what word would you use to *whoop my ass*?" He leans across the table now, his expression daring.

He thinks getting close to me will throw me off my guard, and he might be right, but I pop up on my knees, lean into him, and kiss his full lips before whispering against his mouth, "Chiaroscurist."

He smiles against my lips before pulling back. "Okay. You might have whooped my ass with that one."

I sit back down laughing, pulling my legs under me as he slides the paper across the table. His perfect penmanship flows across the top, "Camila's Gallery Name Ideas." with a big line under it.

My eyes burn. "What is this?" I ask.

"You can't keep calling it *The Studio*. If you want to get a sign made for the front, and business cards you need to come up with a name, so I've been brainstorming anytime an idea strikes me but I've learned I suck at it so let's do it now, together."

My chest tightens as I read the list.

1. Expressions
2. La Vida Art
3. ~~The Art Vault~~
4. Cada Momento

"You've been working on this for me?" He scratches the back of his neck. "Why did you cross out The Art Vault?"

"If somebody mumbles it or has a thick accent of any kind it could sound like The Aardvark."

A shaky laugh escapes me and a single tear falls down my cheek. My finger runs over the letters. "Cada Momento."

"I wrote that one after you asked me to stay with you. I was overwhelmed with pride in that moment and I wanted to remember it. But then I realized I want to remember every moment with you. It doesn't really have an art theme though, so…" I don't let him finish his sentence before I fling myself across the table into his arms, pressing him further into the couch. His arms wrap around me and I kiss him for all the things I can't find the words to say. I kiss him for his unwavering patience and understanding. I kiss him for his selfless support. And I kiss him because I'm in love with him.

"Thank you." I kiss him once more. "Yo también quiero recordar cada momento contigo."

MILES

My balls are frozen.

The house has a wrap-around porch in the back, which was pitched as some incredible selling feature. They forgot to mention you wouldn't actually want to sit out here because it's fucking freezing. Camila is covered head to toe in layers, her leggings underneath a pair of my sweatpants, and a long sleeve T-shirt under one of my hoodies. And fuck if I don't love seeing her in my clothes. She rests between my legs, her head on my chest, my arms wrapped tightly around her, as we lay out on a wooden daybed with a paper-thin cushion on top. I've brought the comforter from the guest bedroom out and wrapped us up in it because Camila wanted to sit out here and *watch the trees*. I'm still not sure what that means but despite the freezing cold, she seems happy so here I am, watching the trees.

"I could get used to this," she says into the darkness. "I feel so refreshed like I really needed this and didn't even know it."

I kiss the top of her head. "We could come back every weekend if you want."

She wiggles her body further into me and I can hear the smile on her face when she says, "I love it when you say things like that."

"I'll buy the whole damn house if you want it, Camila." And I mean it. She must know that I'm serious because she sits up, turning to look at me.

"I just meant, I like when you talk about the future. Our future." She pauses. "I know our relationship started as anything but normal, and when we decided to give this a go we weren't sure what it would look like or what it meant, but when you talk about our future, I'm not afraid of it. I like it. I want everything with you, Miles. I—"

My heart hammers at her words. She's saying everything I've been feeling, and I don't want to hold it in anymore. I can't. I sit up and pull her into a fiery kiss. I kiss her like a man starved. With every piece of my body and soul responding to her. I want her to know and to feel everything I'm feeling for her. Breaking the kiss but not pulling away, my forehead resting on hers, I whisper against her lips, "I love you, Camila." Her heart beats against my hand where it rests on her chest. "I know this is wild, and if you're not there yet, that's okay, but I couldn't go another minute without telling you."

Her lips fall back on mine in a softer kiss, it's slow and intimate. The chill of her fingers locking together behind my neck sends a shiver down my spine. "You're right, it is wild." Her lips brush across mine. "Miles." I can't tell whose heartbeat is whose anymore. "I love you, too."

I force out a breath that was lodged so tightly in my chest it was a miracle I hadn't passed out yet. "Say it again."

She smiles against my lips. "I love you, Miles Cameron."

I never planned on getting married. But at this moment, with Camila in my arms, I couldn't imagine a life not being married to her.

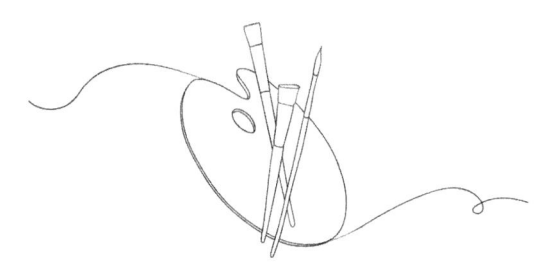

Camila

Miles stands at the kitchen counter wearing only a pair of gray sweatpants. I'm briefly distracted by the V below his waist. But I quickly notice the scowl—that very rarely makes an appearance anymore—etched deeply on his face.

"You really shouldn't be allowed to look so sexy with such a grumpy face," I say.

"Too bad there's nothing *sexy* about this cheap coffee maker," he grumbles.

I know he takes his coffee seriously, so I pull my lips in between my teeth in an attempt to hide my smile but I can't help the mocking tone that escapes me, "Oh no. Not the cheap coffee maker."

I slide up to the counter beside him. His corded arms find the counter on either side of me and I'm wrapped up in his scent. He looks me up and down and his stare sets my body on fire, I'm desperate for his lips on mine. His mouth is now half an inch away from mine and I'm about to close the final gap between us when he grazes past me and nips my ear. The sting both shocks me and excites me until he whispers, "Get dressed."

What? Putting more clothes on is not where I saw this going. My brows furrow together,

"Where are we going?" I ask, disappointed.

"There's a diner about five miles down the road. We'll stop on our way to the airport. It's

got to be better than this instant stuff."

"You got me excited just to tell me to get dressed so we could get coffee?" I blanch.

The short hairs of his beard scratch my skin as he nuzzles his face in my neck. "Are you excited, Camila?" Warm fingers graze my skin when his hand slides under the sweatshirt that drapes loosely around my body. I hold his stare when the pads of his fingers find my bare pussy. I suck up the groan that escapes him. "Fuck it. We'll get coffee on the plane." His arms wrap around my waist, scooping me up.

"Miles," I smile against him but he ignores me and continues to carry me back down the hall to the bedroom.

"Miles," I laugh. "We're going to be late."

"Well since we're their only passengers," his lips find their mark on my neck, "they'll wait."

The fireplace in the corner of the room is still crackling when he sets me down on the bed. The sheets are cool under my bare legs, but the way his eyes penetrate mine causes my skin to heat.

His fingers slide along the waistband of his sweatpants before pulling them down. He towers over me while gripping himself through his boxers. "Lay back, Camila."

His deep voice could command me to do anything. I lower myself to the mattress as his rough hands clasp behind my calves and he settles himself on his knees. The warm feeling of his tongue circles the inside of my knee. "I love how wet you get for me." My back arches off the mattress at the sting of his teeth that nip my inner thigh. "I love how this pussy was made for me." His head drops between my legs and I scream his name as his tongue licks one long sweep up my center. He stops right before he reaches my swollen and most sensitive spot. I push my hips down begging for him to keep going. I feel his lips pull up into a teasing grin against me. And if it were possible to die from aching, I swear, this would be my last breath.

"Miles, please," I cry out. The muscles in my legs flex and I squeeze around him as I try to grind against his mouth. His large forearm spreads across my stomach pinning me to the bed. My breath gets caught in my throat when two thick fingers slide across my entrance, parting my lips and his wide flat tongue rolls over me. My eyes squeeze shut, unable to handle the pressure building inside me. He pulls my clit into his mouth, gently sucking while his fingers dip inside me. My right hand threatens to rip the sheets beneath me while my other holds the back of his head, riding his face as I keep him pressed tightly to me. "Yes. I'm so close," I breathe. His fingers curl to find that spot that has me seeing a burst of light and that's all it takes to send me over the edge.

My heart beats erratically against my rib cage but my body is spent, lying there limp. I press a hand to my damp forehead as he gently sits my legs back down on the bed and stands between them. As I lay there trying to catch my breath I watch him slowly pull down his briefs and the full length of him springs out. I will never get over the sight of him. His thick head is already dripping with precum.

I can't believe there was once a time when sex with a guy was one-minute missionary and when he finished I would force a smile and pretend to be tired. There is no pretending with Miles. Everything about him turns me on. My mouth goes dry as I watch him give himself soft strokes.

"What are you thinking?"

I smile and shake my head. "That if you don't put it in, I'm going to do it for you."

His eyes narrow as he hooks my legs around his waist with one hand and grabs my neck with the other. My pulse beats so hard I can feel it knocking against his palm as he holds me down and lowers his mouth to my ear. "Smart ass."

He stands abruptly before taking his cock in his hand and smacking the weight of it down on me. My legs tremble around him and not even my teeth clamped down my lip can stop the cry that comes out of me. He guides his tip right past my entrance, stretching me, before pulling back out. "What are you doing?" I yell.

"I just like the look on your face when you're begging for my cock."

My eyes turn to tiny slits and my mouth parts in disbelief. He runs his tip up and down my slit and I'm so sensitive from that first orgasm I couldn't pretend to hold out even if I wanted to. "Fuck. Okay, I want it, I want you. You know I do." My eyes snap up to him. "Now like I said, either fuck me or I'll do it myself."

My back arches off the bed when he slams into me in one deep thrust, filling me completely, while a deep rumble forms in the back of his throat. His hands grip my hips lifting me at an angle that has him able to get deeper than he ever has before. With every thrust, he brushes my unbearably sensitive clit while also reaching a new spot inside me.

"Oh God—" I whimper.

"I wonder if he ever gets tired of you calling out to him when you're with me," he grunts as his hold on me tightens and he lifts me higher. His thrusts turn punishing.

The ache in my core is so intense, I can't take it anymore.

Every thrust deeper than the last, the obscene sounds of wet flesh smacking fill the air. "Miles."

His fingers find my overly sensitive spot and he rubs it with such precision. "Come for me." He pinches my clit and that's all it takes.

I cry out as my entire body is set on fire and my orgasm crashes into me over and over again in multiple waves, seeming to go on forever. Only when his lips come crashing down on mine do I feel him twitch inside me as he finds his own release.

We lay in bed, under the covers for what feels like hours. He presses his lips to my neck and down my bare shoulders not giving a second thought to the time and when we were supposed to leave. Our fingers intertwine and dance through each other, and I know in this moment that I will always want this with him. When I look up into his steady eyes, I marvel at this man I get to love and get to call mine.

We missed our flight.

It was impossible to pull ourselves from the bedroom after all the confessions we shared. As a result, we were late to leave and weather hold-ups kept us sitting on a ground plane for most of the afternoon. Miles answered a few work emails while I tried to sort through some of my thoughts about what my trip home will look like.

Now I'm trying not to wrinkle Miles's suit as my hands roam his broad chest. His mouth breaks away from mine, traveling down my neck. "You have to go," I finally breathe.

"Are you sure you don't want me to come with you?" he asks, between kisses.

The truth is I don't want to leave either. The idea of facing my parents is enough to kill any mood, but when Miles does meet my parents I want it to be under better circumstances. I'm only going for two days, and it feels like a short enough trip that if all hell breaks loose, I won't be stuck there for very long.

"I'll be back before you even have time to miss me," I say.

"I miss you already and you haven't even left yet."

Leaving him feels extra difficult after the weekend we had together. But getting this one last issue settled will be the final weight lifted from my shoulders.

I hold his face in my hands, rubbing at his scruff with my thumbs, letting it tickle beneath them. "I love you," I say before kissing him.

"I'll never get tired of hearing that." His head dips down as he rubs his nose against mine. "I'll be back soon to take you to the airport."

"Don't worry about it, Wills is driving me," I plead with him.

"Not a fucking chance am I not going with you. I would have taken the whole morning off but I have to run this meeting. I've given everyone a hard two-hour stop time. So long as Jonas doesn't play class clown, I should be back in about three."

He kisses me once more before stepping into the elevator.

SINCE OUR FLIGHT WAS DELAYED AND WE WERE TOO exhausted to unpack, I'm having to both unpack my Oregon winter clothes and pack my Miami summer clothes. My phone is charging on the nightstand when it lights up with a FaceTime call from Taylor.

"How long do you think a Cubano will stay good for?" she asks before I can even say hello. "Like if you get one right before you get on the plane, and I meet you at the airport? How long is that?"

"Too long," I respond.

She flops down on my old bed. "I've been dreaming about that sweet bread and perfectly seasoned pork. I'm drooling just thinking about it," she groans.

"Taylor, you're literally the best cook I know. You could totally make them." She's shaking her head before I've even finished my sentence.

"It's not the same," we say in unison.

"So, how are you feeling?"

I watch her get off the bed and take the three steps it takes to get from the bedroom to the kitchen. "Surprisingly I'm okay I think. Obviously a little nervous because…well, I am who I am," I say with a shrug. "But I'm confident in my decisions now."

Taylor's phone is propped on something on the small kitchen island, as she dips her grapes in a jar of peanut butter. She looks at me and says, "I'm so proud of you, Mila."

"Honestly, I'm proud of myself too," I say, and I mean it.

I hear the elevator ding down the hall. "Hey, I gotta get going, I need to finish packing and I think I just heard Miles, he must have forgotten something."

"Okay I love you, text me when you land."

"Love you too, I will." I blow her a kiss and she sticks her tongue out and rolls her eyes in the back of her head doing an over-the-top make-out impression. I shake my head, laughing as I hang up.

. . .

"Oh, Camila! Nice to see you, I thought you were on your way to Miami," Talan says when I bounce into the kitchen.

"I am, I leave in a few hours."

"I'm actually heading today too, it will be my first vacation in three years." He beams his signature sweet smile.

"I heard that. Yeah, Miles mentioned he was going to be lost without you this week."

He blushes and nods his head. "I doubt those were his words, but thank you."

I smile at him. "Did he make you come over here to pick something up on your first day of vacation?" I ask.

"Oh, I just wanted to drop off your files. He was very adamant that I get them to you *today*. But I've had this vacation planned for months so I completely forgot, and then when he said you were heading out, I rushed over as soon as I remembered this morning."

I'm assuming they're papers having to do with the gallery. "Well I really appreciate it, thank you, Talan," I say.

He leaves the folder on the table and heads to the elevator, pressing the button, he says, "Enjoy your trip."

"You as well," I shout as the elevator doors close.

I'm about to go back and finish packing but I move to look at the folder first. When I open the manilla envelope my heart stops at an alarming rate.

Record of Dissolution of Marriage, Annulment, or Registered Domestic Partnership hits me in big bold letters. I set the folder on the table and use my hands to brace myself as the room spins around me.

I take a handful of deep breaths, trying to steady myself. Everything is filled out.

Everything from Partner A and B's information to the

marriage license number. And that perfect signature at the bottom,

Miles S Cameron.

My sweaty palms battle with the chill that runs through my body. Why would he just fill these out now after we've started a relationship? After this weekend? And why would he do it without telling me? All too quickly, I'm hit with another realization. I'll be the first to admit I was a little out of it the day Miles told me we couldn't file these papers for sixty days. He told me nothing could be done for eight weeks and I believed him. But if he lied, I'm not sure which option is worse.

Miles

"Should I park, or wait out front?" Wills asks from the front.

"I'm just going to run up and help her with her bags, we'll be right down," I say.

Wills pulls up to the front of my building and I jump out, speed walking through the lobby to the elevator. My heart tells my feet to move so I can get to her quickly, the quicker I get to her, the more time I'll have with her. My head tells me to slow down, the sooner I get to her the sooner she'll be leaving.

Five large suitcases greet me outside the elevator doors. She definitely isn't traveling light. I panic for a moment that maybe she's extended her flight home and will be gone for longer than the two days she had originally planned. Her shoes squeak across the floor as she rounds the stairs into the kitchen.

"Hey, you've got quite the luggage goi—" I stop when I notice the redness around her eyes. But it's not sadness in her eyes, her expression is pure pain. I move towards her and she backs up, causing my heart to lodge itself in my throat. "What's going on?" I ask.

"Our annulment papers were delivered today," she says.

My heart is no longer stuck, it's fallen straight down to my gut. "Camila, let's sit and talk about this real quick."

She holds up her hand to stop me from coming any closer. "When did you sign them?"

"Camila, please. I can explain if we could just sit for a—"

"When did you sign them, Miles?"

"I signed them the day we got back from Vegas. I had Talan order them, he was able to expedite it and I filled everything out that day. Had we gotten them today, I would have never signed them. Fuck, Camila, I wouldn't have even ordered them." The words tumble out of my mouth without a second thought.

"So the papers that you said we couldn't file for eight weeks…you've had." And for the first time in my career, I've fucked up. I spoke before thinking and I fucked myself. "You've not only had them, you've had them filled out, ready to go just waiting for my signature." I stand staring at her, processing what I've done in my head. I instinctively go back to my old ways of saying absolutely nothing.

"You lied to me. You made me think this was all for my benefit when really you could have filed these the next day..." she trails off looking right past me, I can see her putting everything together and it feels as if I've swallowed a rock.

The words finally find me. "I didn't lie," I say hesitantly.

"Don't." Her lips press firmly together and she shakes her head. "Don't use your lawyer bullshit on me."

I stay where I am because I don't want her to bolt, but I'm dying to clear the distance between us, scoop her up, and beg her to forgive me. I need her to understand that I didn't do this to be malicious. That my feelings have changed.

"You manipulated me!" The strangled sob that comes out of her cuts my heart. "You spent weeks making me believe that you did everything for *my* benefit. For what? For your name on that stupid fucking door? This was always about *you!*" Her voice cracks as she yells through her tears and the pressure in my chest becomes unbearable.

"Camila, please just listen to me for a minute." I don't recognize my own voice.

"I should have known. I mean, you said it yourself that day, I think your exact words were *'I might skirt the truth about some things.'*" Tears fall to the floor as she shakes her head.

My feet move to step toward her, and by some miracle she lets me. Her worn-in sweater catches on my calloused hands as I gently hold her shoulders.

Her arms are crossed across her front as if trying to protect herself from me which causes a burning sensation in my chest. To think that only yesterday she felt safe enough to let me in. To tell me she loved me and now she's here in front of me, shoulders hunched and hiding herself from me. She won't look at me and I don't blame her. Her voice is nothing more than a raspy whisper as she tries to hold back her tears. "Was any of it real?"

"Camila, yes. That part is true, I could have filed those papers that same day. Samantha found out and it was selfish, but it was in my best interest that I convinced you to play along. But I didn't know you, and I didn't think I could just come out and ask this of you, so yes, I made you believe it was for your benefit, and for that, I *am* sorry. But I'm not sure I can even bring myself to regret it because had I filed those papers, none of this would have happened. But I swear to you, everything after that day at the pier has all been real.

Everything I've said to you, everything we've shared has been real. I love you, Camila. None of that has changed."

She finally looks up at me, her eyes completely broken and I hate myself for putting her through this.

She bites her lip and nods her head but I don't know what that means. "Tell me something," she says, wiping the tears from her face.

"Anything."

"How can I trust you, again?" I can tell her until I'm blue in the face that I didn't mean to hurt her, but how can I show her, how can I prove this to her? Before I have a chance to respond she steps out of my hands and grabs her bag from the table bringing it up to her shoulder. "I believe you, Miles. I believe that you love me. But that almost makes it worse. Knowing that you love me and you're still able to lie to me." She grabs one of her suitcases and heads towards the elevator. "I have to go, Taylor's downstairs waiting for me."

"Camila—" I reach for her.

"I just need some time, Miles."

Her feet step into the elevator and I watch the doors close on this once-in-a-lifetime woman. I stand staring at the doors for another twenty minutes before I realize she isn't coming back up. I sink into the bench at the dining room table, the table we spend every night at, and my chest hollows out as reality sinks in.

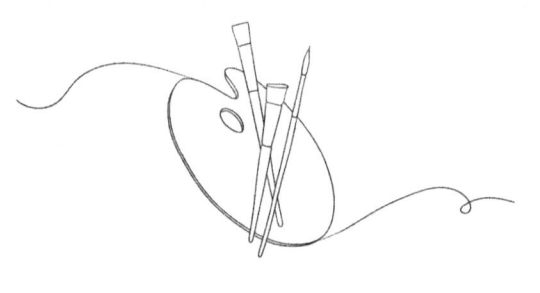

Camila

"Are you traveling or coming home?" The older lady next to me leans over smiling.

Annoyed, I pull my headphones out and give a polite smile. "Uh, both, kind of. Heading home to see my family, but I don't live in Miami anymore."

"Awe, that's so nice. I have three children and nine grandchildren all spread out. They think it's easier for me to travel to them since there's just one of me, and so many of them." She waves a hand of bright red nails around.

I feel like I'm dying inside. My heart is cracked. My anxiety knocked into me like a freight train. I feel like I could close my eyes and sleep for thirty-six hours straight. And it's in these circumstances that I go right back to my people-pleasing ways. So, instead of telling this woman, *'I'm glad you get to see your family but I'm really tired, I'm going to take a nap now.'* I smile and say, "How nice that you get to see them. Are you heading to see them now, or heading home?"

"Oh, I'm a Miami girl for life. I moved here when I was just a girl, and I've been all over the world since, but I'll always come home to Miami," she says proudly. "Where did you move off to?"

"I live in San Francisco now," I reply.

"Ahh! The Golden Gate City!" She beams. "Although not to be rude, I'm one of those people that calls it Fog City," she says with a guilty face.

I fake a small laugh and nod along, "Yeah it can get pretty foggy, I understand."

"So what do you do out there?" she asks. And I have to bite the inside of my cheek and force myself to breathe so I don't cry all over her. *What do I do out there?* I moved in with a man I accidentally married, and then accidentally fell in love with. A man who bought me a studio space so I could live out my dream of owning my own art gallery—that I've spent every waking moment pouring my heart and soul into—and now I've just found out that he used me for his own benefit.

I have no fucking clue what I'm doing.

"I eat a lot of sourdough." Thankfully she laughs and allows the conversation to move on.

I WILL NEVER BOOK A NONSTOP FIVE-AND-A-HALF-HOUR flight again for fear of getting stuck sitting next to someone who wants to talk.

Thankfully I only packed a carry on so as soon as I got off the plane I was practically racing out of the airport. I did pack the rest of my things from Miles's apartment, but I loaded them into Taylor's car and she brought them home for me after she dropped me off.

As soon as I get outside I'm met with that Miami humidity. My face couldn't be more grateful as it instantly absorbs the moisture. I quickly spot my dad's Range Rover in the sea of cars at the arrival terminal and weave my way through them. My mom jumps out of the front seat smiling ear to ear. "Mija!" she beams. "Tu eres tan hermosa!" She pulls me into a warm familiar hug in the middle of the street. "Te extraño."

"I missed you too, Mom. But can we get out of traffic please?" I say, hugging her back.

"Elena, cariño, please get in the car," my dad reasons and she lets me go, grabbing my bag and putting it in the back.

Once I'm settled in the back seat, my dad takes off and my mom is turned around in the front, facing me. "So how was your flight?" she asks.

"It was…long," I admit. "I sat next to a very…chatty woman."

My mom makes the *eekk* face. "You seem tired." Her eyebrows bunch together in concern.

Since it's only been five minutes and I don't feel like divulging every dirty detail just yet, I settle on a safe response. "I didn't get a lot of sleep last night, and with my new best friend on the plane, I didn't get a nap either."

My mom reaches back putting her hand on my knee and gives it a little shake. "We'll be home soon, I just made fresh tortillas, so you can eat and then rest up." Her smile has not let up since I arrived.

"Sounds perfect," I say.

"I'm so glad you're home, mija. We've really missed you," she says, turning back around in her seat.

"Me too."

ART OF CONVENIENCE

I WAKE UP IN MY CHILDHOOD BEDROOM, AND THE MOONLIGHT is brighter than a spotlight casting a dark shadow around the room. The only sound is a dull hum coming from the air conditioning unit. I sit up looking around the room. Not much, if anything, has changed. The matching island tropical wicker bedroom set has held up after all these years. The same pictures still hang in the frames of the gallery wall I made above my desk when I was in high school. The rust-covered duvet with the sandy toupe sheets complements the room in warm earth tones. And I'm reminded of all the late nights Taylor and I spent up in this room, making plans and dreaming till the sun rose.

I pick up my phone, to check the time and find it's 1 a.m. I guess my post-lunch nap turned into a post-lunch sleep. I don't dwell on it, it's 10 p.m. in California, and I'm about to text Taylor when I remember my Do Not Disturb is on. When I open my messages, I'm hit with three texts from Miles and even though I can't get a grip on my own feelings and thoughts, I'm certain the one persistent feeling I have is that I miss him. I don't hesitate to open the message, just to read his words to feel close to him again.

> MILES
>
> I know you asked for space, but I just wanted to know that you made it okay.
>
> I talked to Taylor, she said you arrived safely. I know you said you needed time, and I'm trying to respect that. But I didn't get to say it before you left and I need you to know I'm so proud of you. I know you're nervous to talk to your parents, but you deserve everything good in this world and you deserve everything you want.
>
> I miss you.

I use the inside of my sweatshirt sleeve to wipe away the tears sneaking down my cheek. I can feel the familiar tightness begin to wage a war inside my chest now. I pick up the phone and call Taylor, who answers on the first ring.

"Mila, my little angel baby, how's home?"

"It's...dark," I say looking around.

"Literally or..." she trails off.

I go to speak but I can't stop the cry that falls from my mouth. I pull the phone away and bury my eyes into the neck of my sweater.

"Camila," her understanding voice is so soft as she tries to help me but I just cry harder.

Finally, I put the phone on speaker in front of me, sitting cross-legged with my head in my hands and my elbows on my knees.

"I don't know what to do," I sob.

"I wish I was there to hold you," she sighs. She knows better than to tell me *it's okay* or *you'll be okay*. I know people mean well when they say things like that but, if one more person tried to tell me "You're okay" when I'm clearly not, respectfully, get fucked.

"I wish you were here, too."

We sit in silence for a while because I can't bring myself to ask about Miles calling her.

Miles

I'VE BEEN AN ASSHOLE TO ANYONE WHO COMES WITHIN twenty feet of me. I'm aware it's unfair, but I can't bring myself to care. I almost want to tell Jonas to just turn around and run right back out of my office to spare him from the uncontrollable rage boiling inside me. "You good, bro?"

His frat boy energy and lack of anything ever affecting him just pisses me off today. I ignore him and continue trying to get some work done.

"You wanna dip and go get some bagels?"

I'm going to fucking lose it. I'm trying to think before I speak so I don't say something I'll regret later. I need to just tell him now isn't the time.

"Or we could leave early and grab drinks?"

"Jonas," I warn.

"We could hit Villetta and get our money's worth this month," he continues.

"Jonas," I bark louder.

"Okay screw it, let's just—"

"For fucks sake, shut up!" I shout.

He stares at me but his eyes aren't hurt or upset. They take on the one emotion I can't stand. Pity.

"Look, I've never had to cheer you up," he takes a tentative step towards my desk, "you've always been a grumpy asshole and I've been cool with it. But now you're a depressed asshole, and I'm just trying to help. I'll let you sulk in peace though if that's what you want. When you're ready, you know where to find me." His knuckles knock against my desk before he turns for the door. He pauses briefly with his hand on the handle, "By the way, I talked to Taylor. She said she thinks your girl misses you too."

My head almost snaps off my neck as I lift it so fast, but he's already walking down the hall.

I need to get the fuck out of here.

This is a terrible idea.

The sounds of dishes being thrown into buckets, conversations blending together, and a bell going off every two minutes to let the waiters on roller skates know that more food is up and ready at the counter normally wouldn't bother me, but I'm clearly on edge today.

After my morning blow-up with Jonas, I dropped whatever papers I could off with one of our junior associates. The rest can wait. When I left I was overwhelmed with how lost I felt. I couldn't go home. The idea of stepping out of the elevator to an empty apartment physically makes my stomach roll. It's a neon sign reminding me that Camila left. *She left.* I should have tried harder to keep her from leaving, to talk to me. But we've always had that understanding with each other. The ability to be patient and understand that the other will speak when they're ready. But then she said she needed time. I'm trying to respect that, but I'm losing my mind not talking to her now. I can almost see her little smirk now, how amusing she would find it that the man she had to work so hard to have a few conversations with would do absolutely anything to talk to her now.

I arrived at the diner down the street from my office ten minutes ago and I feel like I'm going to explode out of my skin. I probably should have called Ray and asked him to meet me for a session, but instead, I called the man coming through the door right now.

"I'm glad you called, son." Paul Cameron slides into the booth across from me. He's not as big as I remember. I mean he's tall, 6'4" maybe and he's still in great shape for a retired baseball player. But when I was a kid he seemed like a giant, and in my eyes he was bigger than any superhero. Now if I didn't know him, I wouldn't look twice at him walking down the street.

"It's been a while," is my only response.

He nods and a waitress comes by to take his order. "Just a black coffee, please. Thank you."

I don't feel the anger I expected to feel when seeing him. I don't feel longing for a relationship with him either. I don't feel much of anything. How could I have spent years working towards goal after goal for the sole purpose of rubbing it in his face? To be able to say *'I'm the best and you have nothing to do with it. You get to watch me be great and have no claim over any of it.'* The irony is that everything I have, I've gotten by using him and that anger as my motivation.

"I know better than to tell you that you look well and try to make small talk with you, Miles. So even though I'm grateful that you called, why don't you tell me why you did?"

He's direct and to the point like me, but surprisingly his tone isn't cruel.

My fingers idly trace the rim of my coffee mug that I'm not drinking, but I keep my eyes on him. "I've worked really hard, and been fairly successful these last few years all out of anger and spite towards you." If he's hurt or surprised by what I'm saying he doesn't show it. His face gives nothing away. "But when I think about what I have in my life, none of it matters." The only thing that's ever mattered to me in the last ten years walked out of my arms two days ago. "I just wanted to say that I'm not carrying a baseball player-size chip on my shoulder anymore. I don't expect us to get together for family dinners or anything, I mean shit, if I were you and someone ignored me for close to two decades I'd tell them to go fuck themselves but, I guess just selfishly, I wanted to let you know, I'm done carrying this torch. If she could forgive you in the end, it's not my battle and I'm done letting this consume me."

He takes a sip of his coffee, scrunches his face in disgust, and slides it off to the side. Clasping his hands together in front of him he says, "I am sorry. I'll always be sorry for what I did back then, and even more sorry for how I handled it. I'm sorry I didn't try harder to fix our relationship. I'm the parent and that's on me."

"Why'd you do it?"

The way his arms move lets me know he's likely wiping his sweaty palms on his pants. "Unfortunately if you're looking for some big dramatic answer you won't get it." He blows out a breath before continuing. "I was an idiot. It's as simple as that. I was young, I had fame and success and I let it get to my head, and I fucked up."

That's it. My entire life. From my confused and hurt childhood to my detached and angry adulthood, it all boiled down to a simple *I fucked up*. It seems so trivial now. I want to be pissed at myself for letting something like this consume me for so long. But I recognize that pattern immediately. Beating myself up over it won't change anything. So I nod my understanding and watch as my father folds his hands in front of him on the table.

"And just so you know, you could have ignored me for another two decades and I would never tell you to go fuck yourself. Hell, if you want to start doing family dinners, I'm in."

"That might be a little much right now since I just started talking to you again." The corner of his mouth tugs up as he looks down at his hands. "But maybe in the future," I add.

He smiles as the waiter comes back asking if we'd like anything else, and we both shake our heads no.

When she leaves he leans forward and whispers, "The coffee here is terrible."

And since I'm not ready to be twins with the guy and share similarities, I choke down the rest of my coffee as if it's the best thing I've ever had.

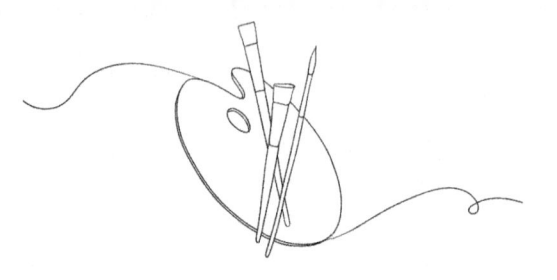

Camila

The incredible blend of spices, vegetables, broth, and wine fills my nose causing my stomach to rumble. Mom is making her paella soup with orzo instead of rice—a childhood favorite of mine. Since I'm flying back tomorrow, we decided to have a family dinner at home tonight. I didn't want to ruin my trip by bringing everything up the day I landed, but I let it sit too long and now the thought of ruining my last night with them is beyond dreadful.

The setting sun dances along the water painting a beautiful backdrop of purple and orange. The sunroom is quiet tonight, unlike our usual over-the-top loud dinner conversations. The sounds of silverware clanking against bowls fill the silence.

"Did I tell you I saw Mrs. Nova a few weeks ago?" my mom asks before she blows on a spoonful of her soup. "She was only in town for two days so I'm surprised I ran into her. She said she was going to try and make a trip out to visit you girls sometime this year."

Taylor's mom has been saying that every year since we

moved. I think I've seen her once, and Taylor's seen her maybe twice. I won't hold my breath waiting for her visit.

I've been blowing on the same spoonful of food for what feels like an eternity. I know I won't be able to eat, until I have this conversation—hell, depending on how hurt and upset they are, it's very likely I won't be able to eat after either. I set my spoon back down in my bowl and my mother's head not so subtly snaps to me while my dad looks at me only out of the corner of his eyes.

"Is something wrong with the soup, mija?" my mother asks, looking down at her own bowl.

"No. The food is good. I just—" I crack my fingers under the table and ask my nerves to call the fuck down. There's no clock in the sunroom but I can hear a faint ticking in my head. I take a breath to steady myself before continuing. "I just wanted to talk to you, and let you know some changes I've made recently."

My mom stops eating and puts her hands in her lap, her full attention on me now. My dad thankfully keeps eating rather than boring his eyes into mine, but he nods to let me know he's listening.

Inhala. Exhala. You deserve to be happy, not a bullshit happy for everyone else, but a genuine happiness for you. Miles's words bounce around my head and I feel stronger because of them.

I keep my eyes trained on my finger where it spins the invisible ring around. "Um, so I guess I should start by saying, I quit my investment banking job a while ago."

I close my eyes, take a deep breath, and when I look at my mom her eyebrows are up in her hairline. My heart rate continues to increase but I keep going, "I hated that job. My boss was horrible, and I dreaded going in every day. And not in a normal *I don't want to go to work* way. More in a *my stomach hurts, I feel nauseous, and I can't do anything on my time off because I'm so physically and mentally drained from my job* kind of way."

Now my dad puts his spoon down and turns his full attention on me.

"Mija, you've been there for over five years. Why would you stay there so long if it made you so miserable?" my mom asks, and her voice is just as shaky as mine.

"I know how proud you were when I got that job, and I didn't want to disappoint you." I feel so small. Like a cartoon mouse backing up into the tiny cut-out in the wall.

My parents both look at each other now, the weight of my father's fist drops to the table and my mom covers her dainty hand over his. I watch her thumb rub lightly at it as if she's trying to calm him down but comfort herself at the same time and my eyes burn as liquid rises. I'm reminded of all the times Miles's fingers brushed my leg or his hands rubbed my back. All the times he was there to comfort me and help me feel brave and I wish he were here now.

"I—" my mom shakes her head slightly, looking at me with the exact same furrowed brow she had when I told her I was going to school in California.

"I'm sorry." My whisper is pathetic as I look down to my lap and two large tears plop into my hands one after the other.

"Camila." My father's stern voice has both my mom and I looking at him. "I've never been disappointed with you a day in your life. Why would you think that?"

I swallow the rock in my throat. "I guess I've just always felt like you expected me to do things a certain way. I know you were upset about my decision to leave for school."

"Camila, I'm your mother. I know you down to your core. I wasn't disappointed, I was worried. You'd never made an impulsive decision like that in your life. For four years you talked about going to medical school here and then out of nowhere you were moving across the country for finance? None of it made any sense."

My fingers rub at the back of my jaw as I try to piece together some of my uncertainty. I had been wanting to move for over a year, I just never told them. It's not surprising that they would be concerned that I decided to leave the way I did.

"Not that it really matters now, all these years later, but it wasn't an impulsive decision. I guess, I was just too scared to tell you before." My mom's eyes are glassy as her lips twist to the side. "Mom," I reach across the table for her, and to my surprise, she squeezes my hand back, tightly. "Not a day goes by that I'm not so appreciative of everything you and Dad have done for me and Seb, and I never wanted what you've gone through to be for nothing. The thought of not making you proud tears me up." I'm surprising myself with the way the words are freely tumbling from my mouth.

"Camila, your mother and I worked hard so that you and your brother could have every opportunity to do what *you* want to do. And we do what we do because we love it. I can't think of a time when I've ever been upset or angry with you for doing something you wanted. So I'm really confused where this is coming from."

I've wondered for a while how much I've internalized my fear of going after the things I want. Putting a mask over them by saying *I can't disappoint my parents or I can't do something because it's not good enough for them.* It's easier to say I don't want to disappoint people than it is to say I'm scared that I'm not worthy of the good things I want. But the reality is, I have so many good things—the best things, in my eyes. The world's greatest friend, my dream art gallery, parents who love me, and a man who…

"Mija—"

I blink away my tears as my chest feels noticeably lighter. "Well, I have some more news." Both my parents straighten in their chairs, my mom inhaling and holding her breath. "I've acquired an art studio that I've been working on for a few weeks now and I'm going to open an art gallery in the city." There is no false bravado in my voice.

The breath my mom was holding comes out while the corner of her lips lift. My dad shifts in his seat, resting his arm on the back of his chair.

"I'm going to assume this is again, something you've wanted for a while and just never told us," my mom says.

"No." I firmly shake my head. "This has been my biggest dream for as long as I can remember."

"Then I have no concerns. I have no doubt that you'll be able to make anything you want work out." Her eyes are soft but her hold on my hand is strong. It's going to take more than a dinner over paella to fix all those worries of doubt but I *am* worthy of good things. I give my mom's hand a tight squeeze and my father offers me a little wink.

"Time for buñuelos?" he asks.

I NEVER THOUGHT I WOULD BECOME A COFFEE SNOB BUT after living with (and making fun of) Miles for nearly two months, I get it now. The coffee steams out of my Selena mug that Sebastian bought me one year for Christmas, but it's bitter. The warmth of the wood seeps into my skin as I sway back and forth on the porch swing, letting my skin soak in the last of the Miami humidity before I have to pack up and head back to the airport.

The screen door creaks open behind me and I twist my

neck to see my mom coming out with her coffee in hand. She sits down beside me on the swing with a smile. I can't help but notice my mom only ever offers real genuine smiles. Never forced.

"I was expecting you to wake up this morning light as a feather," she says, giving me a nudge.

"What do you mean?" I ask, confused.

"I mean, I could tell you were holding something in when you got here and I thought you let it all out at dinner last night," she gives my knee a reassuring pat, "but you're still carrying something, mija. Something is still bothering you."

I look down into my mug unable to meet her eyes. "I guess I have something else on my mind," I confess and she waits for me to continue. "I've been…seeing someone. And it was serious." I take a sip of my coffee to help me swallow the lump in my throat. "But something happened right before I left and in hindsight, I don't actually think it's that big of a deal, but I'm also not sure how to move forward now."

"Did he hurt you?" she asks calmly.

"No," I state. "Not physically. My feelings, my—my heart hurt, yes. But I also know he didn't do anything to be malicious."

"Do you love him?"

"Yes." And that hasn't changed.

"Does he support you? Believe in you?"

Her question catches me a little off guard. But even now, after everything, the one thing I'm still certain of is his belief in me. Not only does he support me, but he believed in me when I didn't believe in myself. "Yes."

"Well, I don't need to know all the details, but it sounds like whatever it is can be worked out."

I vow right here and now to come home more often. I don't want to dwell on the fact that if I had come home sooner, maybe I would have left my job long ago. Maybe it wouldn't have taken me so long to learn most of my issues have been self-inflicted. But if things had worked out any different I likely would have never met Miles. And the world threatens to fall out from under me at that thought. So I won't think about the past, I just make a mental note to call my mom more.

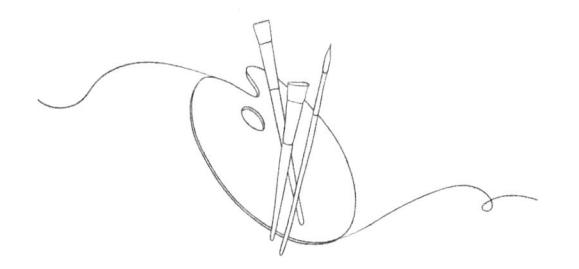

Camila

"This. Is. Insane!" Taylor's voice booms across the luxurious hotel room.

And she's not wrong, the room is absolutely incredible. The large windows overlook the bay. The bathroom is floor-to-ceiling marble with two fluffy robes hanging behind the door and the king-size bed looks like a cloud.

As magnificent as the overpriced hotel room is, it only makes me long for another more extraordinary home. I miss the peaceful earthy textures of Miles's home, I miss being curled up in my little spot on the couch, and I miss the beautiful palm frond paintings. I could list all the things I miss about his home, but what it comes down to is I miss him.

I didn't know where I was going to go when I got back since I still haven't talked to Miles, so going back to his house wasn't an option. I didn't want to go back to my old apartment either, so on my way to the airport this morning, I booked a hotel for two nights.

"Are the cucumbers necessary? They keep sliding off my face," I complain.

"You need them. If your eyes puff up anymore you won't be able to see."

I pick one of the cucumbers off my face and throw it at Taylor. "The cold shower I took since you used up all the hot water when you boiled yourself in there for twenty minutes, was enough, I think."

She sits up on her side of the bed, her face mask dry and cracking on her face. "This is the fanciest place we've been in since we moved out. I had to take advantage," she says.

I pull the other sliced vegetable off and set it on the nightstand as I sit up.

"So, you've talked to him?" I finally ask.

She purses her lips together and nods, "Only twice." She shrugs. "He called me the night you left to ask if I had heard from you, to make sure you got home safely. Jonas texted me *'Sorry'* with the cringe face emoji so I'm assuming Miles probably wasn't very pleasant when he was harassing my number out of him."

"I should have just texted him and told him I made it," I mumble.

"You told him you needed space, he should have expected it," she says casually.

"And the other time?" I ask while fidgeting with the belt of my robe.

She's quiet for a minute like she's debating what she wants to tell me before she finally speaks. "Last night. He wanted to make sure you were still coming home today. He basically just kept saying he fucked up and then he asked me if I thought you would forgive him."

"And what did you say?"

"Do you want the truth or a lie?"

I always want to know the truth obviously, but with

Taylor and the things that come out of her mouth, a lie is probably a better option. "Mostly truth."

She smiles. "The truth is I told him that I don't know but I hope that you do. I told him he went about some things the wrong way, but some people would argue accidentally getting married wasn't necessarily the right move either, but I wouldn't be one of those people."

I stop twirling the belt. "Why?"

She exhales a heavy breath through her nose. "Camila, you've come alive these past few months. And I'm not saying he's the only reason, leaving your job was all you. But I do think he had something to do with your newfound belief in yourself. You've always had people in your corner who love and support you, and you're capable of anything, but it feels like maybe you're starting to see that now too and I can't ignore the fact that started shortly after you moved in with him."

I'm flooded with emotions now and I don't know which feelings to address first. I'm gutted that I wasted so much time. Proud of my personal growth. Unbelievably grateful for my best friend who has always been by my side. And there's another feeling of something I can't place when I think of Miles.

"You miss him." It's not a question.

"Of course I miss him."

"Can you forgive him?" she asks.

And the truth is, I don't think I need to, I was hurt and upset, but I also understand. I know he wouldn't do anything to purposefully hurt me. And nothing has changed in regards to how I feel about him, I still love him and I do believe everything between us was real.

"I keep thinking about a scenario where he meets me at that pier and has me sign those papers, gives me a handshake, and is on his way, and that's the end of the story." Taylor looks at me with eager eyes. "And if that was the end of the story, I would have never known this kind of love existed for me."

There's a knock on the door. "Room service," a woman yells.

Taylor hops off the bed. "Don't forget the orgasms, you wouldn't have known about those either." She points at me and I roll my eyes as she opens the door.

She turns around carrying a tray that's easily three feet wide and filled with boxes of food. "You are so insightful," I deadpan.

She sets the tray down on the bed. "Insight this dick. Up top!" She throws her hand up for me to high-five her.

"That makes absolutely zero sense," I say with a small laugh.

She just shrugs and I high-five her anyway before she falls beside me on the bed.

After we ate our weight in french fries, chicken strips, pizza, and Twizzlers, we watched all our favorite early 2000's movies—well, three before we both fell asleep. The clock by the bed flashes 3:42 a.m. but that doesn't stop me from grabbing my phone as I head to the bathroom.

ME

Can you meet me at the pier later today?

I set my phone on the counter while I go to the bathroom, and plan to set an alarm so I can see when he texts me back in the morning but immediately my phone vibrates. I wash my hands and pick it up before heading back to bed.

> MILES
>
> Any time.

What is he doing awake? I hope I didn't wake him. I can't help but smile at the relief I already feel in my chest.

> ME
>
> 9?

> MILES
>
> I'll bring the coffee.

I put my phone on the nightstand and lay staring at the inside of my eyelids for the rest of the night.

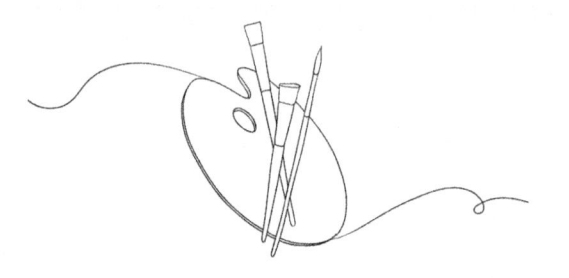

Camila

"How are you feeling?"

"Nervous." I feel jittery and nauseous. Like a water balloon is stuck in my chest while it tries to sink down into my stomach.

"Like *excited* nervous, or *nervous* nervous?"

"Both," I say, twisting my necklace. "I guess I'm just anxious not knowing how the conversation is going to go or what the outcome will be."

"What do you want to happen?" Taylor asks.

"I don't know." And that's the truth. "I want to go back in time and not be duped into a fake marriage."

She nods her understanding, "I respect that."

"But I miss him. I miss everything about him. But I also don't miss how easily it was for me to be hurt by him." And if my heart hurt this bad after two months I can't imagine how much worse I could be hurt down the road.

"Okay well, I'm going to go gorge myself on some Biscoffs and coffee over there so if you need me, you know where to find me." She leans in and gives me a comforting hug. "Good luck," she squeezes tight.

"Thank you, Taylor."

It's not peak tourist time yet, but the wharf is still crowded. It doesn't matter though, I would recognize that back of muscles and that dark head of hair anywhere. He's in his casual clothes again. Black jeans hug his strong legs and a gray crewneck with the sleeves pushed up show off his forearms that are leaning against the wooden railing. Slowly, I approach Miles as if I'm the north and he's the south pole of a magnet. If I move too quickly or get caught up in him I'll likely throw myself right at him. He spins around to face me. Dark circles line the bottoms of his eyes and his hair is soft but ruffled as if he's been dragging his hands through it. I offer a shy smile and take a tentative step towards him.

My eyes glance towards his outstretched hand, hesitating for a moment before sliding my palm into his. The warmth of his hand envelops me—like my own personal heater in the middle of a snowstorm. I take the last few steps closing the distance between us to stand next to him.

"Hi," he breathes. His voice is hoarse like he either hasn't used it in days or he's been yelling. I don't want to know which.

"Hi."

"I'm glad you texted me."

I'm glad I did too if only to see him but words are failing me right now so I just look into his depthless eyes willing the answers to come to me.

"I've missed you, Camila."

I've missed you too, I almost scream at him. I don't know why the words are getting stuck. It's as if I'm working so hard to keep the burning of my eyes at bay, that I can't get the words out. But they're there. Right fucking there. *I've missed you, your face, and the comfort that you provide just by wrapping me up in your arms. I've missed being around someone so supportive, someone who not only believes in me but helps me believe in myself.* I tell my body to relax and I take a deep breath.

"Excuse me, could you take a picture for us, please?"

I drag my eyes away from him to a mother holding her phone out to me. Her family standing behind her against the pier railing.

Miles's jaw ticks and I only smile, knowing he's going crazy inside at all the things unsaid between us, and here's this lady who just wants a family photo.

"Sure," I say, offering her a smile. "Okay ready? Three, two, one…got it!"

"Thank you so much." The woman smiles, already looking down at her phone as I hand it back to her.

I turn back around and I'm met with distressed eyes. His normally strong and assured posture is slack. I can't stand to see him like this, I need to assure him as he's done for me so many times. "Miles—"

"I'm sorry," he blurts, and my eyes go wide. "I should have said it before, but I'm sorry, Camila. I'm sorry I lied to you, I'm sorry I broke your trust, I'm sorry for hurting you, I'm sorry for everything. I didn't plan for this to happen, for *you*, but when it did I didn't think I would regret my choices because all that mattered was we ended up here. I didn't give a fuck about the how. But you were right. I should have. I wish I could go back and find a better way."

My vision blurs from the unshed tears.

"I thought it didn't matter because we ended up together. I would never regret that. But you were right, if I could go back and do it all over I would find another way. I would have given you those papers that day and stalked you like a normal person."

I can't help the small laugh that bubbles out of me.

"I would have found another way because, in this lifetime or any other, I would find my way to you." My tears break free now and he steps closer, his comforting scent filling my nose. He runs his thumb across my cheek wiping away the tears like he's done so many times before. "I've spent every hour of every day my entire life working to be what I thought would be the most successful version of myself, and I thought I got it. But none of it matters. Whether *my* name is on the door or Tom, Dick, or Harry, none of it matters to me without you." His head drops, shaking briefly before looking back up at me. "I don't deserve you, I know I don't. But I will spend every day moving forward working to be the man you deserve." My heart simultaneously hurts and fills. "Because I want it all with you, Camila. I want to make you coffee every morning in our home that you'll fill with beautiful art. I want to share my success with you over dinners and vice versa. I want to be your number one fan through all your accomplishments. I want to be the old grandpa sitting next to you wearing matching silk pajama shorts on Christmas morning. Your goals are my goals and I promise, I'll stop at nothing to make sure you have everything in this world that you deserve. Whether it's a pastry or a goddamn ocean. Nothing will ever be too much for you," he pauses, holding me tighter. "So tell me something."

I smile through the cry that escapes my lips as he uses my words.

"Will you forgive me? Will you come back home and let me love you? Will you let me love you and be genuinely happy with you for the rest of my life?" His forehead drops down to mine and his eyes close as if he's silently begging for a response. "Please. Perdóname, mi esposa."

My fingers brush along his scruff that's turned into more of a beard in the last few days. I watch his lashes flutter and feel his heart thrash under the palm of my other hand that now sits on his chest.

"I don't need to forgive you, Miles." His eyes squeeze tighter before he opens them to look at me. "I already forgave you." The corner of his eyes shines as his body almost collapses on me in relief. His hands find the sides of my face as he pulls me into a desperate kiss. The moment his lips find mine I feel at home again. I feel safe and loved. My arms tremble as I wrap them around him, digging my fingers into his back. His tongue slides into my mouth deepening the kiss and a soft moan escapes me.

"I love you," I manage to get the words out between kissing him. "I love you and—" He lifts me up and I kiss the corner of his mouth, his cheek, his neck. "It's always been you and I would choose you and this strange situation of ours a thousand times over again."

Miles sets me down and we stand at the railing overlooking the bay holding each other for a while. My chest fills with a familiar warmth standing in this spot again and just when I've had enough, when I can't bear to not be alone with him for another moment, he leans down and whispers in my ear. "You ready to get out of here, Camila?"

Miles

JONAS
Bagels?

ME
Not today.

And I'm taking the rest of the week off.

JONAS
😏😏

ME
Jesus. Don't smirk at me.

JONAS
So, your woman found her way home, huh?

ME
Yeah.

JONAS
Nice. Miles Puss Face Cameron was getting on my nerves.

ME
Don't call me that.

> **JONAS**
> Fine.
>
> Miles Simp Daddy Cameron has a much better ring to it anyway.

"Camila!" We haven't left the house in three days. We've barely left the bedroom, save for a few times to refuel.

"I'm in the bedroom." Her voice fills the hallway.

When I find her wearing real clothes I stop in the doorway, coffees in hand. She's tying up her converse when she notices my confused face.

"Hey, Taylor ended up getting the whole day off last minute, so I'm going to help her pack up the rest of my stuff."

I think my face physically falls at the idea of her leaving, which is unbelievable considering only a few months ago I regarded a relationship on par with non-medicated mouth surgery. But Camila still refers to our home as *my* home and I want to remedy that as soon as possible. So I guess the sooner she moves the rest of her things out of her old apartment and into this one, the sooner she might start calling it her home too.

She steps up to me and I hand her a coffee, she takes a sip and moans around the cup with her eyes closed.

"Don't moan like that."

"Like what?" She exaggerates a loud sigh.

"Cock tease."

She lets out a small laugh and kisses my lips. "I'll be home to soothe you and your cock later."

"We'll be waiting." I bite her bottom lip before stealing one last kiss from her.

She hurries past me. I watch my wife look back over her shoulder at me and give me one of those real genuine smiles and goddamn do I love to see it.

CAMILA

"Oh my god! Look what I found," I yell from the back of a very full, very tiny closet. Taylor looks over to me from her pile of boxes and I hold up our sequin shirt. I say *ours* because it was an incredible find years ago, and it turned out to be the sisterhood of the traveling top because it somehow fit both of us and we've both worn it multiple times over the years.

"I knew I didn't leave that gem at some random guy's house," she says, catching it from across the room. "You should keep it."

"Absolutely not." I shake my head. "That shirt is all you." She sits it down in her lap and looks around the room longingly. "Taylor," I whine, "I feel terrible."

Her hands immediately fly up to stop me, "No. I've told you once, I've told you a hundred times, you do *not* need to feel bad."

I nod my head over and over again, trying to will myself not to cry.

"Come here." She pats the bed beside her and I crawl up sitting next to her, dropping my head on her shoulder.

"I'm going to miss you terribly. But it's not like I won't see you anymore," she says.

"I know, I just feel bad leaving you here." I can't help it, but the tear I've been holding in burns so bad now. I blink causing it to roll down my cheek.

"Well, your husband so graciously footed our rent till the end of our lease, so I know you can't feel guilty about that."

"What will you do when the lease is up? My offer still stands," I say, sitting up to look at her. "You can move into the guest room, you would die for the kitchen."

"You're trying to tease me with kitchen porn and it's cruel," she jokes.

"Okay then, I have to know your game plan. It's going to eat at me, Tay. You know this." I wipe away my tears and take a calming breath.

"That I do, my little angel baby, that I do." She reaches across me and grabs a tissue from the nightstand and hands it to me. "Honestly Mila, I'm getting kind of antsy here anyway. Maybe when my lease is up, I don't know, maybe I'll travel for a bit or something."

"You have always wanted to travel."

"See, whatever will be will be." She wraps her arm around my shoulder and pulls me in tight. "Either way, no matter where we are, where we live, or where we end up, you and I will always be good. We'll always be Whisky and Risky, baby."

"Our friendship will always be my favorite," I say through tears, but I'm not crying out of sadness anymore, but out of gratitude.

Epilogue

MILES

THREE MONTHS LATER

"Don't you think this is a little dramatic?" Camila's face is mocking me as I pull out a giant pair of scissors.

"No," I say, kissing the top of her head. "If anything, I don't think it's dramatic enough. If it were up to me, this would be filmed and broadcasted as breaking news to every TV, computer, and phone in the world."

"Well, I guess we can thank our lucky stars it wasn't up to you then."

Tables full of appetizers, desserts, and champagne fill the gallery while pride and awe fill me. I pull the curtains back slightly to take a peek out front. Camila's friends and family are all grinning from ear to ear. Eagerly awaiting the grand opening.

"Oh god." Her fingers twist around her ring for the first time in months, "Half of the city is out there." She slinks back and I let the curtain drop as I follow her to the center of the room.

She poured everything into renovating this place. The first

time she came home with gauze and bandages wrapped around her arm I practically demanded we hire people. But she wouldn't stand for it. Her heart and soul, sweat, and literal blood are in this place and I couldn't be more proud of her.

"You ready?"

She offers a wobbly smile and wraps her arms around herself. I set the scissors down and take her hands in mine, giving her a reassuring squeeze. Her eyelids fall softly as she takes a deep breath.

"It was nice of you to invite your dad," she whispers.

"Baby steps." I shrug. "Now," I wrap her arms around my waist and hold her flush against me. "As much as I want everyone to see how incredible you are, and everything you've accomplished, if you want to head to the back I can think of some ways to calm your nerves."

"Oh yeah? Like what?" Her eyes twinkle and her lips curl up into a small smile.

"I could eat your sweet pussy till your vision blurs." I nip at her bottom lip.

"Don't tease a girl," she whispers against my lips. I unlock her arms from behind me and use them to drag her back to her office. "What are you doing?" I can hear the smile on her face. I sit on a large green velvet couch in the corner of the room and pull her on top of me. With one hand on her hip, my other works the button and zipper of my pants. Her eyes go wide when my cock breaks free of my briefs. She licks her lips and my eyes follow the trail of her tongue.

Holding my shaft I drag it over her underwear that only continues to get wetter with each passing stroke.

Camila's thumb rubs at the bottom of my lip while her hand splays against my cheek. "Thank you, Miles. For everything."

"This was all you, mi esposa." I kiss her lips. "I'm so proud of you." One of those beautiful real smiles graces her lips. Not a shy, nervous, or forced one. A genuine smile. And then her hands tangle in my hair as she kisses me with that full Camila force. I don't bother pulling her underwear down, I just slide them to the side. A breathy little whimper escapes her lips when I push the tip in and I suck it up. I inhale her scent and her sounds, and I relish in the pride she has in herself as I attempt to knock out any nerves. Because I want to do everything with her and there isn't anything I wouldn't do for her. Her knees spread out farther as she sinks lower onto me and now it's me gasping and groaning. I pump my hips forward, harder and faster now and her head falls back exposing the column of her neck that I love to sink my teeth into. I feel her already tight pussy grip my cock and I know she's close. I reach between us and stroke her clit because I'm not going to last another second. Her mouth parts and she cries out my name which always causes me to thrust harder. Her pussy squeezes me and her body trembles under my hands. It's that feeling alone that has my balls tightening and I find my own release inside her.

Camila's panting and sucking in air as she leans down to rest on my chest. I run my hand along the back of her head, trying to tame her hair. "Oh my god. Do you think everyone will know?"

"That I fucked the nerves right out of you?" I ask and she sits up bringing her hands to cover her face but I don't miss the smile beneath them. "If your blushing cheeks don't give it away, my cum dripping down your legs might." Her jaw drops open but I just drop my head back onto the couch and laugh before helping her clean up.

. . .

Twenty minutes later Camila's hands are surprisingly sturdy as she uses the large scissors to cut the ribbon in front of her gallery. Everyone claps and cheers while taking photos. Taylor whoops and screams the loudest. Her mother wipes at the tears falling from her eyes while her father holds her tightly. I hear a loud whistle and find my own father standing a head taller than everyone else as he blows around the two fingers between his lips. I look back down at Camila, beaming from ear to ear and I've never been more proud.

CAMILA

"Having a grand opening is more exciting and exhausting than a night out in Vegas," I sigh as I collapse onto my spot on the couch. Miles drops my shoes that he was carrying on the floor before sitting down beside me. His sturdy hands wrap around my legs as he pulls them over his lap and softly caresses my skin. Even after all this time my skin still heats under his touch.

"Are you happy, Camila?" The smile he gives me makes my heart so full it's heavy in my chest.

I sit up, running my fingers through his hair, and kiss his neck. "Yes, Miles. I'm really, truly, *genuinely* happy." His lips brush over mine. "And what about you? Are you happy?"

He pulls back, his eyes flirting with mine. "With you? It's borderline unbearable how happy I am." He kisses me once more before sliding out from under my legs and heading back towards the elevator.

"Where are you going?"

"I have something for you." His eyes twinkle with mischief and mine narrow in suspicion.

I make my way down to our bedroom to change out of my dress while I wait for him to return. When I look at myself in the mirror I think I'm actually glowing; there's no trace of how tired I am. My eyes only shine with pride. It's hard to believe that only a few months ago I was willing to chain myself to a life I could never be happy in because I didn't feel worthy of anything else because I was tied to the idea of everyone else's feelings mattering more than my own. I still catch myself smiling when unnecessary sometimes, but between Miles and I one of us has to be somewhat approachable.

My head tilts as I take my earrings out, but I pause trying to focus on a clicking sound that echoes through the room. I set the earrings on the dresser and the sound picks up speed, *click-clack-click.* My eyes narrow in confusion when it stops and starts again.

My bare feet pad down the hallway and the sounds only get louder. When I round the corner, a black puppy with huge paws comes galloping and sliding towards me. "Looks like we're going to have to get some rugs," Miles says, scratching the back of his neck.

"Oh my God." I blink back the tears that are forming in my eyes while falling to my knees to scoop the furry thing up. His smooth warm tongue pops out as he licks my cheek. "Miles!"

"The shelter that we donate to had another one of those events last week. I saw it on my way home and I don't know why but I felt compelled to go. When I saw this guy I couldn't imagine him not here with us, so I filled out the adoption paperwork and today, he's officially ours."

There's no blinking back the tears now. The puppy has calmed down and curled up in my lap, not bothered at all by the wet drops that roll off my cheeks and plunk down on his belly. I scoop him up and stand with a smile. "Miles Cameron, are you a dog lover now?"

His arms wrap around me and our new fur baby. "I'm a Camila lover."

I tilt my head back and he kisses me with those lips that remind me how full my heart is and how full my *life* is. He kisses the tears that still break free down my cheeks, and my eyes close tight soaking him in. "I love you, Miles Cameron."

"And I love you, mi esposa."

The End

Coming Soon

What's next for Whisky and Risky? If hot rugby players, small towns, and found family are your thing— you're not going to want to miss Taylor's story coming fall 2024.

Acknowledgments

Dear reader, thank you from the bottom of my heart for picking up Art of Convenience. As a book lover, I know there are a million books in the world I want to read, and it means everything to me that you would choose my book as one of the millions you read.

To the book community, I can confidently say I would not have had the balls to put this book out there if it weren't for all the love and support you've shown me. Especially my bookstagram besties, you guys have been riding with me from the beginning and I can't thank you enough.

To my sweet friend Cassidy, thank you for holding my hand and guiding me through this crazy process. Always there answering my questions and just being an incredible human along the way.

To my girls, Astrid and Francisca, thank you for helping me work through my broken Spanish and answering all my questions so I didn't have to call my grandma.

Thank you to my beta readers- Stephanie, Ely, Sophie, Luna, and Cassidy; I can't think of a more nerve-racking experience than sending my book baby out for the first time, but you ladies made the process so incredible for me and I would choose each of you over and over again.

Thank you to my editor, Kristen. You really went above and beyond for me. Thank you for all your helpful feedback—even if at the time I was overwhelmed, you really helped me create the best version of this story and I'm so grateful. Also, I promise to spell out the word *okay* in the next one.

Thank you, Staci Hart for creating the cover of my dreams. You were incredible to work with and maybe one day I'll write a book based in Seattle so we can put that other cover to use.

Shout out to my favorite barista, Nick, for supplying me with endless amounts of coffee every week.

I'm incredibly lucky to be surrounded by such a supportive family. But a special thanks to all the phenomenal women in my life; My mom, sisters, grandmothers. Thank you endlessly for your support and for promising not to bring up the spice scenes at Thanksgiving diners.

Lauren, my angel baby, best friend, soul sister, emotional support, and personal hype girl. When I said "Might fuck around and write a book," you said, "Great. It's a bestseller and we're going on tour." Your love and support are unmatched and I'm truly the luckiest person in the world to have you. Thank you will never be enough for all you've done for me. For being my soundboard through this whole process. For giving me laughs on the hard days when I thought I would scrap the whole thing and for naming Herbert Preston Jonas the third. This story would not exist without your continuous encouragement. Our friendship will always be my favorite.

Lastly, thank you to my husband. Thank you for being the best partner I could ask to do this life with, for being the HBIC when I needed those extra hours to write, for helping me figure out all the logistics of getting this book out, and for showing me a love better than any book boyfriend.

About the Author

Michelle Carrero lives in Southern California with her husband, two children, and an 80-pound gentle giant, black lab. She found her love for reading one summer while on bed rest and writing her own stories quickly became her greatest dream and passion.

When Michelle isn't reading or writing she can usually be found watching Formula 1, drinking mass amounts of coffee, or having movie nights with her family.